Kat motioned to him with the gun. "Stand up. Slowly."

Sebastian rubbed the back of his head. "What the hell did you hit me with? You could have given me a concussion."

"Next time I'll try harder." With a slight smile, she moved behind him and jabbed him once with the barrel. "Walk slowly. Straight ahead, between that stand of quina trees. We haven't much time."

Sebastian stood his ground. With a self-deprecating grin, he asked, "Can I get my stuff from the truck? I assume you may want to keep me hostage for a while."

Kat shook her head. "I'm not an idiot, Mr. Caine. I let you near the lorry, and you'll disappear. No way. We move. Now."

Thwarted, Sebastian took his defeat in stride. "Okay." He walked first. Katelyn fell into step behind him, and he swiveled his head to acknowledge. "You're good at this."

"You seem to be familiar with being a hostage," Kat returned, narrowing her eyes.

"I enjoy a broad range of talents," he replied smoothly. "Bondage is just one of them."

"Move," Kat growled. She followed closely, waving the gun and willing her cheeks to cool . . .

By Selena Montgomery

SECRETS AND LIES
HIDDEN SINS

Secrets and Lies

SELENA MONTGOMERY

AVON BOOKS
An Imprint of HarperCollinsPublishers

This is a work of fiction. Names, characters, places, and incidents are products of the author's imagination or are used fictitiously and are not to be construed as real. Any resemblance to actual events, locales, organizations, or persons, living or dead, is entirely coincidental.

AVON BOOKS
An Imprint of HarperCollins*Publishers*
195 Broadway
New York, NY, 10007

Copyright © 2007 by Stacey Abrams
ISBN-13: 978-0-06-079851-2
ISBN: 10: 0-06-079851-3
www.avonromance.com

First Avon Books paperback printing: January 2007

Avon Trademark Reg. U.S. Pat. Off. and in Other Countries, Marca Registrada, Hecho en U.S.A.
HarperCollins® is a registered trademark of HarperCollins Publishers.

Printed in the U.S.A.

10 9 8 7 6 5 4 3

*For Carolyn, Robert,
Andrea, Leslie,
Richard, Walter
and Jeanine Abrams.
My family and inspiration.*

Acknowledgments

My debts continue to accrue: I owe Dr. Andrea Abrams for helping me to see the world larger; Mirtha Oliveros for seeding, reading, and proofing; Ben Oliveros for unveiling the mystic life of plants; Jeanine Abrams for scientific accoutrements; my mom, Rev. Carolyn Abrams; my agent, Marc Gerald; and Linda DiSantis, Lisa Borders, and Dr. Johnnetta B. Cole for listening; and my editor, Erika Tsang, for stretching the days. With the deepest and truest love for my sister, Leslie Abrams, for sharp eyes and her terrific magic.

Chapter 1

Nighttime suited Sebastian Caine. In the shadows, he could prowl the quiet streets, invisible to the unsuspecting eye. Dakkar or Paris, New York or New Delhi, the nighttime yielded its secrets to him with a delicate sigh.

Or, perhaps, with the muffled shorting of a cross-circuit alarm system.

"Not nearly as poetic, but effective," Sebastian acknowledged, as sparks cascaded to cobblestones where he knelt. He eased the door open, alarms successfully disengaged. Looking down at the now-darkened keypad, a frisson of awareness tightened his skin. Cutting the alarm hadn't been simple, but an incongruity niggled at the back of his mind. Circuit broken—check. Alarm pad disengaged—check. Brass locks picked—check. He'd done this a hundred times before, stealing inside deserted buildings to relieve unsuspecting owners of their possessions. Still, tonight felt different. Unsettled. But, he reminded himself ruefully, standing outside a mark's house was not the place to figure out what bothered him.

Quickly, he slipped inside the doorway that led into a kitchen most chefs fantasized about. Nearly the size of the walk-up he'd lived in as a toddler, Sebastian thought, but much quieter. As he'd planned, nothing sounded beyond the distant lapping of waves. The perfect spot on the Pacific coast for a thief.

Narrow cobbled streets and brightly colored stucco homes had conspired to give him access to his quarry without the requirements of scaled walls or burrowed tunnels. No, tonight's endeavor required little more than a cooperative quarter moon, his personal finesse, and the absence of the homeowner. By the time Senor Felix Estrada returned home from his buying trip to Buenos Aires, Sebastian would be retired and sunning on a tropical beach. Far, far away from the tiny South American nation of Bahia and his pockets full.

With that pleasant image dancing in his head, Sebastian tucked his instruments into a leather bag and switched the palm light on. Swiftly, he moved through the kitchen to the main rooms. He turned the corner and, instantly, Sebastian flicked the light off and flattened himself against a wall.

According to photos he'd studied, Estrada lived in a sprawling mansion filled with carefully tended objets d'art that rivaled many museums. Tonight, though, those priceless pieces had been flung aside with malicious hands. The place had been torn apart. Apparently, whoever had preceded Caine cared nothing about discovery. Sebastian scanned the room, alert and ready for ambush.

Suddenly, he understood what had bothered him about the alarm. He'd cut the power, he realized, but he hadn't heard the telltale sound to reveal that the line had been active when he severed the wires. Someone had disarmed the house. Someone who might be still inside.

For an instant, Sebastian considered leaving and telling his client that he'd been too late. He could hop a plane to New York and be in bed by dawn. But two thoughts kept him rooted in place.

Of paramount importance was his payoff for tonight's job. In exchange for delivering a sixteenth-century manuscript known as the Cinchona, Sebastian's client offered $500,000. The client hadn't provided any more detail about Cinchona, and Sebastian hadn't pressed for more. Curiosity in his line of work was not appreciated. *Where, when* and *how much* were the necessary particulars. *Why* did not concern him and could be dangerous. He'd worked for this client too often to delve into queries, and a hundred-thousand-dollar retainer wired to Sebastian's Grand Cayman account easily dampened any natural inquisitiveness.

The part of him that might have cared had been ruthlessly trained against that indulgence because prying didn't pay the bills. If his client was willing to shell out half a million dollars for the pleasure of owning some ancient papers another man wanted, who was he to argue?

Standing in the shadows, Sebastian acknowledged that annoyance ran a close second to greed. From where he stood, moonlight crested inside the mansion, highlighting his opponent's damage. Paintings leaned drunkenly against silk-covered walls or sprawled on the floors. Gleaming sculptures of twisted metal had been toppled from pedestals. Books—likely first editions—lay jumbled ignominiously on the floor below high mahogany shelves.

"Philistines," he muttered soundlessly. Even thieves could have an appreciation for art.

A slight noise caught his ear, the sound creeping across polished hardwoods. Sebastian pressed deeper into the darkness, his ears tuned. A nearly unheard *thud* followed the slight bending of wood floors, then silence. He blew out a thin breath. He definitely wasn't alone in the house. But there was only one way to discover who had beaten him there, he decided, peeling away from the wall. Go and find him.

As he slipped into the hallway, Sebastian reached into his leather bag and closed his fingers around the hilt of the knife he carried. The ceremonial dagger had been a present to himself years ago, and he'd so far been able to keep its blade clean. He didn't relish the thought of using the weapon, but he also rejected the notion of dying. Turning the corner, Sebastian peered into the next room and found it empty.

He moved with alacrity through the darkened

house, melting into shadows. Adrenaline settled into a steady pulse of blood that belied the danger. Senses heightened for every aberrant sound thrummed as he cased the mansion. He slipped into the dining room, dagger clutched tight in his hand. Suddenly, he heard the skitter of feet and, seconds later, the *thud* of the kitchen door closing. Sebastian sprinted out of the dining room and toward the rear of the house. He flung open the back door just in time to see a dark form blend into the night. He followed, but by the time he reached the hedges, the thief had disappeared.

"Damnit." The quiet oath emerged as he debated giving chase, but he'd have to guess at whether to go left or right or straight across. He could track him, but the search would take valuable time, and the house had already been breached twice tonight. If his rival had stolen the Cinchona, Sebastian should verify it first, then notify his client. However, he thought, stepping into the house again, the thief could have been searching for other targets. Before he called his client, he decided, he should be sure the Cinchona was gone.

Hand-woven Persian rugs cushioned his quiet footfalls as his weak beam crested over polished woods littered with Estrada's possessions. Sebastian bent over a tumbled Kahlo, the edge of its frame bent by a rough fall. With a gloved hand, he righted the painting. In the center of the capacious room, he noted a second heap of books piled onto the dining-room table.

Observant eyes the color of bittersweet chocolate skimmed the Spanish names, effortlessly
translating titles, courtesy of his mother's intractability on the issue of college. The authors
were unfamiliar, the subjects less so. Bartolomé
de las Casas. *El Diarios de Pizzaro. Nueva crónica
y buen gobierno.* Bernal Díaz del Castillo. More
tomes were stacked on chairs nearby. Whoever
had preceded him into the house hadn't been
after the books or the paintings. They, like him,
hunted for what might lie hidden behind them.

According to the intel he'd received from his
client, the manuscript would probably be in a
safe upstairs; but Sebastian didn't trust other
people's intelligence. He stepped over a toppled
chair and around more haphazardly tossed
paintings, including one he recognized as a
Henry Tanner, a tear in the canvas visible beneath his light. His cool rush of blood heated
with indignation.

Sebastian took pride in his ability to admire
the magnificence of the collections of his prey,
and wanton destruction offended his sensibilities. Estrada had built a fantastic collection, one
that Sebastian might have envied were he a different sort of man. However, envy, like sentiment, had no place in the life of a recovery
specialist—Sebastian's glorified term for his life
as a thief.

He and Felix Estrada had chased the same
treasures for as long as Sebastian had been in
his line of work. Sebastian considered his tus-
sles with Estrada to be the results of friendly

rivalry, especially given the fact that Estrada had once saved Sebastian's life. Unlike Sebastian, though, Estrada was a collector, willing to pay any price to possess the beautiful and rare.

Stepping into the next room, a wide great room drawn in golds and creams, Sebastian froze. It appeared Senor Estrada had finally paid too much.

The body of Felix Estrada lay sprawled on the glossy hardwood, blood pooling at his side. Shocked, Sebastian dropped into a crouch and eased over to the still form. The gaping wound in Estrada's abdomen held a pearl-handled knife. A look told Sebastian that the knife had staunched the flow of blood, while it had simultaneously severed the artery that poured Estrada's life onto the floor. The internal bleeding would be severe and fatal. He lifted the limp hand and found a weakened pulse. Abruptly, Estrada's eyes flashed open.

"*¿Donde es* cat?" he rasped, his question interrupted by a harsh cough. "Where is cat?"

Sebastian ignored the broken inquiry about the missing pet. The blood soaking into his black pants concerned him more. Rage welled, unfamiliar emotion for a thief and a liar who prided himself on limiting his emotions to ironic resignation and smug indifference. But Sebastian knew from the pallor beneath the brown skin that Felix Estrada was a dead man. Fifteen minutes ago, Sebastian could have saved him, but not now. All that was left was to find out why he was dying. And who killed him. "Do you know who did this to you? Who stabbed you, Senor Estrada?"

Estrada thrashed his head back and forth. "No. No. Cat. Where is she?"

I can't believe the poor dying bastard is worried about his damned pet, Sebastian thought grimly. He continued to hold Estrada's wrist, feeling the pulse slow. "Tell me who hurt you, Felix. There isn't much time. Tell me, and let me call the ambulance." But he knew Canete would not have an ambulance swift enough to save Estrada's life.

The feeble hand twisted beneath Sebastian's to take his larger one in a fierce hold. *"No ambulancia.* Find her. Find cat. *Muy importante.* Promise me." The hold tightened. "Promise me."

"Sure," Sebastian lied, stunned by Estrada's burst of strength. "I'll find your *gata.*"

"She knows the answers." Estrada gasped for the breaths that slowed.

"Smart cat." As his words sank in, Sebastian's eyes narrowed. "Knows the answers to what?"

"To the secret you are here to steal."

Sebastian rocked nimbly on his heels, ready to bolt. "You know what I'm looking for?"

"The Cinchona." Estrada managed a weak smile, his grip loosening. "A fine goal, Sebastian. You took the Oglasi from me in Ségou. And the statue from the temple of Malay. Too often, you have sneaked away my treasures with elegance. My latest find is what you would steal. You have been an excellent pupil."

"Pupil?"

"You have found much by—" A hacking cough racked the thin chest and the vibrations traveled up their joined hands. "By following me. You have an eye for beauty. For history. Perhaps in this, you will find the balm for your restlessness."

"I'm not restless," Sebastian protested, slipping his hand free to test Estrada's pulse.

Estrada frowned, in annoyance rather than pain. "Do not lie to yourself, Sebastian. You no longer steal for money but to find purpose. Meaning. Redemption for our sins. We all seek such, no? Few of us succeed. I—I almost did." He stopped, dragging air into weakened lungs. "You still can."

"Stop, Senor. Save your strength," Sebastian urged. Now was not the time for meditations on his life, such as it was. For now, the path he'd chosen years ago suited him. Instead, he delicately probed the area around the protruding knife. Crimson spilled around the blade. Definitely, removal meant instant death. "We need to get you help. Tell me who did this."

Ignoring the urgent question, Estrada continued with effort. "Remember the favor you owe me?"

An image of a vault and Samurai sword flashed in Sebastian's memory. "*Sí.* You saved my life."

"Yes, then I ask the same of you," he extorted harshly. "You must find cat. Protect her."

"Sure."

Estrada lifted his head, captured Sebastian's

evasive gaze with a hard, determined look. To emphasize, he grasped the wiry wrist near his death wound. He had no more time, not to finish what had destroyed him. But here was his final chance. He fought off the muzziness that crept into his thoughts, fighting for the last seconds of lucidity. "Promise me, Sebastian. Protect cat. Swear it."

"I swear. I'll protect your cat."

The broken body shuddered with pain, yet he patted Sebastian's cheek proudly. "*Gracias.* Thank you." Felix gasped, taking in gulps that seemed to accomplish nothing. The death rattle of failing lungs filled the room. "You want. The Cinchona. I. Did not. Intend to die. For it."

"Art isn't worth murder, *Señor.*" He'd never taken a man's life, by God. Certainly not for a manuscript, the piece he'd been hired to "recover" for his latest client. His last client.

Estrada awkwardly patted Sebastian's hand where it lay near the gaping wound. "Wrong, *mi amigo.* Art is life. Cat knows this. She knows how to find life, how to save it."

Sebastian focused on Estrada's irrational claim. "Your cat knows how to save lives?"

Before the dying man could respond, the strong grip on Sebastian's hand fell away. Estrada coughed, struggling to draw in air.

Sebastian lifted the gray head and urged air into lungs wet with blood. "Senor Estrada? Who did this to you?" His voice was low, ragged. The strangled airways hissed with effort. Sebastian pressed his ear close to the parted lips that curled against death throes. "Senor! Tell me who did this!"

"*Cat.*" The whispered confession barely reached Sebastian's ear, though it pressed close to Estrada's cheek. "Cat." A shudder, a rasp of noise. Then silence.

Minutes, seconds later, Sebastian uncurled his six-foot-plus frame and started toward the phone to ring the police. He closed the distance with long, angry strides. Grief threatened, stirred compassion. An ornate ivory receiver perched on a round base with old-fashioned rotary dial. Elegant and beautiful and anachronistic. Wholly fitting. Sebastian reached for the receiver, then he stopped himself, quelling ruthlessly the prick of conscience that demanded he seek justice.

Estrada was dead now, Sebastian reminded himself coldly. And Sebastian Caine was no altruist. He was a thief and a damned good one. One who had a job to do.

"The manuscript." Sebastian spun away from the phone. "Find the manuscript, first, then you can call the police. They'll find the killer . . . when you're not here."

He stalked over to one of the overstuffed chairs and lifted a length of Egyptian cotton dyed a somber black and returned to the body. Carefully, Sebastian draped the fabric over Estrada, a fitting shroud. He muttered a prayer taught to him decades ago by his mother. "Farewell, Senor. May God have mercy on your soul."

* * *

In the heavy black of evening, unbroken by streetlights, Katelyn Lyda rushed down the cobblestone walk, head down, the burlap sack clutched to her chest. She could feel her heart pounding beneath her ribs, her lungs aching to breathe without sobbing. Every few seconds, she lifted her head, as though scenting danger. When none materialized, she ran on, tears blinding her vision, but her feet sure on the uneven ground.

At the edge of the postage-stamp-sized town, she reached the gravel road that led to Canete's valley. She'd hidden her Jeep in the dense tangle of verdant green and brush, per Tio Felix's orders. Quickly, she descended into the wash, oblivious to the scrape of rock and sand against her skin.

Nothing could be sharper than the pain of grief, so her mind focused on escape only, on reaching safe ground. To think of anything else would be fatal. She needed desperately to believe that the ambulance she'd summoned had arrived and would save him. That leaving the knife in place had held his lifeblood inside, but she knew better. Had known when the blood poured out, despite her ministrations. Tio Felix was dead, and she had run, leaving him to the mercies of another madman.

Katelyn clambered inside the cab, slid against the cracked leather of the seats. She struggled to start the ignition in the aged vehicle. After a couple of sputters, the Jeep left the valley floor, climbing toward the foothills of the Andean mountains that ran parallel to the coastline, on the eastern edge of Bahia. Wild sounds pierced the evening—bats waking for their nocturnal journeys, the call of macaws to their mates. More subtle sounds caught her ear as well. She could hear the wind rustling through the muña and scattering the white flowers of the Cabello de Angel. Guided by memory, she sped along the trail.

When she had pressed high up to the formations of stone creating cliffs and sheers and crevasses that swallowed people whole, Katelyn stopped. She bounded out of the truck and carried her pack and the burlap bag to the campsite she'd set up earlier. Felix had forbidden her to register in town or to come too close until he called. With her caramel skin proclaiming her African-Latina heritage, she was what the locals called a *morenita* and, therefore, memorable. At the time, she'd chalked up his cryptic instructions to the mild paranoia she associated with her favorite relative, but she knew better now.

If she had been in town, had arrived earlier, would he still be alive? she wondered miserably. But Kat doggedly pushed the thought aside. Anguish and remorse could wait, she thought, until she'd figured out her next move. When a moan caught in her parched throat, she pressed her eyes shut.

"Don't give in, Kat, not yet," she murmured to herself. "Focus." Opening her eyes, she fumbled in her pack for her canteen and took a deep swig. She nearly reached for the cell phone in her pocket, but she wouldn't be able to reach her parents in Africa, and talking to anyone else was more than she could manage. Besides, what would she say? *I've stumbled into a sixteenth-century nightmare. Come and get me?*

Exhausted, she sat with her back propped against a quina tree, which she found sadly fitting. After all, it was stories like the legend of the quina that had brought her to Bahia. Days ago, she had been delivering a lecture to a crowd of hundreds at a medical conference in Halifax. Her topic, the medicinal properties of blue cohosh, hadn't exactly wowed the gathered doctors, but she was used to the glazed eyes and suspicious scowls from physicians. Native plants as legitimate medicine were only a step above witchcraft and voodoo in their estimation.

But Katelyn knew better. From the time she was two, she'd studied the shape of flowers, the sap of trees. Flora and fauna were her life. Because of them, because of Tio Felix, she had become Dr. Katelyn Lyda, an ethnobotanist. And what she had been given by her dying uncle might prove to be her undoing.

Slowly, she opened the burlap satchel she carried everywhere and removed two items, which she laid gently on the ground. A small, leather-bound notebook was cinched tight by a length of string. Reverently, she lifted out a larger manuscript, also bound in worn leather, the frayed pages stained by the passage of time, its cover scrawled in Latin. Katelyn read the words she'd been too frightened to examine earlier, and she gasped.

In faith, thou shalt find salvation. In devotion, thou shalt find peace. In the least of these, He places eternity.

With shaking hands, she opened the pages, the musty smell rising to her nostrils, telling her of history and agelessness. The Cinchona.

She'd heard the name before, from Tio Felix. But not as the title of a manuscript. No, to her, the cinchona was a plant, one described in the books on botany he'd gifted. Summer visits had stoked a child's love of nature, and her fascination with the cultures she'd encountered grew as she devoured stories of people she'd never heard of. Catholic scholars and histories of Spanish conquest and fables from ancient lands crowded on tall library shelves in the magnificent house Tio Felix built in Canete. There, he'd taught her about her mother's native land and taken her on treks across its face, from the craggy beaches to dense jungle and towering hills. Bahia.

She'd been summoned a week ago by a telegram containing the words: *Fides. Salus. Studium. Quiesco. Aevum. Venga rápidamente.*

Faith. Salvation. Devotion. Peace. Eternity. Come quickly.

Now, Tio Felix lay dead on the floor of his house, and she hid in the forest with an ancient diary and a centuries-old manuscript etched with familiar words.

And his blood on her hands.

* * *

In Washington, DC, a short, squat redbrick building hid in the shadows of taller spires of chrome and glass. The spindly, gray-haired man keyed in his code, and heavy metal doors swung open on airless hinges. He rushed inside, not waiting to sign the logbook or chat with the security guard. The guard did not stop him, too used to the pell-mell pace of the building's inhabitants. She recognized Dr. Clifton Burge, a researcher for the National Institutes of Health. Quietly, she scratched his name onto her pad.

Oblivious, Burge sped along the tiled corridor, his heels striking in uneven syncopation. At his office door, he entered another set of digits and slid his pass through the crease in the black security panel. Once inside the tight, claustrophobic space loftily described as his office, Burge ignored the reams of pages that spewed from his printer. He'd once dreamed of gleaming laboratories and miracle cures, but fate and his own limitations had intervened.

But he had one last shot at glory, at finding what he required to survive. Unless he failed in that too. With trepidation, he reached for the telephone, where a red light blinked furiously, and lifted the receiver with a shaking hand.

"Once more chance," he begged of the caller on the other end.

"We had a deal, Dr. Burge. You have failed to deliver."

Burge felt the salami roll he'd eaten lurch greasily in his gut. "We're close. I swear it." He stared at the printer and its rows of data, incomprehensible to most. Fear had bile rising in his throat, and he choked back a plaintive wail. "Please. One more chance."

"Why?"

"Because I know the truth." Burge turned a sickly green and sank into his chair, but he made the threat. "Cut me out, and I'll tell," he whined.

"Good-bye, Dr. Burge." The line disconnected.

Chapter 2

"It's not here." Sebastian resisted the urge to smash the black-and-white photograph of young Japanese children taking calesthenics. The photo by Ansel Adams had concealed a lead safe tucked into the wall in Estrada's bedroom. The contents had been riffled through and only personal effects of no discernible value remained. Sebastian had no doubt his manuscript had been there not an hour ago.

Now, the manuscript that was supposed to pay for his retirement was nowhere to be found. Instead, what he had for his endeavors was a dead body and a missing cat that might have the answers he needed.

A cat that he could find no evidence of in Estrada's house. No cat food, no drinking bowl, no cloying hairballs. Only the empty safe, the dead man and bloody red footprints tracked throughout the house.

For the second time in as many minutes, Sebastian cursed himself for letting the killer slip away. Had he been even fifteen minutes earlier, he would have been able to save Felix's life and secure the manuscript. Sebastian had little doubt the knife would have found a more suitable resting place. Now, his only lead was a phantom cat.

Turning, Sebastian caught sight of himself in a skinny mirror hanging opposite the safe. Blood had been transferred to his cheek, and he swiped at the darkened patch, his throat constricted. Murder pissed him off. Killing a mark was the stuff of amateurs or the sport of miscreants. He was neither, and he didn't work with those who were.

Grimly, Sebastian pulled out his phone and quickly dialed. The clicks on the other end signaled that his call was being routed through a couple of substations, following his client's normal protocol. No calls at the office. A clean phone for every job. A new e-mail account with untraceable IP addresses. She was a stickler for security and privacy. Sebastian appreciated the mild paranoia, respected it.

When the call abruptly dropped, he disconnected the phone and punched in a new series of numbers. After four rings, he terminated the call. Thirty seconds later, the phone shrilled for his attention.

"Caine." Sebastian propped his hip on the dining-room table, his long fingers drumming against the wood. "You didn't mention there'd be company."

An ocean away, a terse oath singed the air. "What?"

The imprecation spoke volumes, Sebastian realized. Helen Cox wasn't given to displays of actual human feeling. In fact, in their years of collaboration, he'd never heard more than a succinct "good," which often passed for effusive praise. Once, he'd managed to elicit a more satisfying response, but he made that kind of mistake only once.

The lack of praise didn't bother him. He required little else from his employers than a timely payment for his troubles and quality intel on his target. He'd gotten the first, which made him wonder what happened to the latter. "The package isn't here. And the previous owner is dead. Something you want to share?"

"Your implication?"

Sebastian looked at the red stain on his fingers, the smudge on his cheek. "The implication? That you don't trust my services and decided to hire a secondary team. If so, that's your prerogative. But I don't do murder for hire, and I don't play with those who do."

"Please don't tell me you're developing a conscience, Sebastian. I'd find it hard to believe you," the creamy voice drawled.

Sebastian smirked, an unamused slash of white in the darkness. "Conscience has nothing to do with it. I'm a firm adherent to the principle of survival of the fittest. People in my line of work are less inclined to kill you if they know you won't kill them. Having a dead body turn up on one of my jobs will damage my reputation." He didn't add that the murder of a good man had the galling ability to edge into that space where his conscience had once resided. Like vertigo, it was a sensation he didn't care for particularly. "If I've got company, we need to renegotiate the terms of our partnership."

"I didn't hire anyone else, Sebastian. I thought you were the best. If my confidence has been misplaced . . ."

The threat wasn't lost on Sebastian. Again, he thought about the invisible cat and the bloody footprints. The murderer had substantial lead time and his target, but Sebastian was an excellent tracker. "No, your investment is well placed. I promised you the package by Sunday, and I'll deliver."

"Sunday, Sebastian. I'll expect an update in two hours." The line went dead.

With a click, Sebastian shut the phone and tucked it into his pocket, not quite satisfied but having little choice. Given the manuscript's apparent value, Helen Cox probably wasn't the only person after it, which made his job infinitely more difficult. What should have been a routine grab had become a treasure hunt. He frowned, considering his options. Other than breaking into Estrada's home, how exactly was he to go about finding a sheaf of papers when he had no idea what was written on the pages and who else wanted to possess their contents?

Start with the last person to see Estrada alive. The owner of the bloody footprints, who appeared to have also taken off with the man's cat. Time to go.

With quiet, competent motions, he checked for any trace of his visit. Thin black leather gloves separated his skin from contact with surfaces hungry for prints or human oils. The cropped black hair curled beneath a black ski cap. He could do little about the blood that had soaked into his cotton pants until he returned to his truck.

The stains on the floor were another matter. To erase evidence of his presence and to limit clues, he swabbed at the hardwoods where his ministrations to Estrada might have offered a hint as to body weight or height. He used a bleach solution to wipe away the footprints as well. Satisfied, he prepared to leave the mansion where Estrada grew colder.

The black-draped form lay still and damning where he'd found him. Estrada was expected to be gone for another two weeks, according to Sebastian's intelligence. Two weeks before a nosy neighbor discovered his remains. Two weeks too long.

Cursing himself for the weakness, he fumbled on the table for another piece of cloth. He wrapped it around his gloved hand for extra protection and lifted the landline. An operator with a lilting greeting offered assistance. "Senor Estrada is hurt. Send an ambulance," he told the operator in easy Spanish.

"We have already dispatched," the operator replied quizzically. "We have unfortunately been delayed. What is his condition?"

"Dead." Before the operator could press him

for details, Sebastian disconnected the call. What kind of murderer called for an ambulance? He replaced the receiver and, as he spun away, caught sight of an answering machine. Realizing the messages had already likely been erased, he started to leave.

"What the hell?" he said softly. With his hand still covered, he pressed the PLAY button on the answering machine.

Two messages played, one reminding Estrada of a dental appointment and a second offering him a seat on an excursion to the Yucatán. Sebastian heard a long pause, then a third message played. The voice that spilled into the dining room was female and feminine, strong and heady and filled with the mysteries Sebastian preferred to avoid in women. The lightly accented voice slid out of the machine like silk, winding around Sebastian and sinking into him. Disregarding the punch of desire, he focused on the message. "Tio Felix? It's Katelyn. I'm leaving Lima now. I should be arriving as scheduled tonight, probably by seven o'clock. I can't wait to see you. It's been too long."

Katelyn. Kat. "Damned Kat," Sebastian muttered as realization dawned. He jabbed the delete button and hastily checked his watch. The digital readout told him that Felix's niece had probably been around for his murder. More than likely, she'd been holding the knife.

No wonder the dying man had begged him to find her, Sebastian realized. Find Kat, and he would not only get his retirement back, he'd be able to hand Estrada's killer over to the authorities. Maybe even collect a reward.

In the distance, Sebastian heard a car backfire and remembered his ill-advised call to the authorities. The ambulance would be there in a few minutes, with the police soon to follow. Quickly, he moved past Estrada's body, murmuring an apology for the sacrilege. The wet stains from his cleanup glistened. The police would have to use special equipment to find the residue and link it to the murderer's escape, and Sebastian didn't doubt that they would. Especially with the stink of chlorine to warn them. But erasing the footprints would give him a lead on the missing Kat and her ill-gotten gains.

Sebastian retrieved his rented truck from the alley three blocks away. He climbed into the cab and rummaged through his duffel bag for a change of clothes. Reaching over the seat, he snagged a discarded plastic bag and brought it to the front of the vehicle. The sticky patches of his blood-soaked clothes peeled away with effort. Sebastian yanked his shirt free, oblivious to the play of muscle that had enticed more than one woman. He wadded the dirty shirt and shoved it onto the floorboards. Squirming a bit, he shucked his jeans and awkwardly pulled on a fresh pair of pants. The bloody clothes went into the bag, which he shoved inside the duffel's interior. He'd keep the clothes until he had a chance to incinerate them. DNA had become too effective a trace to run any risks.

"I hate murder," he muttered to the empty

car. Killing was messy and led normally sane people into the trap of revenge. Not him, he reminded himself as he turned over the truck engine and aimed for the beach. He'd find Katelyn and take the Cinchona and escort her to the nearest authority. Let the people paid to care about justice sort out her punishment.

Without clear tracks to follow, Sebastian took a guess that she'd probably flee toward the uninhabited parts of town. He drove swiftly, competently, down near the beach, where the sand slid into valleys that rose into the edges of the mountains. There, his astute brown eyes caught where footprints became tire tracks, despite the gathering dark. He jerked the steering wheel, aiming the truck at the base of the mountains. Even with her head start, there were only so many places to go.

As the truck bounced over rocks and gripped at the rocky soil, Sebastian wondered how he'd come to be chasing a murderess in the Andes. Recovering the manuscript should have required picking a few locks, cracking a safe or two, and catching the next flight out. Instead, he was chasing a—was there a word for a woman who killed her uncle, he thought absently. He cranked down the window, the cool night air providing a little respite, and he cursed the elusive Kat.

He despised when simple became unnecessarily complicated. This job was to have been his last hurrah. A final, straightforward caper to send him into glorious retirement. Maybe find another way to fill his time. To relieve the restlessness Estrada had accurately identified.

In recent days, he'd been forced to reexamine his life, a habit he hoped to break soon. He made it a policy not to be too introspective. Still, after watching two of his friends struggle to regain control over their destinies, he'd become preoccupied with the irksome notion that his line of work might not be as fulfilling as it once was.

For both Erin and Mara, love, an affliction he still planned to avoid, had figured heavily in solving their problems. Love required steadiness and perseverance and paying attention to someone else's needs, none of which were in his genetic coding. But the contentment he'd seen in both of them had caused a reaction that felt too close to longing for his taste.

On the ground, mud tracked over rock, a sign that someone had recently driven out of the valley and up the drier terrain. Sebastian steered the truck to follow, his eyes sharp on the land revealed by the high beams of the headlights. He wished he'd taken more time to study the topography of Bahia. That he hadn't was a sign he was getting too settled for a life that demanded constant alertness.

Not, he cautioned himself, that he regretted the past fifteen years of petty larceny and grand heists—twenty, if he wanted to get technical. He enjoyed the thrill of finessing the tumblers of a lock, the ingenuity of jury-rigging a rappel to escape from a Swiss chalet with a million dol-

lars in bearer bonds. At thirty-five, he appreciated the style to which his line of work had
permitted him to become accustomed. His penthouse on West End Avenue in Manhattan was a
far cry from the sixth-floor apartment in Harlem
where he'd lived as a child.

"All courtesy of flexible morals, a genius for
acquisition and a keen eye for the bottom line,"
Sebastian congratulated himself aloud. He lived
a life most men only dreamed about. No cares,
no commitments, and ample money to stay that
way as long as he breathed. Snorting, Sebastian
dismissed the minute ache that had taken up
residence just beneath his breastbone. *Probably
just indigestion.* Seconds later, a loud *pop* signaled
the blowout of his right front tire.

He jerked the wheel hard to the left, just in
time to hear the rear tire on the passenger side
explode, rock spurting beneath the shredded
rubber. Stone bounced against metal, and the
truck listed dangerously. Slamming on the
brakes, he guided the truck to a skidding stop.
He killed the engine, but left the headlights on
to break the dark. Beside his duffel bag, he kept
a toolkit with his tricks of the trade. Gathering
the bag, he leaped out and circled the truck, bemused. Two blowouts in as many seconds meant
either his truck was crappier than his supplier
warned him or his ascent had been discovered.
The tingling at his nape warned him that Luis
had not sold him a bad ride.

Crouching, he crept around the vehicle to
catch sight of his assailant. Beyond the ragged

tires, shadowed hills mingled with slate gray rocks and stubbornly green bushes clinging to rock face. Sebastian scanned the hills and the thick nests of trees, but in the heart of night, even his excellent vision had its limits.

After almost three minutes of steady observation without another incident, he reconsidered the possibility that his natural alarm had failed him. His skin still prickled with suspicion, but he had no proof. No more shots had rung through the valley. He cast for signs of movement in the clumps of green but heard nothing but the rustle of wind and light movement that could only be the most graceful of animals. He knew of few humans who could melt into the scenery so well and move quietly enough to fool even the birds.

No, he decided. The assailant he had to contend with was Fate, which left him with two flat tires in the middle of the night on a hillside. With a sigh, he moved with a fluid stride to the rear of the vehicle and started to rummage for a jack and a spare tire. He circled the truck to the front flat.

The tingling became a terrible itch seconds before a blunt, heavy object hit the side of his head and he went down, toolkit flying a few inches in front. Just out of reach.

"What the hell?" To evade the next blow, he scrambled forward, abrading his palms on the rough terrain. He managed to surge into the glow of the headlights and began pushing himself up, ears ringing. Before he gained his feet, a warm weight landed on him, corralling his hands and blocking his arms. "Ooof!"

In the next moment, three things occurred to him. One, he always needed to trust his instincts. Two, Bahia was not a soft country. Rocks and other pointy objects littered every free surface, as the jagged edges digging into his abdomen attested. And three, he was 90 percent certain that Estrada's Kat was straddling his prone body and had a gun to his head.

"Who the hell are you?" the dusky voice demanded against his ear.

"Sebastian Caine," he answered quickly. "I am a friend of Felix's. Who are you? Kat?"

The cool metal pressed firmly against his temple. "I'm asking the questions," came the hard retort, but the gun wavered at the mention of her name.

As punishment, she shifted her weight, and Sebastian gasped as stones pressed into his kidney. And lower. He spat out a curse. "If you plan to castrate me, there are more humane ways," he muttered.

"What?" she asked, startled by his accusation.

"There is a particularly spiky rock that's close to limiting my family options," Sebastian explained brusquely.

Mortified, Kat scrambled to her feet. "Slide over, facedown." When he started to move, she cautioned, "Remember, I've still got a gun."

"I haven't forgotten," he muttered. After he'd found a comfortable spot, Sebastian exhaled in relief, then glanced up at his captor. Even from his awkward vantage point, he could see that she was tall, willowy, and lushly curved. In the light, she was pale brown, a sun-kissed shade; her face had been composed of broad strokes with an artist's delight. Toffee-colored eyes glared at him from beneath winged brows that arched into natural distrust. Beneath the wary eyes, diamond-edged cheekbones drew his gaze to a wide mouth that was bold and deliberately unpainted. No classic beauty, Katelyn was a gorgeous Amazon, a true femme fatale with a fierceness to match.

Sebastian invited smoothly, "Feel free to climb back aboard."

For the umpteenth time, Kat realized she was out of her depth. She had been perched on a cliff, watching the dark truck scramble higher into the foothills, eerily following her exact path. She'd used Felix's gun to shoot out the tires, as she'd seen raiders do once in Uganda. Like it had there, the truck spun out, and the driver left the vehicle for safety. A stout branch had taken care of the rest. She wasn't trained for interrogation or espionage or guerilla warfare. She was a scientist and a scholar, whose most exciting adventure had been eating supper with the Rom in Hungary. Now it was up to her to figure out who the very tall man sprawled on the hillside was and what he had to do with Felix's murder.

As she thought of her uncle, the grip she held on the pistol tightened. Adrenaline mixed with sorrow, and the combination fueled the fury that had kept her upright.

She'd seen the faces of her uncle's killers, but she didn't recognize the man who called himself Sebastian Caine. All she knew at that moment was that he had look of a dark lord—tight, sexy, and remorseless. He reminded her of a younger Merlin she'd seen in a movie once, where he had whipped the sea into a frenzied storm upon command. Watching Sebastian, she imagined that should she come too close, he would cast a spell over her, binding her to his fate. Instinctively, she took a couple of steps away.

"Who sent you?" she demanded urgently. When his gaze followed her retreat, she forced her feet to move her closer, to stand near his prone body but a safe distance away. Shrugging off the fanciful thoughts of wizards and warlocks, she leveled the gun. Better this way, she told herself. Superior positioning, in case he tries to make a move. Holding the pistol steady, she barked again, "Who sent you?"

"Felix. He told me to find you." Sebastian figured the truth couldn't hurt. The moon hung high in the mountains, illumining the woman who had taken Estrada's life. She didn't strike him as a killer, but he'd been wrong about women before. "He told me to look for Kat. Just before he died from that stab wound you gave him."

The news of Felix's death nearly buckled her knees, her vain hope that her call would save him snuffed out. Only her promise to him kept her upright. *Play it out, Kat,* she warned herself silently. *Tio Felix is depending on you.*

The man who had snuck into the house as she crept out had not been one of the men who tortured Felix, but she didn't trust him. But he seemed to believe she was the murderer. She had to know why. Trying for bravado, she nudged Sebastian's hip with her booted foot. "Felix is dead. Which should remove any lingering doubt from your mind about what I'm willing to do to you," she snarled.

"Given the handy way you shot out my tires, I have no doubts about you at all," Sebastian retorted, watching the play of emotion across the mobile face. "So, what kind of niece are you, exactly?"

"Niece?" The word startled her. *How did he know so much about her?*

"Your message on the answering machine. You called him *Tio* Felix. Is that the Spanish equivalent of a sugar daddy? Did he owe you money or something?"

Katelyn sputtered. "Are you accusing me of being his whore?"

"Not with a gun to my head, no." Sebastian decided to risk looking at her directly. His attacker was turning a lovely shade of pink. "We're both adults. If Felix was your lover, that's between the two of you. If, however, he was related to you, I have to wonder why you killed him."

Reminding herself to play along, Kat prompted, "Why do you think? I'm sure you have a theory, since you followed me up here. After all, if I am a murderer, you've taken a terrible risk. Why?"

Sebastian narrowed his eyes, all traces of humor vanished. "Because I think you know where the manuscript is. I think you stole it from Felix."

The condemnation in his tone lured Kat. Perhaps he, like her, had stumbled into this mess. He used Tio Felix's name as though they'd been acquainted. Even friends. Kat took a hesitant step forward, the vise on her chest easing for the first time in hours. Maybe Sebastian Caine knew what Tio Felix had given her, what he'd entrusted to her care. Intrigued by the unexpected possibility of an ally, she leaned closer, and asked softly, "Why do you care? What does it matter to you if I did?"

"If you've got the Cinchona, I'll pay you $250,000 for it."

Disappointment tumbled against a sudden wash of sorrow. He was not a friend, Kat realized. Which made him an enemy. "You'll buy the manuscript? The one I stole from a dead man?"

Sebastian heard the disgust, but refused to be discomfited. After all, the lady had stolen it and likely killed to get it. How dare she be disappointed in him. He had a job to do, and he'd gladly part with a share of his fee to get this entire gig over with as soon as possible.

With a nod, he confirmed his offer. "Give me the manuscript and after I pay you, I'll forget Felix Estrada and his entire family, nieces included." Rolling onto his side, he propped himself up on a bent arm and smiled winningly. Overhead, bright stars danced in a clear indigo sky. "Come on, Kat. Do we have a deal?"

Chapter 3

Taking a chance, Sebastian eased into a sitting position, his hands above his head. She seemed distracted by his offer, yet her grip on the .22 millimeter remained steady. "Felix Estrada was a good man, but he's dead now, God rest his soul. You have something I need, and looking at you, I expect a cool quarter of a million dollars wouldn't hurt you." The faded khakis shorts she wore hugged generously rounded hips and framed sleek thighs. Her tank top was frayed around the edges, the indiscriminate color of its origin now a dingy gray. Whatever she did for a living, it didn't pay well. As good an explanation as any for murder.

"And all you want is the manuscript?" Kat repeated. *My uncle's life for your fortune.*

"That's it. Plus, I swear not to mention your name to the authorities. Money and anonymity. It's a great offer." He didn't mention that the only name he could offer the police was

Katelyn. A small clue—not worth the breath. Besides, Sebastian didn't voluntarily speak with cops. Ever.

"You're the type of man to make this kind of offer, aren't you?"

"What? The lucrative kind?"

"No. Amoral." Kat cocked her head, examining him. The hollowed cheeks, the clever, brown marble eyes, the arrogant curve of a mouth that seemed to permanently smirk. Beautiful, she thought, but empty. "You barter with a murderer for paper? No pesky conscience?"

"Getting a lecture about conscience from a woman who, at the very least, left her uncle to die seems a bit absurd to me," offered Sebastian pointedly. He was the first to admit that his moral code contained very few lines. But the lady had no right to judge him. Still, the slight pang he felt reminded him vaguely of chagrin. "A conscience is inconvenient in our line of work, isn't it?"

"Convenient?" Kat waved the gun, as though to beat back his pronouncement. More to herself than to her captive, she whispered, "There wasn't time."

Dropping his hands, Sebastian propped his elbows on his knees. His toolkit was within reach, and he had a knife in the bag. Assuming he could distract her. Keep her talking, he decided. "Time for what? To wait for him to die? Or to at least cover the body before you made a clean getaway? Even those of us of flexible honor make time for the niceties."

"I didn't—that is, I don't—there wasn't time." Kat shook her head. "Oh, God."

Sebastian watched as she slowly began to tremble, her body silhouetted against a cropping of trees. Kat, the murderer, fascinated him. In one instance, she blushed at the thought of being Felix's lover, and in the next, she calmly admitted to deserting the dying man. Now she trembled like a leaf. A trickle of warning skittered along his spine. Complicated women had an appalling effect on him—he became distressingly forthright, honest, and dependable. He frowned. "Why did you kill him, Kat?"

I didn't. The protest caught in her throat, and she could hear her uncle again, demanding her promise as she knelt by his side, trying to stop the rush of blood that seemed endless.

The Cinchona, Kat. Take it. Finish my work, gata. And return it to its people. Tell no one.

I have to call the ambulance. I have to get help.

No! Finish this and return the Cinchona. Do not fail me. Swear it.

I swear.

She'd called the ambulance and retrieved the manuscript and diary from its hiding place, only to discover another intruder in Tío Felix's house. He'd warned her to go, and, because she'd promised, she ran.

Stop it, she told herself sternly. Perhaps she could have done more, but she hadn't. The only way to make it right was to fulfill her promise and finish his quest. And find the men who killed him.

She had one lead to follow. One other human being who knew the name of the Cinchona. Sebastian Caine. He would tell her where she could begin.

"We're not going to talk about this here." Resolved, Kat motioned to him with the gun. "Stand up. Slowly."

Sebastian gained his feet and rubbed at the back of his head. "What the hell did you hit me with?" As soon as he asked, he saw the stout limb lying behind her. "You could have given me a concussion," he accused.

"Next time, I'll try harder." With a slight smile, she gestured him toward the thicket of trees. "It's going to rain soon. We need to move."

Sebastian stared up at the clear, cloudless sky. "No way."

Kat didn't argue. Instead, she moved behind him and jabbed him once with the barrel. "Walk slowly. Straight ahead, between that stand of quina trees. We've haven't much time." She inhaled deeply, nodding to herself. The unpredictable weather of the Andean range in the summer meant brief but powerful thunderstorms that rarely made it beyond the mountains to the ocean. Rains appeared suddenly, then disappeared in a flash. They had twenty minutes, she guessed, to make it to the cave where she had set up camp.

Sebastian stood his ground. If she didn't want the money, he had no idea what she'd do with him the higher they went into this remote section of the Andes. He'd rather take his chances with a disabled truck and the Canete authorities. Luckily, the keys were still in the ignition. If he could get to them. With a self-deprecating grin, he asked, "Can I get my stuff from the truck? I assume you may want to keep me hostage for a while."

Kat shook her head. "I'm not an idiot, Mr. Caine. I let you near the truck, and you'll disappear. No way. We move. Now."

Thwarted, Sebastian took defeat in his stride. "Worth a try. Can you at least grab my toolkit?"

She bent to retrieve the bag, eyes trained on Sebastian. Feeling its weight, she decided to hold on to it. "Let's move."

Obediently, he began to hike over the hilly soil, following a trail of sorts. His captor moved like a gazelle, leaping over the snarled branches and treacherous stone at an admirable pace. He fancied himself in excellent shape, but within minutes, his breathing was heavy, tightened by the altitude. Behind him, Kat barely sounded winded.

"Are you from the mountains?" he puffed, as they scrambled over a ridge. "You haven't broken a sweat."

"I've lived in many places," she admitted. "I'm adaptable."

Sebastian stopped his climb, turning to face her. "Are your parents missionaries or something?"

"A naturalist and an anthropologist," she

responded without thinking. When she realized what she'd revealed, she glowered at him.
"No more questions. We need to move quickly."
Kat gestured to him with the gun again, and
he began to hike faster.

Minutes later, they emerged from the trees
into a clearing. Her Jeep stood in the middle of
the open space, shrouded by the surrounding
foliage. At the edge of the clearing, a cave hollowed out the sheer wall of stone. Branches had
been readied for a fire, which would have to
wait.

"I assume you plan to tie me up somehow,"
Sebastian offered. "Tell me where the rope is."

"You're very cooperative," Kat said, suspicious of his good nature. "Why?"

"I believe in honor among thieves, Katelyn.
We do what we must to survive." He shrugged
philosophically. His good humor was part cunning, part nature. Anxiety clouded the judgment and made a man act sloppy. If the sleek,
gorgeous Kat found him agreeable, they'd
reach a mutually beneficial arrangement all the
sooner. "Obviously, Estrada did something that
made you think you had to kill him. My goal is
to not give you a reason to shoot me. So, where
do I go to be bound?"

Bemused, Kat pointed him inside the cave. A
pallet of a sleeping bag and a thermal blanket
was neatly laid out at the rear of the cave. Closer
to the entrance, a camp lantern sat on a natural
ledge that jutted out of the rocks. A dark blue
backpack leaned against the cavern wall, bulg-

ing from its contents. She dropped his toolkit next to her items. "Go over there."

Sebastian scanned the cramped quarters. At six-three, the ceiling barely cleared his head. And while he couldn't touch the side walls with his arms spread, it was a close thing. The cave was longer than it was wide, he noted, the lantern barely piercing the dark far wall. Probably thirty feet in length, the cave had burrowed deep into the mountainside. Depending on where she put his toolkit, he would be on his way inside twenty minutes. Unless she gave him cause to stay. And given the day he'd had and the endless legs on his captor, he could be persuaded. He made his way to where she indicated, muscles loose and ready. "Okay."

"Open the backpack," Kat instructed as she lit the camp lantern. "There's a length of cord inside. Tie one end around your right wrist. Tie the other end to your ankles. No more than six inches of give."

Sebastian followed her instructions, impressed by her sangfroid. Maybe she had done this before, he conceded. He moved to the pallet to sit and quickly wrapped the cord around his wrist. The bungee cord had clips at both ends, which he left free. "Done."

Kat walked over to where he sat, tethered. She laid the gun behind her, out of his reach, and swiftly looped the remaining cord around his left wrist. She leaned in close to wind it behind his back. At that angle, her body brushed his, and a slow burn began in her belly.

Sebastian remained perfectly still, with only the thud of his pulse an indication that he was aware of her presence. He had no intention of remaining trussed up for long. As she assumed, he had been held captive once too often to be held for long. But for his plan to work, he had to focus on something besides the feel of her pressed to his side, a yielding of firm softness he found quite appealing.

Clipping the ends together at the base of his spine, Kat eased away from the strong, warm body that seemed to pour off heat. With a furtive look, she met his eyes, which were two points of fiery dark. She swallowed hard, and whispered, "I think that's tight enough."

A scent that reminded him both of the outdoors and sultry, sexy nights invaded his senses. He leaned close, the space between them disappearing. "You might want to check it again," Sebastian suggested, the words a low rumble of sound.

"Ah, no," Kat managed as she jerked away from temptation. Sebastian Caine was quite possibly the most beautiful man she'd ever seen. And the most dangerous.

Like the urge to sink in rather than run away.

He lured her, his body warm and alive. And she was cold. So very cold. Suddenly, the weight of the past hours crushed down upon her. She had to get out of here, get into the air to breathe. The fear and apprehension and grief wouldn't let her breathe. Kat clambered to her feet, tears pressing behind her eyes.

Once again, she could hear Tio Felix's voice pleading for mercy. A mercy the men refused to show him. Pursued by the sounds, she rushed out of the cavern and into the night. *Everything was wrong!*

She stood on the ledge, memories crashing through her, rending her. Burning sobs caught her hard, and she shook with grief for endless minutes. Then Kat noticed that the wetness on her cheeks was also coming from above. The summer storm she'd predicted had arrived on time. Fat drops of rain fell from the sky, drenching her in a matter of seconds. Kat stood in the torrent, her heavy mass of hair coming unbound to cascade around her shoulders. The thick skeins of chocolate brown fell to her waist, and she felt the weight of them at her back.

Abruptly, she felt something cool and hard press against her. A sob strangled out on a terrified laugh. "I left the gun inside, didn't I?"

Sebastian nodded, though she couldn't see him. "Yes, you did. And I carry a knife in my toolkit. You should have searched it. A rookie mistake, but you've had a hard day, Katelyn. Why don't you come inside so we can talk?"

With a forlorn sigh, she turned to him, and he saw the silvery glimmer of tears. His hand lifted to wipe at the moisture, a tenderness that disturbed him. Women and weeping didn't move him. Mata Hari had tried similar tricks, learned from her forebears. All the evidence pointed to Kat as a murderer, not a hapless young woman way out of her depth, shaking from the force of her grief.

Suddenly, though, he had to know for certain. "Inside, Kat. Now," he instructed gruffly.

Having little choice, Kat led the way inside the cave. The cool air inside chilled her wet skin, and she shivered. "Can I build a fire?" she asked quietly.

"Sorry, no. But you can wrap the blanket around you." Sebastian tossed it to her, and he tried not to stare at the damp tank top. But the effect of the night air on the sweetly rounded curves the top attempted to conceal was having an equally potent effect on him. As were the tracks of the tears that were drying on her flawless skin. Though he knew better, Sebastian had a hard time believing a woman so despondent could be a cold-blooded killer.

Kat didn't notice his attentions, focused instead on how miserably she'd already failed in her task. Resigned, she sank to the cold, hard ground and tucked her bare legs beneath her, scraping the skin. She'd lived in worse places, with more dangerous men. Still, more than likely, he'd kill her here, and no one would notice.

Eventually, her parents would miss her, but it would be weeks before they knew anything was amiss. Her e-mail from Canada had told them that she was on her way to her uncle's home in Bahia. Though her parents' home base remained in Miami, they were traveling through Gambia. Her mother had decided to trace the family roots in western Africa, and her father was investigating the sighting of a presumed-extinct insect in nearby Mauritania. They might pick up the message in a week, long after Sebastian had killed her and left her body to rot.

As though he'd read her mind, Sebastian took a seat on the cold ground beside her and offered, "I don't plan to kill you, Katelyn. But you have something I need. I'm still willing to pay you for it, provided you tell me whether or not you killed Felix."

Kat glanced at the gun beneath his hand. "No."

"No, you won't tell me?"

She shook her head. "No, I didn't kill Tio Felix. And yes, he really was my mother's older brother."

Sebastian disregarded the surge of relief and focused on ferreting out the truth. He leaned back on his left hand, the muscles in his forearm bracing to support his weight. The right one remained on the gun. "You were there, Katelyn. I saw your footprints. You tracked his blood out of the house."

She flinched and insisted, "I was there when he was stabbed, but I didn't kill him."

He arched a brow. "Didn't try to save him either."

The images swamped her again, jagged and painful. "No. I didn't. I hid and did nothing to stop them from hurting him."

"Them," Sebastian repeated, stretching out his legs and crossing them at the ankle. He relaxed, knowing that the deceptive posture often lulled the frightened into comfort and confession. It held the added advantage of letting him block her should she try to run. The gun would serve as a prop only, with the safety on. "Who is 'them'?"

"Three men." She shuddered with the recollection and scrubbed briskly at her skin beneath the warmth of the blanket. From the hidden closet in the hallway, where she used to play hide-and-seek in the great house with its secret rooms, she listened to her uncle's murder. "Two men held his arms while the third one stabbed him. He was such a slight man. They hurt him, squeezing his arms. I heard one break." She caught her breath, refusing to break down again. "I hid. While they killed him, I hid."

Straightening, Sebastian nodded. "Smart. You don't engage anyone who has better firepower or more strength unless you've got some other superiority."

"I let Tio Felix die."

With a shrug, he countered baldly, "And you survived. That's a net gain, kiddo. If you'd tried to help him, I'd have found both your bodies tonight."

"Maybe you should have!" She snapped out the retort, her shoulders taut, hands emerging from the folds of the blanket to gesture anxiously. "I hid until they left, called an ambulance that never arrived. When you came, I stepped in his blood and ran away. I'm a coward."

"You were smart." Sebastian gripped her restive hands, always a sucker for a woman's bravery. He released the butt of the gun, unconcerned. "Don't be an idiot now. There was nothing else you could do. Try to play the hero, and they'd have killed you too. And I could have been one of them, coming back for the spoils. You called for help, then you did what you had to do. You got out alive. It's the best any of us can do." He watched his words slide over her, seeing that she didn't believe. Sebastian knew from experience that she wouldn't. Not yet. Instead, he focused on what he could accomplish. "Did they find what they were looking for, Kat?"

"No," she murmured, lost in her self-flagellation, her shoulders bowing beneath the weight. She'd failed Tio Felix, so quickly. Now, Tio Felix's death would go unavenged, his life's work sold to the highest bidder. Despite everything, though, Sebastian's words brought a modicum of comfort. "I found it first."

Sebastian froze. *She found it first?* Her admission brought a swell of relief, the first he'd felt since he stumbled over Estrada's body.

As he suspected, Kat had found the Cinchona in her uncle's safe. But he hadn't seen it in the cave. He'd searched her gear when he'd freed himself, but all he'd come across was an old diary, which surely wasn't the ballyhooed Cinchona. The Spanish on the pages was Castilian and some dialect he didn't recognize. Still, he

understood enough to know the journal contained the mundane ramblings of a priest unhappy with his assignment to the New World.
Those writings were valuable to a nerdy histo-
rian, but not nearly worth what he was being
paid to recover it. Since the diary wasn't the
prize, the Cinchona was still out there, somewhere. He was sitting with the one person who
should know.

Keeping his voice gentle, he shifted toward
her, probing, "Where is the Cinchona, Katelyn?
Where did you put it?"

Katelyn heard the question, realized what
she'd admitted. She glared up at him, eyes
drenched but blistering. Jerking her hands free,
she bit out, "I won't help you."

"Help me what?" he asked artlessly, eyes
measuring her reaction. The high color and
murderous look she aimed at him spoke volumes.

"I won't help you steal the manuscript," she
spat, scooting away from him. Her spine brushed
stone where it curved into the entrance. Sebastian sat feet away, tantalizingly close to the prec-
ipice. How had she fallen for his charade, the
show of understanding cloaked in camaraderie?
The brief surrender incensed her. She'd taken
Psychology 101, understood the basic premise of
befriending your prey. And had tumbled with
the first good line.

Luckily, she hadn't capitulated. Completely. If
he killed her now, all he'd be able to show for
her death was the diary of a priest named Father

Borrero. Hardly worth her life, but obviously, she and Sebastian had different values. Still, he didn't strike her as the type of man who would murder for profit. More likely, he'd try to charm her into submission, just like before. No doubt, given sufficient time and barriers as fragile as hers, he'd be a great success. The Cinchona would rot in the tree where she'd stuffed it before she told him where to find the manuscript. Feigning a bravado she didn't feel, she demanded, "Do your worst. I won't help you find it. I've put it where you'll never find it."

Her declaration had Sebastian revisiting his conclusion about the Cinchona. Surely, she didn't imagine her childish game of hide-and-seek with a diary had worked. Hoping he misunderstood, Sebastian quizzed, "The diary? That's the Cinchona?"

Katelyn startled. She'd stashed the manuscript near where she'd ambushed Sebastian and hidden the diary among her belongings, to read later tonight. Had hidden well, she'd thought indignantly. Crossing her arms, the blanket slipped off her shoulders to pool around her in waves of deep blue. She leaned forward, annoyed. "You found the diary? How?"

"It's what I do." Had done, in fact, as soon as her back was turned. At her look of pique, he complimented, "Clever, though, using the torn lining of your satchel. But I'm a pro."

"What are you going to do with it?"

"With the diary?" He focused on her question, on the tension threading her words. "Is the diary the Cinchona?" Sebastian lost his smile of indulgent humor. "Is it?"

He had no idea. The realization struck her like a thunderbolt. Sebastian had no clue that the diary wasn't the manuscript or that a second document existed. Latching on to the first glimmer of hope she'd had all day, she forced herself to nod reluctantly. "Yes," she conceded.

"You hide a manuscript worth half a million dollars in the lining of your bag?"

The tone of professional consternation nearly broke her outrage. "I didn't have much time to plan," she apologized automatically. "If you hadn't tracked me so quickly—"

"That's no excuse. If you're going to be in the business, you've got to take your job seriously."

"My job?" Kat shook her head. "This isn't my job, Mr. Caine. In fact, it bears no resemblance to what I do for a living."

The sneering condescension rankled, but Sebastian dismissed her contempt. Few accepted his line of work as a reasonable means to the ends he preferred. "I steal. So do most people, but when you tell a person she's being taken, it's called commerce. Is that what you are, Kat? A capitalist?"

Despite the maelstrom churning inside her, Kat found herself biting back a rueful smile. The man, for all his faults, was effortlessly charming. Almost funny. Steeling herself, she retorted, "What I do for a living doesn't require fleecing anyone."

"Good for you." So, she wasn't in business.

That left thousands of other options. Seemed he'd have to spend some time figuring out exactly what Katelyn Lyda did that paid her so poorly. Lucky for them both, he wasn't one for idle or unasked questions. "Then why did your uncle bring you here? What exactly could you have contributed?"

She started to respond, then remembered abruptly that they weren't acquaintances getting to know one another. "None of your business. In fact, none of this has anything to do with you. I have the Cinchona, and you don't."

"Technically," Sebastian corrected, "I have the Cinchona. And the gun." He lifted the black metal in sympathy. "I've got all the cards, Kat."

"Will you kill me if I don't answer?" Kat scooched farther away until her back hit the wall. "Or will you wait for your friends to join you?"

Sebastian started to move toward her. She flinched, a subtle movement that scratched at his underused conscience and bothered his ego. Women rarely recoiled from him, never in fear. "They weren't my friends, Kat."

"So you say," she taunted.

Clear dark brown eyes shifted to shadow in an instant. Sebastian rose to his feet lithely, no movement uncertain. "So I say, Katelyn, so I mean. I am not a killer."

"Then let me go."

Sebastian spun on his heel and gestured to

the cave opening. "Fine. You can go, but I'm keeping the Cinchona." He looked down to where she sat cross-legged on the ground. The sight of the frayed shorts and shabby tank top disturbed his sensibilities. Fair was fair—she found the diary, she shared in the pot. "But the offer is still on the table. How does $100,000 sound to you?"

Though she had no intention of taking the money, the cut-rate offer galled her. "Sounds like less than half of what you offered earlier," Kat protested. "You said two-fifty."

Sebastian shot her a disdainful look. "That was before I found it myself. Price went down."

"You found it in my bag," she argued heatedly. "You're a cheat."

He scowled, disliking the description. Thief and liar, he didn't mind, but a cheat was a lower form of life. Like a killer. "I'm a businessman. So we'll split the difference at $175,000. Deal?"

"No." Tired of staring up at him, she scrambled to her feet. "I don't want your money. I want to do what my uncle asked of me."

Coldly, he reminded her, "Felix is dead. Any promises made are null and void."

"Not to me. I keep my word."

"Bully for you. I don't give mine." Often. He kept the rest of the sentence to himself, remembering with a pang the promise he'd made to Estrada. Sebastian lied with impunity, but he was a scrupulously honest broker. He didn't take jobs he couldn't do, didn't seek payment when he failed. And he rarely gave his word because he didn't break it. Ever. "What did you promise your uncle?"

"That's none of your concern."

"Then we're at an impasse."

Knowing she was losing the battle, Katelyn cast about for a way to get the diary. She had the Cinchona, but Tio Felix seemed to think they were connected. She stepped forward, closing the distance between them. In the darkened space of the cavern, lit only by lanterns, the light threw shadows into every corner. She halted just out of his reach, her eyes somber, her voice steely. "You don't know what the Cinchona manuscript is, do you?"

He shrugged. "My client hired me to find a rare manuscript and deliver it. I don't delve too deeply into the nature of my targets. That's not my style."

"Perhaps it should be," Kat recommended.

"A difference of opinion." He didn't care for the details unless the details mattered. Her snide tone grated at him, but he resisted the urge to retort, with effort. Instead, he shrugged again. "Fine, enlighten me. I assumed the Cinchona was an obscure Spanish manuscript about the conquistadors or something."

"Or something." Because she knew so little herself, she chose her words carefully, spinning a story out of thin air. "Do you know the legend of the Incan gold mines?" she asked quietly.

Sebastian propped a booted foot flat against

the cave wall and leaned back, the gun held lightly in his grip, the safety on. "No."

"When the Spanish came to the continent, they tried to barter with the Inca. They wanted the Inca's gold."

"And they enslaved them to get it. So?"

"The Cinchona is reputedly the history of Pizzaro's band of conquistadors and their agreement with the Incan priests. In return for sparing the lives of the women, the Inca promised Pizzaro mountains of gold."

He'd skimmed the first lines of the diary, and the priest had indeed mentioned Pizzaro. "There were no mountains of gold."

"Technically, you're correct. There were no mountains of gold. But there were mines. Secret mines where the Incan royalty hid their treasure, waiting for the Spanish to leave. The Cinchona is supposedly the recitations of one of Pizzaro's priests, telling of the last sighting of the Incan gold."

Sebastian pushed away from the wall, eyes focused on Kat, skin humming with anticipation. "That's the Cinchona?"

A gifted storyteller, Katelyn leaned forward, inviting Sebastian to believe her lovely lies. "Yes. My uncle found the Cinchona, but he obviously told the wrong person. They killed him to get it."

"Ancient Incan gold?" He rubbed at his chin thoughtfully. A gold mine would be enough not only to retire to an island but to buy a whole chain. The image of warm, golden sand and warm, golden women shimmered before him. That the women looked hazily like Katelyn was a thought he didn't probe too deeply. "How long would it take to find it?"

Katelyn hesitated, not sure how long it would take to find imaginary gold. "Four days," she temporized. "We use the diary to find the mines. I need time to read it and decipher the Spanish and any codes. Four days and it's all ours, if we work together." Four days to find what the diary and the Cinchona actually led them to.

Four days to redeem her soul.

Sebastian smiled grimly. "And why do I need you?"

Her smug look should have warned him. "Because I'm the one who can read the diary's version of Spanish. Unless you studied Spanish with a native of Peru or Bahia, you don't know Quechua. The priest encoded his diary by writing in the tongue of the conquered. I learned Quechua from my family. Without me, you've just got a bunch of paper. Unless you find another partner."

"And why do you need me?"

This time, Katelyn spoke the truth. "There are men who murdered my uncle to get this secret, and I don't think they plan to stop. You strike me as one of their kind, and I am not as good at this as I need to be."

Trying not to be insulted, Sebastian considered her offer. He had the diary and at the first sign of trouble, he'd take it to Helen. Plus, he could keep his eye on Kat, as he'd promised Felix. Sebastian tucked the gun into his waistband and held out his hand. Patience had never been one of his two virtues. "Well, come on, partner. Let's get started."

Chapter 4

"You're tying my hands."

Katelyn checked over her shoulder and found her "partner" standing at the cave's entrance, legs apart, arms crossed. The slow tapping of his booted foot warned her that his patience was wearing thin. Tendrils of dawn broke through the copse of trees beyond the cave and sprinkled yellow and orange around him. He blocked the exit like a sentinel, his face about as welcoming.

"I'm going out to take a bath, Sebastian. That's all." She crouched three feet away, shoving a change of clothes into her satchel. Finished, she clipped the metal fastener and turned. Unused to looking up at men, she cocked her head back to look directly into the irritated eyes. "I'm your partner, not your prisoner."

"Then tell me, partner, where you've been trying to go since last night? And don't tell me you desperately desired a bath at two in the morning."

Her excuse blown, Katelyn opted for a partial response. "I need to think. Alone."

"Why does thinking require a bag?" Sebastian replied through gritted teeth. They'd been arguing since his eyes had opened and sunlight had pierced the cavern walls. He'd slept sitting up, propped against the rocky walls, and his temper had taken on a similar mien. After their truce, she'd tried to slip out into the night twice, and both times, he'd returned her to the cave. This was her third attempt at escape. He was tired and cranky and in no mood to bargain. "Do you understand the concept of partnership, Katelyn?"

"Yes, Sebastian, I do." She mocked his slow drawling of her name. "And I understand that you have something I want and I have something you want. More importantly, we both have information we have no intention of sharing with each other."

"Such as?"

"Such as who you're working for." She crossed her bare arms in front of her and watched in fascination as his dark eyes shifted from stormy to steely. The hard look in them made her take a step back. "I'm sure there's some agency out there that would love to know your whereabouts."

"Are you threatening me, *gata*?" Sebastian asked the question softly.

"No." Kat nearly took another step back, feeling stalked like hunter's prey. Part of her admired the effect, given that the man who spoke hadn't moved an inch. "No, I'm not threatening you. I am merely pointing out the obvious. You have secrets to keep, and I respect that. Why can't you?"

"Because only one of us seems hell-bent on sneaking away from camp." In a flash, the velvety baritone he used as a voice slid from hard to cajoling. "Kat, honey, I know you don't trust me. I don't expect you to. You haven't a reason in the world. Neither do I. So, excuse my concern and intractability when you keep trying to light out of here as though you already know where the gold is."

Through sheer force of will, Kat didn't react to his accurate guess. Twice during the night, she'd tried to sneak out to the grove of olive trees where she'd secreted away the Cinchona. She couldn't afford to leave it hidden, not with the unpredictable weather and native denizens of the mountains. The oilskin she'd wrapped around the centuries-old leather would protect it for a night, but no longer. More importantly, she had to have it when they reached their destination. And to know where in the world they were going.

Unfortunately, she couldn't tell him what she was retrieving, and she had no other good reason to leave the campsite. But once he announced at dawn that they needed to head into the city for supplies, she realized she had to recover the manuscript before they left for the oceanside.

Fixing her most agreeable expression into

place, Kat tried once more to reason with him. "Look. I need to go out. I'm leaving everything behind except for my pack. You've got the diary. What more do you want?"

"An explanation." The terse response was accompanied by a quick movement that left her arm empty and had her pack dangling from a wide, elegant hand.

Kat grabbed for the bag, but he simply pivoted away. "Give it back," she demanded vainly as he unzipped the seam and dumped the contents to the ground.

Before she could protest, Sebastian knelt to itemize the contents he had searched the night before. "A wallet. Passport." He flipped it open, flicked at the crowded stamps of the world traveler. "Benin. Cook Islands. Forgive my skepticism, Dr. Lyda"—he skimmed the bold name typed below the photo—"but you do get around."

"I travel for work," she explained thinly. Her posture stiffened, and she refused to bend to his level, literally or figuratively. "Give me my passport."

"Not yet. I didn't get a good look at your photo in the light last night. Lovely likeness of you." He lifted the folder slightly, comparing the picture and the living, livid reality. Enjoying her slippery grasp on her temper, he mused aloud, "I think I prefer your hair the way it is now. A river of chocolate silk."

Sighing, Kat reached for the document, trying to ignore the compliment and the warmth in her cheeks. "I want my passport, Sebastian."

"Of course you do. A passport will let you board a plane." Amused by her growing ire, Sebastian continued his inventory. "A padlock. I did find this interesting." He sifted through the tangle of clothes to the heavy object beneath. "You should try a better brand. I had it off this lockbox in four seconds flat." He flipped open the metal lid and exposed a plane ticket for one to Miami. "Ah, yes, the ticket to get you on your plane."

"Why do you care if I leave? You've got the diary."

"As you pointed out yesterday, my Spanish is good, my Quechua is lousy." He kept half an eye on the small brown boots that were within easy reach of his face. Once or twice, he thought they aimed at his teeth. Above his head, indignant breaths hissed in and out of the bag's owner. He snagged the tickets and shut the box. Satisfied and curious, he gathered the remaining items and dumped them inside the tan canvas pack. Swiftly, he closed the bag, rose, and draped one strap over her tense shoulder. He held the plane ticket, passport and wallet in one hand, above his head and out of Kat's reach. "What are you a doctor of, Dr. Katelyn Lyda?"

"That's none of your damned business. Give me my passport, my ticket, and my wallet. Now."

"I don't think you're a medical doctor," Sebastian pondered thoughtfully. He ran his eyes over the trim, toned body and the sturdy fingers curling into a fist. Last night, when those hands had cinched the cord around him, he'd felt the light edge of callus at the palm. "You must be a scientist, though. You know the weather, and you move like a mountain goat."

Before she could stop herself, Kat snarled, "You compare me to a goat?"

"No." He grinned at the very female annoyance. "I said you move like one. But I was more accurate yesterday when I thought you moved like a gazelle."

"A gazelle." For a moment, she absorbed the second casual compliment of the morning, and the answering heat from the eyes that studied her. Then her eyes fell on the black of her wallet. "Those are mine," Kat insisted. She refused to reach for the purloined items, too proud to jump up and miss. Instead, she opted for dignified anger. "You have no right."

With a dismissive shrug, Sebastian retorted, "I told you not to tie my hands." He tucked the wallet and passport into his pocket and tapped the ticket against his palm. "You can have them as soon as we find the gold. Not before." The arrangement seemed reasonable to him. She could traipse about as she pleased, but no one would put her on a plane to the U.S. unless she had contacts even he didn't possess these days. He peered out into the strengthening light. "If you want to clear your head, better make it fast. I'm breaking camp in an hour."

"Fine." Kat squared her shoulders and

shrugged the pack fully onto her shoulder. She'd be damned if she was going to fight with an overgrown thug who made his questionable living by stealing from old men and hapless women. She took a couple of steps forward, then her own description of herself as a hapless woman swirled in her brain.

She'd traveled for nearly a day without sleep, and had to watch helplessly while her favorite uncle was brutally murdered. She was hungry, exhausted, and in way over her head. And, damnit, she wanted her passport back. With a muted cry, she spun on her heel, dropped the bag, and launched herself at Sebastian.

Because he had turned to gather his own gear, Sebastian didn't seen the warning signs—at least that's what he told himself later. He heard a low sound and felt his knees buckle under the tackle. In a flash, he found himself for the second time in as many days sprawled on rocky terrain with an angry woman sitting on him. Precipitously close to being unmanned. Again. Rocks jutted out of the ground and poked him in excruciating symphony. Kat distributed her weight unevenly, most of her settled on his kidneys. And lower.

His normally even nature tilted screamingly toward exasperation. A simple job had become a wrestling match with a doe-eyed shrew with ungodly curves. "That tears it," he muttered, temper boiling over. In a deceptively languid move, he glanced over his shoulder. "Kat, you've got to the count of three to get off me. One."

Kat paid the soft warning no mind. Instead, she leaned forward to hold him still as she dug into his back pocket for her wallet. When her hand curved around taut, firm flesh covered by denim, she struggled not to give in to the unusual urge to pinch a stranger's butt. Hand burning, she closed her fingers gratefully around the leather square and jerked free.

Sebastian tensed at the feel of the questing hand, his blood pooling in more than anger. Dangerously, arousal surged to mix with fury. "Two."

Triumphant, Kat felt for her passport and tickets. Secure that she had him pinned, she followed the pump of adrenaline and instinct and reached beneath his whipcord lean body for his front pocket. The wrinkle of plastic heralded her find. She slipped her fingers inside to snake the tickets free. These were her things, and no one would take anything else from her without a fight.

"Ah-ha." She grasped the paper corner, but the tickets were wedged tight beneath their combined weight. Digging deeper, her fingertips grazed something harder and warmer than rock, and her breath hitched in her lungs, her skin sang.

"Three."

In a blur of motion, Kat found herself no longer astride a captive Sebastian; instead, she lay firmly beneath a looming, furious man. She tried to breathe, tried to think. But he filled her lungs, her vision. Smooth brown skin stretched taut over a face molded from fantastical, erotic dreams. Hot demon eyes bored into hers, coming impossibly close. Like the mouth hewn of stone, slicked with an unexpected softness. Close, wonderfully, terrifyingly close. So close, their breaths mingled in the cramped space between their lips.

Oh, my, she thought dimly. *He's going to kiss me.*

Damnit all, Sebastian realized, *I have to kiss her.* What he had intended when he flipped her beneath him vanished as he watched the lush, wide mouth part in anticipation. All he could remember was the incendiary brush of searching fingers against him. Beneath him, along every inch of him, the strong agile body pressed painfully, delightfully. "I warned you," he whispered. He reached between them and brought her eyes to his, the brown luminescent in the filtered sunlight. "You should have moved."

"I didn't." The tacit agreement fluttered out before Kat could reason. Unwilling to give herself time to think, she lifted her head.

The first contact singed and burned and sang through Sebastian. He recoiled, unwilling to accept. But he lived to take what he shouldn't have.

Sebastian caught her mouth beneath his and tested the delicate seam between her lips. With gentle forays, he coaxed them apart, and when she opened to him, he sank inside. There, he found tastes too heady to resist. Sweet yielded to tart, melded into spices nature had not conceived. He shifted, gathering her to him, feasting.

Free to lift her arms, Kat curled them around his broad shoulders, her fingers sinking into the coils of black curls at his nape. How had she lived for thirty-two years without knowing that a kiss could be so—much? Overwhelming and tempting and satisfying and endless.

She angled her mouth, eager to explore this new experience, to understand the questions sifting through her hazy thoughts. The kiss was frenzied and desperate and tinged with a sweetness that fluttered in her belly. When his tongue touched and captured, she sighed, the exhalation becoming a moan when rough satin swept her mouth fully. "Sebastian."

"Katelyn."

The answering whisper of her name shivered through Kat, and she twined her arms tighter, determined to know every part of the hot, wet cavern of his mouth. Deeper and deeper, they tasted each other, both determined to sate longings neither had known.

Sebastian rolled, pulling Kat with him, her lithe body draped along him, her thigh brushing his turgid length. She shifted and the crackle of plastic echoed through the cave like thunder.

Her ticket.

As though struck, Kat jerked free and scurried off Sebastian. In her haste, she dropped her recovered wallet, not stopping her backward retreat until she smacked against rock.

Unable to believe that she'd been sprawled across a stranger, ready and eager, she fought against waves of mortification. And the spirals of desire that danced still.

Sebastian propped himself on one elbow and reached down to pick up the leather holder. He stuffed it into his pocket and drew up one leg to prop his other elbow against. The movement brought little relief, and now, he understood that nothing short of Katelyn probably would.

With a voice that sounded like flint striking stone, Sebastian offered a narrowed smile that spoke eloquently of their embrace. "Go on, *gata*. Run away. Clear your head. I won't try to stop you. But be back in one hour, or I'll come hunting."

"You mean looking," Kat corrected in a husky whisper.

The lean smile disappeared. "Whatever."

Kat scurried down the trail, checking behind her every few steps. Sebastian wasn't following her, but she found it hard to take any comfort in the fact. Her mouth tingled from his kiss, and her skin seemed to tremble wherever he'd touched. She felt bruised, battered, and utterly alive for the first time in her life.

The errant thought brought her up short, and she stopped at the base of the hill. She didn't consider herself boring. Maybe she paid her taxes in January and knew her bank balance to the penny, but she lived a life that most would consider thrilling. Traveling to exotic locales to study plants and people few ever encountered was far from unexciting.

But she'd never met anyone like Sebastian Caine before. He was gorgeous, infuriating and the last man on earth she should rely on. By his own admission, he was a thief, and a very good one.

Her pocket began to buzz and Kat fumbled inside for her forgotten cell phone. She glanced at the name on the screen and flipped the cover open eagerly. "Shelby?"

"The one and only." In Miami, Shelby Daniels reclined on a bed piled high with pillows, her foot propped on one as she painted her toes. She cradled the phone against her shoulder and sipped at her second white tea of the morning. "I called the hotel yesterday, but they said you'd checked out. I thought you were in Canada until next week."

"I decided to take a detour." Kat saw a fallen log and lowered herself, squinting against the sun. She desperately wanted to tell Shelby the truth, but caution had her hedging her story. "I'll be out of touch for a week or so. I probably won't be able to answer the phone again until I get back." Until Kat knew for certain who was after the Cinchona, it was probably safer to limit her contact with anyone close to her. But she needed the familiar, if only for a brief moment. "How are you? How was the audition?"

"I got a call back, but we'll see. Lyssa Weaver is also up for the part, and you know how much directors love the way she can disappear by turning sideways. God, I'd love to strap her to a gurney and force-feed her ice cream." Shelby scowled, then relaxed her forehead deliberately. She had another screen test that afternoon, and every wrinkle showed. "I can't wait until fluffy hips are back in."

Kat smiled, familiar with her next line. "I heard a rumor they were coming back this fall."

"You lovely liar, you."

"Can you stop by my house and water my orchids?"

The request reminded Shelby of Kat's earlier pronouncement. "Wait a second. You decided to take a trip on a whim?" Her dearest friend hadn't had an impulsive moment in all of her thirty-two years. This was the same woman who had planned a detailed itinerary for their senior spring break trip that included the numbers for all local police stations in Jamaica and the quickest route to the embassy. Intrigued, concerned, Shelby probed, "Did you meet a dark, handsome stranger and decide to elope?"

"Not exactly," Kat muttered. "But close."

"Close?" As a woman who made her living in sound, Shelby was alert to nearly every nuance in Kat's voice. She could hear tension, sadness, and a husky note that had her capping her polish and sitting up straight. "What is going on, Kat?"

"Nothing. I finished my lecture series early and decided to take a trip to clear my head."

"Clear what out of it?"

"Cobwebs. Thoughts." Casting about for a good excuse, she added, "Alan Granger."

Shelby pounced. "Alan? You two broke up three months ago. And you did the breaking. I believe your exact words were that he was as predictable as allergy season and half the fun."

"He was a good man." Solid. Dependable. Mildly handsome without being overwhelming. Nothing at all like Sebastian, with his fluid morals, dangerous eyes that saw everything, and a sinful mouth to make her forget herself. "Dark, handsome strangers are overrated."

The note of exasperation came across the phone clearly, and Shelby demanded, "Where are you, Kat? Do you need help?"

Annoyed by her slip, Kat replied quickly, "I'm okay. Really. I've got some family business to take care of, and I had to do it now. I'll be home next week." *I hope. Assuming I survive until then.* But she kept the fears inside her head and forced a light tone into her voice. "I just have to finish up a project, then I'm back."

"Kat, you'd tell me if something was wrong, huh?"

Lying to her best friend for the first time in twenty years, Kat replied, "Absolutely. Now get off the phone, finish painting your nails, and break a leg. Love you." She pressed the end button before she was tempted to say more.

A glance at the time showed that she had to hurry if she was going to make Sebastian's deadline. Even after only a day in his presence, she had no doubt he'd make good on his threat. She scrambled off the log and ran along the path, oblivious to the rising heat. As she jogged, she thought about the choices she had to make. For now, she'd keep her deal with Sebastian and use his help to figure out what she was supposed to do with the real Cinchona. He'd told her not to trust him, and she wouldn't. But for now, she'd have to rely on him to survive.

Survival was her primary objective. And for once, she had no idea what would come next.

Chapter 5

Sebastian remained stretched across the cavern floor, watching as Katelyn hurried out of sight. Bright sunlight broke through the murky interior, scuttling the night creatures to their hiding places. The night's rain had washed the valley clean, leaving behind the ripe smell of piñon to tease the senses.

Normally, he would have tailed her to find out what she was hiding, but he didn't move. In the first place, their brief romantic tussle had him hard and ready and in no shape for a hike. Plus, he was fairly certain the little liar had hidden the real Cinchona away in some niche in the mountains and needed to retrieve it. When she returned in twenty minutes—and he was certain she would—her pack would be heavier, and she'd shield it like a mother bear protecting a cub. He'd gotten his last look inside her belongings for a while, but the aftermath had certainly been worth it.

Yes, he determined with a slow nod, she was

hell-bent on going out alone because the diary he couldn't read wasn't the Cinchona manuscript. After she'd fallen into a fitful sleep, he'd used his palm light to pick through the good father's ramblings. The tales of Spanish conquest had been mercifully vague on details but starkly clear on results. The Incans had been slaughtered from Ecuador to Peru, or conscripted into Pizzaro's army. Borrero hadn't found his new occupation as a junior conquistador compatible with his holy orders. Sebastian had waded far enough into the text to learn about Borrero leaving the order and wandering into the Bahian jungle.

That was the second time Kat woke up weeping. When he tried to offer comfort, like the first time, she tried to evade him and go outside. He thwarted that, and instead, she crawled back into her sleeping bag, the intermittent shudders his only signal that she didn't sleep. Part of him felt guilty for keeping her inside, but he didn't have many options. And she'd come out of the night as feisty as ever.

His erstwhile partner had survived the kind of trauma that drove grown men to their knees. Shaking his head, Sebastian stood up. Katelyn Lyda was definitely one of a kind, as strong inside as she looked from the outside. Grief had been redirected, fueled into a righteous indignation, and a passion that found its echo in him.

He needed to know more about her, he realized. His easy, last hurrah had been transformed into a tangled mess, with Dr. Katelyn Lyda at the center of it all.

When he was finally able to move, he strolled to his gear and removed the PDA that he'd linked to his throwaway account. He depressed the power button and waited for the little antenna to show him his mail. Soon, though, he discovered that accessing a server in the mountains of Bahia was no mean feat, and tucked inside a cave, the unit lost its signal.

He wandered out to the ledge, eyes scanning the scenery. Movement in the trees below had him craning forward, only to realize the figure was a grazing deer, not Kat.

With her speed and stamina, she was likely miles away by now, recovering the Cinchona from wherever she'd concealed it. Come to think of it, she'd probably hidden the manuscript from him while she watched his truck climb the mountains.

If he'd been in her position, he'd have left the papers secreted away until he'd shaken her loose. But with the sudden rains in this part of the country and her surprise partner, the smart move was to take the Cinchona with them. And the lady was plenty smart enough to know he'd be an excellent bodyguard as she took the manuscript somewhere into the wilds of Bahia. She had a mission she didn't intend to clue him in on, but she thought she'd manipulate him into helping.

Sebastian grinned at the young woman's cunning. Clever plan, he conceded. It's what he would have done. Turning away from the ledge, he reentered the cave and sat cross-legged on the hard floor, back against the wall, body out of sight from an intruder.

Slowly, he drummed a tattoo on his raised knee. What he hadn't figured yet was whether the Cinchona truly led to a king's ransom or not. Tales of an Incan mine filled with gold whose secret had been squirreled away in a priest's manuscript were fantastical. But what he'd seen of the diary gave her story credence. Borrero spoke of a treasure worthy of kings. In the sixteenth century, only gold commanded that kind of panegyric. And it explained Helen's urgency to recover the Cinchona. He rarely followed the market, but her company, Taggart Pharmaceuticals, was reeling from a bad drug that had made it to market and made millions of users violently ill.

A fortune in gold would go a long way to covering Helen's pretty ass.

If Katelyn was telling him the truth, there was nothing in his contract that said he couldn't find the gold himself. All through the night, the plan had appealed to him more and more. Spend four days traipsing through the Andean mountains with a smart, beautiful woman whose layers seemed to have layers. Find the gold, figure out the woman, get the manuscript, and make it to the airport in time to catch the red-eye to New York. His client would get her Cinchona, and he would jet off to Bimini to start spending his loot.

Perhaps he'd convince the mystifying Katelyn to join him, he mused. Sebastian drew his denim-covered legs into his chest and draped his arms across, elbows jutting into the quiet, shadowed space. Figuring her out would take some time, but he had a suspicion she'd be worth the effort. Obviously, Katelyn wasn't a pro—he could tell that much from her rookie mistake of leaving the gun behind.

Plus, finding her sitting in the rain, her face wet with tears, had moved something inside him. Something familiar and alien—the urge to comfort and protect, to soothe away her grief and assuage her guilt. He'd resisted the compulsion to join her in her bedroll simply to hold her last night, too aware that beneath the desire to comfort was a very male interest in the lovely scientist.

Though she had yet to tell him any more about herself, he fathomed that she spent her time thinking for a living. There was the telltale groove that appeared between her almond-shaped eyes as she contemplated her next move. The preternatural ability she had to predict the weather. Her ease with the terrain and her well-stocked hideaway in the cave. And the notebooks he'd found riffling through her belongings. The pages of graph paper recited formulas and referenced chemical compounds and some genus of plants he vaguely recognized. Definitely a scientist.

Probably a naturalist, given the gorgeous, fit body. As they bedded down last night, he'd had more time to examine his new partner. Her nimble, lushly curved form had the type of strength that did not come from hours aerobi-cizing or running on a treadmill. Her fitness climbing the mountains spoke of a life spent outdoors. She had stamina and grace and an al-lure that had made sleeping nearly impossible.

Instead, he'd perused the notebook he'd found, when he couldn't make sense of the di-ary anymore. According to her notes, she was trying to prove that some plant did something that pharmaceutical companies were eager to create artificially. He didn't understand most of her analysis, but there was enough to get the general drift. The notebook had him wondering once again why Felix Estrada had summoned his niece to Canete.

When he would have woken her to interro-gate, Sebastian found he couldn't. She'd slept fitfully, probably exhausted by her bout of tears and the crash that followed a rush of adrena-line. In repose, the stunning face settled into a serene beauty that echoed her heritage of Afri-can and Latino ancestry. A mélange of features that had culled the best of both worlds.

Of course, when she awoke this morning, he'd been struck by the fierce determination that fired her bravado as she bargained with him. She had an ulterior motive for wanting his help. Sebastian had less than a week to accom-plish his task, and he had no issues with spend-ing four days traipsing around Bahia with a lovely and suspicious Kat.

Particularly one who could kiss like she did.
He shifted, desire returning in a flash of memory. Hell, it had been a while since a single kiss
had rocketed through him like that. A frown
furrowed between his brows and, never one to
lie to himself, he admitted silently that his reaction to Kat's kiss had never happened before.
Ever.

He respected women. Adored women. Enjoyed the mystery of steel and satin that was
the essence of the sex. His best friends were of
the fairer gender, and God bless his mother
for her infinite supply of patience and bail
money.

Sebastian loved women, and they shared a
fondness for him. But never had one so quickly
spun him into heat and oblivion. Not until Dr.
Katelyn Lyda. He could still taste the mixture of
fascination and fear that clung to her. And the
grim determination to avenge Felix's murder.
He had to admire her and her attempts at subterfuge. She was playing in a dangerous game
she barely understood, and so far, she was holding her own. In another life, if he were a different sort of man, she was a woman he could fall
for easily.

In this life, though, she was the woman he
was about to swindle out of her uncle's dying
bequest.

With an ease of movement that spoke of his
time scaling less arduous terrain than mountains, he gained his feet. He'd conducted a swift
search last night to yield the diary, her wallet

and stuff, and her notebooks. While she ran her errand to retrieve the Cinchona, he would inventory the rest of their supplies.

The cave had been laid out with the rations used by experienced hikers who spent days away from civilization. Water, trail mix, and dried foods were neatly stacked near the bundle of sticks that could be quickly set to burn. A camp stove lay disassembled, a trio of metal sticks that appeared to expand into a tripod. Her sleeping bag was obviously well used, its army green pockmarked and worn. The lantern had a trimmed wick, and it rested beside a wide-mouthed flashlight that could cut through gloom with ease.

Then there were the books. Sebastian reviewed the spines, a mix of fiction and academic treatises on the medicinal uses of certain native plants. Five volumes had been tucked into her second bag, which held a few changes of clothes. Pairs of khaki hiking shorts and tops of faded color nestled against more filmy items that captured his attention. Dr. Lyda preferred silk and lace beneath her sturdy gear, he noted with a contemplative smile. Another of her intriguing contrasts.

"Why the hell are you pawing my underwear?" The tense accusation came from the opening of the cave.

Sebastian glanced up, his broad hand closed around a wad of pink silk. Kat stood in the shaft of sunlight, arms akimbo, eyes flashing. His duffel bag at her side. He smiled, unconcerned about the livid glare she aimed at him. "Thanks for bringing my things."

"Answer my question."

"I'm investigating you, Dr. Lyda. Trying to figure out exactly who you are."

"By rummaging through my underwear?" She hurried into the room. Sebastian knelt on the ground near her bag and didn't move. The man had no shame. Embarrassed and irritated, she squatted down to snatch the fabric from his hands. It was of no consequence that she'd done the same thing to him at the truck. She hadn't been caught. "If you want to know something about me, just ask. Stay away from my things."

"You decided to leave me here alone. Your mistake." She snagged his wrist, and Sebastian released the pink bra with its lacy border. "Pretty."

Kat started to rise until she realized that he continued to sift through the duffel bag's contents. "Cut it out." She reached for his wrist again to halt his search. Smooth muscle and sinew shifted beneath her grip, the skin warm and strong, and she nearly jerked away. The sweet ache she'd thought to have run off during her trek returned with a vengeance. Because she wanted to hold on, she let go. Instead, she turned her head, which was only a breath away from his, and hissed, "Stay away from my belongings."

Sebastian missed the feel of her cool fingers against his skin. Angling his head to watch her, he offered, "We're partners, Kat. And I don't work with people I don't know."

"Going through my underwear won't tell you anything important."

"To the contrary, darling. I already know a lot about you. You have five books with you but only three changes of clothes. Which means you didn't plan to be here very long, but you don't take chances on being bored." Sebastian lifted crimson panties designed to make a man beg. "This tells me that despite the rugged life you lead, you have a sensual streak and excellent taste." He murmured the last, his voice a low ebb of sound.

Her stomach tightened, and Kat found herself drifting toward the lure of Sebastian's voice. Abruptly, she realized what was happening and pulled herself back. "Stop touching my stuff!" Kat shoved the bag away from his hands. "Do you have any respect for privacy?" she demanded tightly.

"In my line of work, privacy is overrated." Realizing that he had pushed her far enough, Sebastian rose to his feet. Katelyn shot up beside him, anger flushing her caramel skin. The crown of her head skimmed just below his nose. An unusual but alluring match in height that he rarely encountered. "You are quite tall, aren't you?"

Katelyn resisted the urge to hunch her shoulders as she had growing up. Instead, she squared them and tilted her head back to meet his eyes. Around them, the air had grown heavy and still, no breeze coming in from the mountains. "So are you," she retorted.

"That I am," he agreed softly. Something arced between them, and Sebastian recognized the feeling. Pure, sweet desire. But they were on a rushed schedule, and any exploration of Katelyn would take several luxurious hours, hours they could ill afford. Grappling for slippery control, he offered wryly, "And I'm starving. Is that something else we have in common?"

In response, her stomach rumbled, the sound amplified by the cave. Unsteady, intrigued, she could only smile ruefully. "I think so."

"Good. That's something we agree on." He folded his arms across the black T-shirt. "One for one."

Kat nodded. "But I'm serious about you staying away from my things."

Sebastian tilted his head in a gesture of contrition. "Occupational hazard. One I will try to curb for the next few days."

"Thank you."

"You're welcome." He grinned again, his teeth a slash of white in the dim cave. "I'll do my best."

Kat thought the warm smile more dazzling than the sunshine that streamed outside. Once again, her stomach did the flip that had become ubiquitous in his presence. She blinked slowly, mahogany lashes fanning across her skin. When she opened her eyes, his were staring intently, and the smile had vanished. In its place was a look she recognized from that morning. A look that turned the stomach flip into a somersault. Recognizing the need for retreat, she inched away from the tall, hard man and turned toward the camp stove. "Um, I can make us some breakfast before we head into town."

"I'd appreciate it." Sebastian took a step away, too. "I'll be back in a minute." With that, he whirled around, stopping to scoop up his bag, and strode out of the cave and into the morning air.

Kat found herself releasing a breath she hadn't realized she'd been holding. "Oh, my. What am I doing?" The silent cave offered no response. Figuring she wouldn't get one, she moved to her stored equipment and retrieved the camp stove. With practiced moves, she set up the contraption, laid and lit a fire, and filled the pot with water. While it heated, she gathered ingredients for breakfast. Packets of oatmeal were stirred into the heated water, and the grains began to plump and thicken.

She left the oatmeal to cook and turned to her duffel bag and satchel. Swiftly, she scooped out the Cinchona, still wrapped in its protective oilskin. The slicker had turned away the worst of the rainfall. Reverently, she opened the manuscript, lifting her head every few seconds to check for Sebastian's return.

If she'd had her druthers, she would have spent her time alone this morning comparing the Cinchona to the notes in the diary. But her new partner had confiscated the diary, she remembered with irritation. Of course, he thought it was the real Cinchona. If she was to finish her mission, she'd have to keep him believing it. Kat lifted her head again, listening for the scrape of boot against stone that would signal his return. Hearing nothing, a plan formed.

She wrapped the manuscript in its oilskin and tucked the wrapped package into the base of her satchel, which she carried at all times. Then, after a glance at their bubbling breakfast, she did a quick search of the cave, looking for her stolen items. First, she opened his toolkit, rummaging through the interesting collection of metal rods and a wicked-looking knife with a serrated tip. Coming up empty, she turned to the rock face, wondering if he'd shoved anything inside.

"You're not going to find them, honey." Sebastian walked back into the cave, skin damp from his bath.

"Sebastian!" She dropped her hands from the crevice near his toolkit. He was dressed in the khakis and white T-shirt she'd found in his bag. The casual outfit highlighted the sheen of his skin and the exceptionally fit body beneath. "I was just—" She trailed off as he entered the cave, his eyes intent and focused on her.

Sebastian had no doubt what she was looking for. The wallet, passport, and plane ticket were safely stowed in his pocket. As for the diary, he did what the best thieves had done for centuries—he hid the diary in plain sight. The small book was within a few feet of Kat's searching hands, inside her duffel bag, but she was poking into the craggy rock, looking for their hiding place. "First rule of stealing, Kat. Never get caught."

With a sputter of frustration, Kat scrambled up from her search of the crevice near where he'd bedded down for the night. She leaned against the wall. "I wouldn't have if you made noise like a normal man. How did you do that?"

Sebastian wandered over to the wafting smell of oats cooking. He picked up a spoon and stirred the meal. Kat had set a stick of cinnamon and a miniature grater on the lip of the tripod. He gathered the tools and began to add the spice to the mixture. "How did I do what?"

Kat watched as he seasoned the oatmeal. *God, he has beautiful hands.* Remembering his question, she muttered, "How did you come in without me hearing you? I have excellent hearing." Annoyance mixed with approval. "You move like a shadow."

Finished with his task, he set the items down and turned to face her. "You're not exactly a noisemaker yourself, Kat. In fact, you are quite aptly named. I didn't hear you return this morning. Silent as a *gata*."

Kat flinched. "Don't call me that."

Instantly contrite, Sebastian crossed to where she stood. How had he forgotten that the young woman had lost her uncle yesterday? The uncle who called her *gata*. Stopping in front of her, he laid a gentle hand on her arm, rubbing along the chilled skin to soothe. "How are you doing?"

Kat felt tears threaten at the show of concern, but she willed them back. Instead, she let herself absorb the comfort of human contact and clung to her promise to Tio Felix. "My uncle is dead, and I'm partners with a thief." The last escaped on a strangled sob. "I don't know what I'm doing."

"Hell, you're doing better than a lot of people, Kat. At least you've got a thief for a partner. Better than an arsonist or a mime."

She chuckled involuntarily and swiped at a stray tear that escaped. "You can't be nice and funny. You're one of the bad guys."

"No, I'm in gray. But you are clearly a white hat." Giving in to impulse, Sebastian shifted her into a hug that brought her to his chest. She stiffened, then her arms slid around his waist to hold tight. Pressing her head into his shoulder, he whispered gently, "Felix would be proud of you, honey. You survived last night. And that's all you can do. Survive each day."

"It hurts. Knowing I failed him. That I didn't save him."

Sebastian brushed a soft kiss over the crown of her head. His hand stroked the long line of her back, pressing her closer. "Don't be a moron, Doctor. You did what you could. Felix played in a game he understood, where men and women will kill to get what they want. In that game, someone has to die."

At his stark words, Kat shivered and

squeezed him tighter, grateful for the warmth of his embrace. The sweep of his hand against her spine lulled her, reminded her that she hadn't been so close to anyone in too long a time. The questions bubbled inside, spilled out. She tilted her head to watch him. "Do you kill? To get what you want? Would you kill me?"

Sebastian's hand stilled. His hold tightened. Above her head, he stared out of the cave into the distant hills. "No. I don't kill. I've never had to. But I understand survival, Katelyn. I believe in it."

She inched away, and his arms permitted the movement. Kat raised her head to meet sable eyes that were hard and focused. "What does that mean?"

"It means that I won't die for a noble cause." Sebastian slackened his grip but left his arms in a loose circle around her body. To comfort and to prevent retreat. He kept her eyes locked in his, making sure she understood. "I play in a dangerous world, one I'm ready to get out of. Finding the Cinchona and this gold is my ticket out. I've stayed alive this long by following three simple rules."

Knowing he expected it, she whispered tightly, "What are they?"

"One, I don't sacrifice myself for anyone. Two, I don't put anyone's happiness above my own." He paused.

When the silence lengthened, Kat did what he expected, and asked, "What's number three?"

"Number three is simple. Stay the hell away from anyone who might make me forget one and two." With that, Sebastian released her completely and walked over to the stove. "Breakfast is ready."

Chapter 6

Katelyn lingered where she stood. *Stay the hell away from me.* The warning from Sebastian Caine couldn't have been more explicit. This wasn't a man to rely upon, to care about. At the wayward thought, she shook her head as though to clear it. *Care about?* She'd just met the man, and she didn't particularly like him. He was a thief and a liar and everything she abhorred in humanity. Men like Sebastian were the reason she'd chosen to study ethnobotany. His ilk made their fortunes destroying cultures and raping the land. With no respect for history or the people destroyed by their actions.

Trouble was, Sebastian didn't fit neatly into the category of callous pillager. An admitted thief who slid from cajoling to comfort to maddening in an instant. Who had been genuinely outraged by Tio Felix's murder. Whose kiss wound her up so tight, she could still feel his imprint on her mouth.

"Are you coming?" From across the cave,

Sebastian lifted a bowl and spoon expectantly. "We need to get moving soon."

"Sure." Adopting his air of nonchalance, Katelyn quickly joined him at the makeshift table composed of a jumble of stone that had fallen from the cave ceiling long before they had arrived. She sank down onto the opposite side and extended her hand for the oatmeal. Steam rose from the dish, reminding her that she hadn't eaten since she got off the plane in Lima. Suddenly, she was ravenous. Katelyn tucked into the bowl, oblivious to the hiss of heat. "Perfect."

"Not quite."

She glanced up, eyes quizzical. "What's wrong?"

"I didn't see any coffee in your bags."

The hopeful note in Sebastian's voice made her mouth curve into a rueful smile. "I don't drink coffee. Caffeine has its medicinal uses, but I prefer not to become addicted to stimulants."

"Don't let Starbucks hear you." Hopes dashed, Sebastian settled instead for the canteen of water and two small cups he'd located. He filled one for Katelyn, then drank deeply from his own. After a few minutes of silent eating, he decided the time had come for information. "So, Dr. Lyda, what does the doctor stand for?"

"I'm an ethnobotanist," she explained after a quick swallow. "I study the native uses of indigenous plants. My specialty is pharmacognosy." At his raised brow, she expanded, "Pharmacognosy explores medicinal and toxic products

from natural plant sources. Like cocaine from
the coca plant used by the Cogi tribes in Colum-
bia. Or the original uses of the poppy plant in
Afghanistan."

"You study how cocaine and opium can save
the world?"

"Not exactly," she demurred, reaching for the
tube of honey he'd set out. She opened the top
and squirted a thin, sticky stream into her bowl.
With a quick stir, she expounded, "Cocaine and
opium are narcotics that have particular uses no
longer tied to their original medicinal natures. I
study cultures that have forgotten or forsaken
the underlying, historical uses of plant life."

Sebastian appreciated the straightforward
reply, no hint of arrogance. Her kind had a tendency to overcomplicate in order to sound even
smarter. He smiled and added a squeeze of
honey to his meal. Apparently, Kat had a sweet
tooth. "A plant detective. Interesting. Do you
work with medical doctors or in a lab?"

Hearing genuine interest, Kat warmed to her
subject. Her day job didn't always lend itself to
cocktail conversation. Not everyone cared about
the exciting life of an ethnobotanist. "I do a bit
of both," she replied, swallowing her oatmeal,
the plump, sticky grains sating her hunger. "Before modern synthetic medicines, pharmacol-
ogists and medical researchers worked closer
together. We looked to the native uses of plants
for clues on best remedies. The best researchers
understood the connection between nature and
health care."

"What happened?"

"We advanced." She lifted her spoon and chewed thoughtfully. "Like everything, once we found a quicker, cheaper way to save lives, most researchers abandoned plants as the source of health care. Industrialization supplanted information and we—" As she wound up as she always did for this particular lecture, she glanced up when she realized her audience of one was laughing at her. "What's so funny?"

"You take this seriously, don't you?" Sebastian noted.

"Of course, I do," she began, until she noticed that she was waving her spoon emphatically and that a glob of beige oatmeal clung to the side of Sebastian's cheek. "Oh, I'm so sorry!" She came to her knees and bent across the stone table to wipe at the oatmeal just as he reached up to remove the offending mess.

Sebastian trapped her hand beneath his, pressed against his unshaven cheek. He moved her palm to his mouth and calmly sampled the food that had migrated there. "No apologies necessary. You are obviously very passionate about your work."

"Yes." The answer was a bare whisper of sound. Tingles shot along nerve endings Kat hadn't known were connected to her hands. The gymnasts that had taken up residence in her belly seemed to be aiming for Olympic gold. "What are you doing?" she murmured.

"Cleaning us up." With slow, firm strokes, he licked away the oatmeal spiced with cinnamon and honey. Taking his time, he explored the bold tracery of lines that swept across skin that was firm without being rough. And held her eyes captive in his. "Tell me about your favorite plant, Kat."

"My favorite plant?" she repeated dumbly.

"Anyone who loves her work as you do must have a favorite. What made you choose ethnobotany?" He drew her hand along his cheek again, held the trembling palm there. "Tell me about it."

"Cinchona."

The name slid out and Sebastian frowned, tightening his grip in reflex. "Cinchona? The manuscript?"

Kat stiffened and jerked her hand free, and Sebastian released her. Sitting safely on her side of the table, she scrambled to come up with a plausible explanation that would not reveal too much. Thinking quickly, she explained, "Cinchona is the scientific genus of a tree. The one that produces quinine."

"The treatment for malaria?"

With a short nod, Kat expanded, "Among other purposes. It was a favored remedy to treat fevers. The priests called it 'Jesuit fever bark' and exported it back to Europe."

Sebastian considered the likelihood that her favorite plant and his ticket out would carry the same title. Especially when she watched him so steadily, as though measuring his reaction. He drained his cup of water and poured more from the canteen that lay between them on the stone. "Why would a manuscript about Incan gold be named after a tree that produces a malaria treatment?"

"I don't know. I suppose the value of the tree to the Incas and to the Jesuits made the cinchona worth its weight in gold." She held her breath, hoping he'd accept the fabricated response. During her visit to recover the Cinchona, she'd read more of the text, and she wasn't ready to admit to herself what she had read. "I guess."

"Good explanation." Rather than challenge her, Sebastian gained his feet and reached down to stack her empty bowl inside his.

She studied his face, unable to tell if he believed her or not. But the bold sweep of planes and angles held no clue to his thoughts. "No more questions?"

"Not yet." From years of practice, he balanced the cups atop the pile, shoved the spoons into the bowls.

"You do that well."

"A recovery specialist has to be versatile, darling." To show off, he lifted the pile with one hand, balancing the stack with ease. "Ta da."

From her vantage point on the ground, Kat smiled at the display. "What else have you done?"

"Waiter. Curator. Executive chef. Assistant to a philologist," he responded, and smiled. "I've been a jack of most trades. Occupational perk."

"Then why become a thief? If you can do so many other things?" Clearly, he was intelligent and multitalented. She didn't understand why a man with so many options would choose the most dangerous one.

Giving her an appraising look, he lowered the dishes. He rarely explained his choices. To himself or anyone else. "My mom was a housekeeper in New York. A good family. But I wanted more. So I got it."

"By stealing?"

"It's a living." He shifted the stack and plucked up the honey and cinnamon to drop into her lap. "I'll go rinse these out in the seep. Break down the camp. We still need to go back to my truck before we head into town."

Katelyn rose to join him. Sable strands escaped the braid she'd twisted into a knot at her nape. Moving so they stood toe to toe, she folded her arms and captured his impassive gaze. "So we're clear, Mr. Caine, I don't take orders from you."

Sebastian appreciated the picture she made, fierce and determined. And wrong. "You are free to do as you wish, Dr. Lyda. But in fifteen minutes, I'm leaving for my truck, and I'm taking the diary and your passport with me." Because his hands itched to brush back the wayward strands that curved around her cheek, he turned on his heel and strode out of the cavern.

Katelyn stared after him for seconds, annoyed. "He'd leave me in a second," she muttered to the open air. Poking her tongue out at his retreating form, she did as instructed. Not that there was much to do. She was an expert

camper, and she always kept her gear in ready-
to-move shape.

Her two bags, the army duffel and her satchel,
quickly joined the camp bag where she stored
the stove and lantern. That bag stood open,
awaiting the bowls and utensils Sebastian was
cleaning.

Which shouldn't have taken so long. The
seep was near the truck and filled with rain-
water. Maybe he'd left her, she thought abruptly.
Had hidden the diary outside and was going to
leave her behind. The thought lodged in her
mind, and she felt her ire rising. Crossing the
cave, she imagined what she'd do if he tried to
desert her. Bahia was full of fun plants that
could make a grown man beg for mercy.

As she exited the cave, she smacked into Sebastian's still form. Without turning, he reached
behind him to steady her, then drew her unre-
sisting form to his side. In companionable silence, Sebastian draped an arm around her
waist. Katelyn stood stiffly at first. When he did
nothing more, she followed his lead and stared
out across the valley.

Though both had been out already that
morning, she too was captivated by the scene.
Outside, the morning sun had already begun to
bake the brown earth of the foothills, light
dancing among the piñon and sage. The russet
hills descended to black rivers that snaked
through the valley floor. Ripe green vineyards
dotted the banks closer to Canete, but she had

chosen a site that was miles from the homes and farms. The blue canvas of sky had been sketched with pure white clouds, a dance of alabaster and azure that met the Pacific Ocean at the horizon.

"Tio Felix loved Bahia. Mom and Dad tried to convince him to join them in Miami when they moved, but he always refused." Katelyn spoke softly, the ache of sorrow winding through her.

"Why wouldn't he leave?"

"He told them that God had carved heaven from the mountains and named it Bahia and that he would be a fool to abandon heaven. He said it was probably his first and last visit."

Sebastian understood the sentiment. "Some of us stake out our paradise on earth. Avoid the rush."

"That's rather cynical of you," she protested, turning slightly against his arm.

"Realistic."

"I miss him." She swallowed around the lump that formed in her throat. "I didn't see him much lately, but he was always there for me. I used to spend the summers with him, hiking around the countryside."

Stroking her arm soothingly, Sebastian offered, "I knew your uncle. We met up more than once. Estrada was a tough little bull, cunning. Could talk his way into anywhere. Once, we were after the same clay ocarina from the Shang Dynasty that had found a new home in Seoul.

While I cut my way into a vault, Felix had tea with the owner's wife and convinced her to sell it to him for a song. Madame Cho and Felix found me standing in her husband's vault, surrounded by treasures the Chinese government would have gone to war to recover. When the lady would have had me slit from ear to ear, Felix not only saved my life, he got an excellent deal on a set of fifteenth-century celadon bowls from the Korean Goryeo Dynasty. And an offer to tea the next time he was in town."

Knowing she should be appalled at Sebastian's brazen admission, Kat couldn't help but laugh. "Do you have any sense of—"

The rest of her sentence never emerged. In a blur of motion, Sebastian tucked Katelyn to his side and dived to the rocky ground.

"What?" The gasp from Katelyn was drowned when Sebastian covered her mouth with his hand.

"I saw something. In the ravine," he explained tersely. With careful movements, Sebastian eased Katelyn deeper into the shadows of the cave. The jut of rock served as a shallow awning and offered little cover, but its gloom was a damned sight better than the spotlighted target they presented standing near the lip of the cliff. The sheer face of the mountain would disguise the presence of the cave until their hunters drew flush, but he didn't figure that would be too long now.

"We've got company. Probably your friends from yesterday." Against Katelyn's ear, he explained in hushed tones, "I saw three figures moving in the brush. I don't know if they saw us, but I don't want to take that chance. Down here, we're safe for now, but I need you to be still. Don't move a muscle."

To show she understood, she caught his look and did not blink.

"Good girl." Sebastian waited the space of two breaths, then slid slowly along her taut, still length. Near her feet, the cavern entrance waited. Their only weapon, Kat's gun, lay inside. As did the bounty their guests were hunting. He needed to get to the gun, get their stuff, and get them down the hill while the getting was good.

Ear pressed to stone, Katelyn listened in tense anticipation as heavy footfalls scrambled against the terrain. The trail she'd taken up the mountain had been intentionally difficult to trace. And with the rainfall yesterday, any tracks had been swept away by the deluge. Still, the grunting of men grew uncomfortably close and her heartbeat sped up in concert. From the echoes of sound, they were five minutes away at best. A clutch at her throat joined her too-rapid heartbeat. Cold shuddered over her skin as she recalled the brutal scene she'd witnessed the night before as they'd tortured Felix to gain his secrets. Now they'd find her and take his legacy.

No! The denial screamed through her mind. Her uncle had not died in vain. She'd be damned if his killers would profit from his death. Pushing the stultifying fear to a corner of her mind, she focused on the peril at hand. Men, three by her estimation, were coming.

Once they crested the lower ledge, the hidden cavern would be an easy target. Which meant she and Sebastian either needed to stop them from making it up the mountain or needed to be gone before their unwanted guests arrived.

Beneath her prone form, jagged stone dug into flesh, and her arms felt sticky and sore. Turning her head only slightly, she noted for the first time that Sebastian's tackle onto the rock had ripped at her bare arms. Torn skin oozed trickles of blood, the red stains streaked with dirt. Sebastian had probably saved her life, though. The thought bothered as much as it unfurled a tendril of warmth. Despite his disdain for rules and honor, he at least cared about her survival.

Speaking of which, she wondered, cutting her eyes to the left, where the hell he was.

As though he could hear her, a form appeared on the edge of her peripheral vision and tapped her booted foot and pressed the toes flat. Understanding the silent sign, she inched forward, remaining on her back. The terrain shredded the thin tank she wore, and more shards poked at her aching skin. Inch by interminable inch, she eased her way forward. When she felt Sebastian's hand grip her thigh, she stopped.

The rush of coming battle churned in his gut, and he cursed himself for having waited so long to leave. He knew better. Should have known better. A fortune in gold and one dead body already.

But, this time, he might be able to pay his debt to Felix Estrada, which meant protecting Kat and the Cinchona. He spoke in a tight whisper, the words disappearing almost before they could be heard. "On the count of three, I need you to turn over onto your stomach and crawl around the side of the cave to the seep. I'll be right behind you. Take the keys, get in the truck, and be ready to move." He lifted her hand, which lay near her side, the palm abraded by the ground, and closed her fingers around the satchel strap and car keys. "Do you understand, Kat?"

She whispered as low as he, "Yes."

Satisfied, he adjusted the duffel bags and secured her camp gear beneath his arm, unwilling to leave a trace of their presence. He started the countdown. "One." The sound of the men grew louder, as the thin air forced them to breathe harder. "Two." By Sebastian's calculations, they had mere minutes. "Three."

With a tumbler's grace, Katelyn moved into position and was soon crawling down the slope where the Jeep was hidden among the piñon bushes. Her movements barely disturbed the earth. Sebastian followed quickly, keeping an eye on his back trail. Using his foot, he tried to brush out signs of their passage, but the effort was clumsy at best. By his count, they had thirty seconds before she would have to drive them out of there.

He heard the men come over the ridge and spun on his heel, jogging for the truck. "Start the engine, Kat," he instructed, tossing their gear onto the rear bench. Climbing inside, he yanked the gun from his pocket and knelt on the seat to watch for their visitors. They popped over the ridge in quick succession, the first one bearing a rifle bigger than himself. A volley of bullets struck the trees around them, and one shattered the Jeep's glass, the shards spraying outward.

"Drive!" Sebastian yelled, aiming his gun. The bullet leaped out but missed the rifle's holder. "Now, Kat. Go now!"

Rock churned beneath the wheels, and Kat shifted into drive. Turning in a tight circle, the Jeep pitched over the ridge and into nothingness. For endless, weightless seconds, they hung in the air, then dropped like a two-ton stone. Gunfire erupted behind them, coming closer and closer. Shouting punctuated the scatter of bullets, and Sebastian waited for a good shot.

The Jeep struck ground, the tires slipping as they tried to find purchase. Katelyn spun the wheel hard and floored the accelerator. The engine growled in agreement, and the vehicle jumped forward eagerly. Restrained only by their seat belts, the pair shook violently as the Jeep rattled along a stony path that had been hidden by the ledge. Rock yielded to trees, whose broad leaves whipped at their faces. Dense stands of vegetation blocked their path, but Katelyn expertly weaved the Jeep between the obstacles.

Sebastian spared a glance at his companion. She drove with speed and precision, and not a small hint of recklessness. As they crested a rise, he saw the outlines of three men standing on the ledge they'd abandoned. One held a rifle, but the Jeep was out of range. "You can slow down, Kat. We lost them."

When the Jeep continued to barrel forward, he checked her profile and found her jaw clenched, an echo of the fingers clamped around the steering wheel. The topaz eyes stared unblinkingly at the forest, and he realized she was driving on instinct alone. "Kat, honey, slow down. It's okay. They're not following us." He slipped a hand along her nape, tracing soft rings on the taut muscles. "Come on, darling. Let it go."

The sound of Sebastian's voice broke through the haze of fear that surrounded her, consuming her thoughts. Kat felt the light touch on her skin, heard the gentle voice that urged her to stop. "Are they gone?" she whispered. Looking at him briefly, she searched his face for reassurance.

"Yes, they are. You did good, Kat. Real good." Concerned, Sebastian used his free hand to cover hers on the wheel. The shocky look in her eyes warned him that she wasn't as tough as she pretended. And much tougher than he'd imagined. Katelyn Lyda was a hell of a woman.

The realization stirred him, made him remember dreams he'd discarded years ago. Dreams of happily ever after and other nonsense. Sebastian pushed away the hazy image, and said tersely, "Why don't you stop the car and let me drive?"

Chapter 7

The Jeep rumbled along the valley floor, heading south, away from Canete. Kat noticed the detour, and finally asked, "I thought we were going for supplies?"

Sebastian swigged from the canteen he'd rescued from their gear. "Canete is probably crawling with cops by now."

"Because of Tio Felix."

"Right. We go back there, someone is bound to recognize you. They'll bring you in for questioning, and it will be a month before a judge sets bail." He'd given the matter a great deal of thought, especially when she went on her jaunt. "Besides, I want to read the rest of the diary, figure out where we're headed."

"Headed?" Kat asked blankly.

Sebastian turned his head sharply. "To the gold. Remember? The Cinchona. Incan gold."

"Oh, yes." In the rush to escape their visitors with her life intact, she'd forgotten momentarily the story she'd made up about Incan treasure.

Kat sat back, closing her eyes to escape Sebastian's inquiring look. Keeping lies straight was hard for her under the best of circumstances. As a child, she'd invariably gotten caught. Lying didn't come naturally for her, and she had the worst poker face in the world. "I'm still a bit frazzled," she temporized.

And she was lying through her straight, perfect teeth, he noted. The tan satchel rested between her feet on the floor of the truck, heavier than it had been when he first went through it. Unfortunately, their guests hadn't given him adequate time to search through the contents and check for new additions. He'd been forced to scoop up everything, pausing only to grab the gun. Kat had followed his instructions to the letter, and he owed their safe getaway to her lack of histrionics. Still, the events had to have taken their toll, as evidenced by the shadows smudged beneath her eyes. "You should take a nap. I figure we'll head south for an hour or so, then pick a nice little hotel for the afternoon. Read through the diary and plan our expedition."

As though waiting for permission, her lids felt heavy and drifted down, lashes fanning out. "Wake me if you want me to take a turn." The husky mumble faded quickly as Kat drifted off.

Sebastian smiled approvingly and laid his arm across the back of the seats. Within seconds, her breathing lengthened into steady, even drafts. Too heavy, her head lolled against the headrest, and giving in to temptation he knew to ignore, he tipped her over to relax against his shoulder. Soft, warm breaths puffed along his skin, followed by a quickening of blood that had become reflexive in her presence.

Scenery flashed outside the car in photogenic succession. Mountain peaks disappeared behind wisps of white clouds, and dark water twisted through the countryside. Beneath the Jeep, brown earth, rutted and uneven, jounced the axles until he found a trail that led out of the valley.

With controlled speed, he guided the Jeep onto a rural highway, really no more than a slap of tar over poured concrete. Sebastian hadn't been in Bahia before, but his research had been thorough. Like Peru to the south, Bahia had been carved between the Pacific and the Andes, with an Amazon tributary running straight through the center. The resulting landscape yielded part tropical rain forest and part desert sierra. The real mountains and the broad river skated just outside Bahia's compact borders.

According to the history he'd read, Bahia had been an accidental country, grown from a family's civil war. The supreme Incan leader, Huayna Capac, died and left three sons. His eldest son Atahualpa headed the Incan imperial army, based in what became Ecuador. Atahualpa's half brother Huáscar ruled the capital city of Cuzco, which became Peru. However, Capac's sons didn't know he had an illegitimate child,

Chalcucha. By the time the Spanish set their sights on Peru, Huáscar and Atahualpa were engaged in a bitter civil war. When Pizzaro arrived, Atahualpa had defeated Huáscar and become the Inca. He allowed Chalcucha to live and installed him as the puppet ruler of Bahia. Centuries later, Bahia still formed a natural barrier between Ecuador and Peru.

On the side of the road, a llama led its grizzled master, the shaggy white back saddled with a bundle of indiscriminate purpose. The man watched Sebastian, who tipped his head in greeting. An answering nod was the man's response, and Sebastian swerved the Jeep around the area where the two walked.

Kat stirred against his shoulder, and he murmured softly, urging her to rest. The next few days would sap her energy unless she stored it up. Grief, he knew, was enervating and debilitating. Which was why he admired how well she'd stood up so far. In his life, loss had been fairly contained. His father had died before he was born, and neither of his parents had relatives to speak of. Sebastian had found a little sister in his best friend Erin, the daughter of the family his mom kept house for.

Sebastian thought about Kat's earlier query. Why did he steal? The answer wasn't too complex. He liked shiny stuff. His childhood hadn't been marked by deprivation, though he did remember the time before his mom went to work for the Glovers. The husband and wife and their only child, Analise Erin Abbott Glover, had been good to him. He had no doubt they'd treated the servant's kid better than his counterparts. Still, peering into their monied lives hadn't been sufficient. So, instead, he discovered young an aptitude for parting fools and their money, a skill he had honed into a profession.

The memory of his first big job remained with him that day. He'd been hired by an oil magnate to recover the man's gift to a mistress who had deserted him for a computer tycoon. The sapphire necklace in a platinum setting rarely left the lady's neck. But a little finesse and her overindulgence in prescriptions had netted him a paycheck that rivaled his mother's salary for a couple of years.

She pretended to believe him when he said he'd won the money in a bet.

God bless her, Mrs. Caine didn't ask too many questions of her son. Like Erin. And his occasional collaborator, Mara Reed. The best friends, he supposed, accepted you—without too much hand-wringing and philosophizing. They came to your aid and left you to your own devices, unless interference was absolutely necessary.

Katelyn didn't strike him as the noninterfering type.

"What are you thinking about?"

The sleepy question wafted against his cheek, and he offered a half smile. "How I plan to spend my gold."

"Hmm." The curve of his lips spoke of mysteries, and his casual response jabbed at Kat's inconvenient conscience. She should tell him there was no gold. After all, he'd just saved her life. However, she hedged silently, there had been nothing altruistic in his rescue. Without her, all he had was the diary, which he couldn't read. Saving her had been necessary for his plans, and keeping the truth about the Cinchona to herself was essential too. Sitting up, she blinked at the changing scenery, the Andean hills giving way to the lush vineyards that stretched along the tributaries. "Where do you plan to stop?"

"Ballestas, I think. According to the road signs, the town is about ninety kilometers away. I figure we can grab a hotel room, eat, and plot our treasure hunt. Ever been there?"

Kat drew her feet up to prop against the dashboard, dropping her chin to her knees. "I haven't really traveled around Bahia. Tio Felix and I mainly stayed in Canete during my visits."

"You stayed with him a lot?"

"Nearly every summer. Mom and Dad taught college, but they used the summers for travel."

"Must have been lonely, being dumped on your uncle."

She hadn't really thought about it before. "No, I wasn't lonely. Not at all. I'm an only child, like my dad. And they didn't dump me on Tio Felix. I asked to come. He was larger than life, told the best stories." Kat angled her head toward Sebastian, considering. "I hadn't thought about it before, but I think I found my parents boring. College professors who didn't watch television and who actually read my homework. Visiting

Tio Felix seemed much more exciting than traipsing behind either of my parents doing fieldwork."

"Understandable. Which one is the anthropologist?" Sebastian prodded.

"Mom. My dad is the naturalist, and I appear to be a combination of them both." She laughed quietly. "A therapist would have a field day."

"You seem fairly well balanced, all things considered."

Her smile faded. "I keep waiting to fall apart. I should, you know." Kat bit at her lip, eyes troubled. "I saw him murdered, Sebastian. My favorite relative, who took such good care of me. But I'm not curling into a hysterical ball and weeping. What's wrong with me?"

Because he had been pondering the same, Sebastian had a ready answer. "Absolutely nothing, as far as I can tell," he responded honestly. "My take on you is that you don't wallow well. What would change if you spent the day crying?"

"Maybe I'd feel better." Maybe the leaden weight that had settled on her chest would lift some. "Maybe I'd be able to forgive myself."

His eyes hardened. "You didn't do anything wrong, Kat. And we'll both feel better when we beat the men who killed Felix. I promise you that."

"I thought you didn't make promises."

He caught her expectant look for a split second, the deep brown intense and serious. "Count it as an exception."

* * *

"We lost them." Enzo delivered the news via satellite phone from the ledge where his targets had stood. "By the time we reached the top, they'd taken off."

"Then find them," Helen demanded. "I hired you to find the Cinchona and keep on eye on Mr. Caine. So far, I am very disappointed."

On the other end, Enzo shook his head. "We didn't know about the girl. You didn't tell us Caine was working with her."

I didn't know, Helen thought. The news of Dr. Katelyn Lyda traveling to Bahia had come hours after Sebastian accused her—accurately—of hiring Enzo's crew as an insurance policy. It seemed that her practiced paranoia had come in handy. Enzo tracked Sebastian to a camp with the woman she believed to be Estrada's niece. However, years of collaboration with Sebastian had her doubting betrayal quite yet. "Caine might be playing an angle, so I want you to find him. Let him know who you are. See if he needs assistance."

"We will. Given the tire tracks, I assume they've headed south to another town to re-coup."

"Then go on. And do not disappoint me."

At the hotel, Sebastian left Katelyn in the car while he registered them under one of his pre-ferred aliases. The clerk debited Jim Hasson's credit card and handed Sebastian a key to his second-floor suite with twin beds. Sebastian retrieved Kat, sheltering her under his protective arm, their bags stacked on a bell cart he borrowed from the lobby.

They stepped into a creaky elevator that groaned its way up a single flight. Kat preceded him down the hall and unlocked the wooden door. Inside, gauzy eyelet curtains billowed in the open French doors that doubled as windows, and a narrow balcony protruded from the floor. The wrought-iron grate around the balcony held firm as he tested his weight on the railing.

"What are you doing?" Kat asked, as he leaned over the metal bar, his weight hanging in space.

"Planning our escape. Our friends tracked us to the cave, which means they've got a good eye. We didn't exactly obliterate our trail out here. I'm not taking any chances."

Kat accepted the explanation but didn't care for the escape route. She crossed the gray-carpeted floor to stand near the doors. "How do you intend to get down there?"

"Quickly." Sebastian entered the suite, brushing past her. "Second floor. Not too far down. I'll go first, and you'll come after me."

"You plan ahead," she responded dryly, stepping out to look over the balcony. Palms swayed in the breeze, and spring flowers dotted the beds beneath the window. Despite years of climbing mountains and her avid love of skiing, she'd never had occasion to rappel from a hotel room, let alone leap to what looked like certain death. Kat relaxed against the rail and watched as Sebastian quickly unpacked the essentials and left his bag primed and ready to move.

He, on the other hand, appeared to take the idea of their demise in his stride, a trait she found intriguing. Then again, she found almost everything about Sebastian Caine intriguing. He was smart, sly, and quite possibly the sexiest man she'd ever known. From the cool, dark eyes to the hard, toned, athletic body, to his rather startling view of the world, she found it impossible to peg him. Or to think of hardly anything else.

Men like Sebastian rarely entered her world. A raw awareness of him shivered through her, and she accepted the dizzying sensation. Like his kiss, he wasn't a safe man to want, to be tempted by. Smart girls like her steered clear of his kind. But, Kat acknowledged, she no longer felt like being safe.

"Hungry?"

Kat's eyes flew up to meet his questioning look, a flush building. "For what?"

"Lunch." Sebastian rubbed at his stomach, smiling slightly at her confusion. "Oatmeal is filling, but I'm starving. You ready to eat again?"

"Sure. Give me a minute." Kat hurried forward and snagged her satchel to carry into the bathroom. The door shut behind her with a snap.

Sebastian muttered a quick curse beneath

his breath. He still hadn't found an opportunity to see what Kat had added to her bag during her walk. Plus, she'd gotten antsy all of a sudden, as though she were hiding something. While she washed up, he closed the windows and secured the latch. Habit had him angling the remote on the television and positioning the clock radio to face the bed he'd claimed and hang slightly over the lip of the side table. He set the leg of the desk chair perpendicular to the front of the desk. The paranoid trick would alert him if anyone came into the room in their absence.

"Ready." Kat emerged from the bathroom, her hair brushed and wound into a braid that hung down her back.

She'd dabbed something shiny on her wide mouth, Sebastian noted with a twist of desire. His hunger for lunch transmuted instantly into a need that was more basic and immediate. He closed the distance between them, his pulse drumming. "I don't think I am as hungry for food as I thought," he murmured, running a finger along her freshly scrubbed skin.

Kat felt the simple touch as a lick of fire against her face. "What—what do you want?"

"A loaded question, Kat. Do you really want my answer?" He flexed his thumbs along her collarbones, laid bare by her top. "Think fast."

She tried, but runners of sensation coursed along her too-heated skin and twisted her logical thoughts into a jumble. Lifting a hand to his chest, she felt the quickened beat beneath her palm and sighed. More than her next breath, she wanted his mouth against hers, his kiss to sweep her into the tangle of mindlessness she'd found with him before. But his warning and her promise dropped her hand. Kat stepped away and pasted on a friendly smile. "Lunch. I think we should have lunch."

Without waiting for his agreement, she eased around him and scurried out the door. Sebastian watched her hasty retreat, his hand balled into a tight fist. Deliberately, he relaxed his fingers and waited for the sharp bite of desire to subside.

She made a wise choice, he thought ruefully. Kat wasn't ready for what he would take, and he wasn't prepared to give her what a woman like that needed in a lover. He wasn't the tomorrow type, and definitely not happily ever after. Moving forward, he grabbed his key from the table and headed for the elevator.

Kat waited at the closed doors, wary. "Okay?"

He punched the call button and nodded once. "We're fine. We're partners, Katelyn. That's our deal."

The hotelier directed them to a hole-in-the wall down the street, where a plump woman and her rounder husband plied the *Norte Americanos* with ceviche, ripe, fresh-picked corn, and sweet potatoes. Sebastian tucked into his meal with relish, helping Kat finish hers. By mutual consent, they avoided conversation about the Cinchona or Felix or Incan gold. Instead, Sebastian entertained her with stories of his exploits she hoped were exaggerated. In turn, she told him about her work and the many places stamped into her passport.

To walk off the meal, they wandered around the seashore town of Ballestas and pretended for a few hours to be the tourists everyone assumed them to be. Sebastian remained watchful, constantly scanning the areas for signs of their visitors from earlier. Their path took him around the town, and he scoped out the best exit routes.

Kat wanted to visit the water, so they stood on a pier that jutted out over the blue-green waves. Sebastian shifted to stand behind her, his arms draped around her. She started to move away, but she remained in place, unwilling to break the skeins of comfort and something more that surrounded them.

A breeze came in from the water, and he rubbed her arms to warm the chilled skin. "How are you holding up?" he asked quietly.

Kat stiffened, then relaxed into his ministrations and sighed. "It seems unreal. I keep expecting to wake up. To find myself in bed at home, coming out of some terrible dream."

Because any words he might offer would sound pithy, he dropped his chin to the crown of her head, and asked, "Where exactly is home? Miami?"

"For now, yes. I'm on a fellowship there for a couple of years." She angled her head to study him. "What about you? Where's home?"

"New York. Upper West Side. My mother

lives in Harlem, a brownstone near the park. Likes to walk her two ugly bull terriers there every night." The truth slid out, easy and comfortable and unexpected.

"What are their names? The two ugly dogs?"

"Law and Order." When Kat turned her head in surprise, he gave a rueful grin. "She has a sense of humor and an endless supply of hope."

With a delighted laugh, Kat curled her fingers over his. "I always wanted a dog, but my family traveled too much. I had to settle for a stuffed walrus I called Quentin Xavier."

"A walrus?"

"I read *The Jabberwocky* and had to have one," she confessed.

"You're an interesting woman, Dr. Lyda."

"Interesting is usually a euphemism for something less than flattering."

"What about fascinating? Brave? Intrepid? Beautiful?"

Kat felt warmth creep into her cheeks, and she stared determinedly out over the rising waves. "I have a hard time remembering that you're a thief, Sebastian."

"A recovery specialist," he corrected with a chuckle. "I take from the wealthy and give to the even richer. Less moral ambiguity that way."

Turning, she lifted her face to his. "I'd think you could do so much more with your life. You're smart and charming. Resourceful."

"The hallmarks of a Boy Scout, I'm afraid. Not nearly as fun as my current day job."

"But safer." Before she could stop herself, she lifted her hand to touch his cheek. She barely knew him; and yet, she'd placed her life in his hands. Without regret. "I shouldn't rely on you."

"No, you shouldn't." He pulled her hand to his mouth, pressed his lips to the cool palm. "I'm not a good man, Kat. I'm not a thief with a heart of gold looking for redemption."

"Then why are you helping me?"

He didn't have a glib answer for her, and the realization terrified him. Fulfilling his pledge to Felix and finding a trove of Incan gold were the proper answers, but neither held the whole truth.

"It's getting late," he demurred. "We should get back."

Kat watched him, saw a glint of emotion that looked like fear and longing. She leaned away, still held in his arms, and smiled. "You spend a lot of time telling me not to trust you."

"Fair warning."

She stroked his cheek. "For who? You or me?"

His hold tightened. Somehow, he'd started to forget his rules. When her scent rose between them, sea and sunshine, he could barely remember why he should let her go. "I don't know."

He lowered his head, his mouth finding hers

with an impatience belied by the gentle play of his fingers against her skin. Again and again, he kissed her, each time diving deeper, seeking more. She wrapped her arms around him, and he dragged her closer, needing the feel of her in his arms.

Kat moaned softly, losing herself. Never before had a man taken her so quickly with a kiss. Her head spun, her eyes closed tight as she savored the changing angles and textures as he seduced her mouth, her heart.

Before she was ready, he drew away, lifting his hand to brush at her hair. Taking her hand, he led them back to the hotel, following a different route than the one they'd taken to shops. He sneaked them in the rear door and guided her to the elevators.

"Are you up for taking a look at the Cinchona?" Sebastian asked once the elevator doors slid shut.

Kat swallowed, fighting off the compulsion to tell him everything. She hugged her satchel guiltily. "Sure."

Sebastian unlocked the door and motioned for her to wait in the hallway. The remote control hadn't moved, nor had the clock radio. But the desk chair was flush against the desk, shoved beneath the desk. He stalked into the room soundlessly, gun drawn, and did a survey of the bathroom and the closet. Both were empty, the doors opened wide as he'd left them.

"Damnit," he snapped. "They've tracked us here."

Kat's eyes widened in alarm. "How do you know?"

"The chair. It's been moved." He headed for his bags and hers, gathering them in one hand. "Let's go."

"Hold on," she urged. "Couldn't it have been the maid? Look at the beds."

Sebastian started to argue but checked the bed anyway. Two mints had been laid upon their turned-down sheets. A harsh laugh rumbled out and he exhaled deeply. "False alarm. Sorry."

Walking slowly inside, Kat teased, "At least I know I'm safe with you. Even from renegade maid service." She sat on the end of the nearest bed and grinned. "Why don't you go down and check with the front desk? You won't be satisfied until you do."

She was right, Sebastian admitted. Pleased by her calm acceptance, he instructed, "Bolt the door behind me and stay here until I return." He opened his kit and removed his knife and sheath, strapping it to his ankle. Finished, he handed her the gun he'd confiscated. "Try not to use this on me or our tires, all right?"

"Be careful."

"I always am, darling." He grinned and slipped out the door, then took the stairs down and tapped the bell at the front desk. The manager appeared. "Ah, Senor Hasson. You have a message."

"For me?" The hairs on his neck stood on edge. No one knew his aliases, and he hadn't checked in with Helen all day.

"The man, he asked if we had a young woman staying with us. A lovely *morenita*. I answered yes, and they wanted to leave a message for you, sir." He extended his hand, a yellow slip of paper between his fingers.

Sebastian accepted the missive and read the line quickly. *Outside. Come alone.* Expecting a trap, he tried to decide whether to grab Kat and run or to meet the note's writer and get some information. As long as Kat stayed in the room with the doors locked, he could spare ten minutes, he reasoned. This way, he'd either learn something more about the Cinchona, or he'd find out who had killed Felix and on whose orders.

"Please ring my room and let my wife know that I'll be up shortly." He moved quickly out the doors, the feel of his knife comforting against his shin. The parking lot was nearly empty of cars, except for a scattered few close to the front. Hotel lights illuminated short distances, leaving darkness between the old-fashioned poles. At the fifth pole, Sebastian saw a figure. He covered the distance with long, solid strides, temper flaring.

"Did you go into my room?" he demanded without preamble, his hand snaking around the man's throat. "Did you?"

"No." Enzo answered, raising his hands,

palms out. "Senor, I believe we have mutual interests."

Sebastian did not reply. His fingers tightened reflexively, slowing the flow of air into the man's lungs. In the dim light, he studied the man. He was shorter than he and trim, rather than solid. In a fight, he'd best him easily, but Sebastian preferred to leave physical bouts as a last resort. Wits mattered more. "Who are you?"

"John Doe." The name gasped out as the man scratched at his wrists, struggling. "Stop it."

With each swipe, Sebastian's fingers tightened in warning. "Keep playing games with me, and you'll pass out. Make me angry, and you won't wake up." He squeezed tighter. "What is your name?"

"John." The rattle of air warned Sebastian that soon the man would black out. "Doe. I work for the same woman you do. Mr. Caine."

Sebastian loosened his grip but kept his thumb pressed tight. Just as he suspected. Helen had hired muscle to come in after the Cinchona. To his knowledge, this was the first time she'd taken the extra step, which meant the manuscript was more valuable than he realized. To suss out exactly why it was worth a second team, he probed, "When did she hire you?"

"A week ago."

A week after hiring him. "Did she tell you about me?"

Enzo nodded. "Yes. My team and I arrived in town ahead of schedule and thought we might be able to wrap up the retrieval quickly. Estrada proved unwilling to cooperate, and my associates were overzealous."

"You gutted an old man for nothing."

"So it seems, but you appear to have developed a better method with his niece."

So Helen knew about Kat. Which meant their lives had gone from in danger to terminal. Helen Cox was nothing if not ruthless when she wanted something. And Kat was the key to the Cinchona. Dropping his hand, Sebastian shrugged. "Katelyn has proven less than useful so far, but I am hopeful that she'll reveal more in time."

"Your deadline is coming quickly."

"That's my problem. You can tell our employer that I appreciate the support, but I've got this under control. Dr. Lyda and I are reaching an understanding, and I will make my delivery on schedule."

"My methods are faster."

Sebastian resisted the urge to break "John Doe's" neck. A man like him didn't travel alone. He scanned the lot, assuming one of the darkened cars contained his associates. "Your methods leave dead bodies and unnecessary clues."

"I can help."

"I don't need it. Tell our employer that I work alone. If she wants me off this job, she should tell me. But I doubt your tactics will work any

better on Katelyn than they did on her uncle."
Sebastian narrowed his eyes and his teeth bared
in a slash of white. "Come near me again, and I
will be very unhappy. Understand?"

"Sí, Señor." Enzo spun on his heel and faded
into the shadows.

Chapter 8

"Kat?" Sebastian spoke from the doorway. "We need to move."

"What's wrong?" Kat stopped her pacing near the bed and turned. Her stomach hitched, and she squeezed the handle of the gun tightly. "Did they find us?"

"Not yet," he lied easily, walking into the room. "Your maid theory was correct," he told her. With gentle hands, he loosened her grip on the gun. "But I don't like sitting still with people looking for us. We should leave."

"Where do you want to go?"

He'd thought about it on the way up to the room. Helen Cox didn't hire two teams for an old sheaf of papers connected to rumored gold. "The Cinchona has a history, Kat. I want to know what that was. How Felix came to know about it."

Guilt swirled inside Kat, but she held her tongue. She wanted to confide in him, but a tendril of doubt held her silent. However, she did know one person who might be able to give them both answers. She began to gather her things and jerked her head at Sebastian. "Let's go."

Outside, Kat circled to the driver's side of the Jeep and held her hand out for the key. Sebastian dropped it into her palm and stored their gear. Without a word, she climbed inside, and he followed suit. She gunned the engine and peeled out of the lot.

"Where are we going?" he shouted over the rush of noise.

Katelyn whipped the Jeep toward the north. "You said we needed answers. That's where we're going."

"Where?"

"An old friend of the family. Hang on."

She whipped the Jeep onto the road, and Sebastian inhaled sharply as a low-hanging branch took aim at his head. Ducking low, he considered whether he'd made a tactical error in letting her drive. He blew out the deep breath on a string of epithets as more lethal boughs poked and jabbed at him. "Just to be clear, are you trying to kill me or just maim me beyond recognition?"

"Stop being such a baby." Katelyn retorted, but she slowed the barreling charge to a more sedate pace.

"I'd like to arrive at my destination alive." Sebastian groused, though he had to admire the tight control with which she drove. The speed inched up steadily, but she handled the aging vehicle well.

"Sebastian, who shot at us?"

"I don't know. Felix's find made news in the wrong circles. More than one collector will want to get his hands on it." And her. Like John Doe would if Sebastian didn't protect her. He'd finally recognized the man beneath the lamp as Enzo Selva. Back in New York, the thug was renowned for his ferocity and his willingness to rip his prey apart. Sebastian had never tangled with him, but he'd been unfortunate enough to stumble over one of his victims. He'd never forget the sickly-sweet odor of blood that clung to the walls and the carpet of the tycoon's penthouse in Long Island. Or the broken bodies that had him rushing into the bathroom for relief.

At the moment of recognition, he'd altered his plans. Slightly. No, he wouldn't throw in his lot with Enzo or his companions. Even he claimed more of a soul than that. But if he could get Katelyn onto a plane back to the States, he'd salve his conscience and fulfill his pledge to Felix. Besides, after she was safe, he could decide if he'd keep the Cinchona or sell it to the highest bidder.

As though she'd read his mind, Katelyn asked quietly. "You were downstairs a while, Sebastian. What were you doing?"

"Talking to the manager." Sebastian looked away, over the mud-stained window. "Trying to find out if anyone else had been in town looking for you or the manuscript. He hadn't heard anything."

Katelyn accepted his explanation, dismissing her qualms. Focused on her destination, she drove through the night in silence. Eventually, they crested another rise, and the river basin spread out before the Jeep. In the moonlight, modest wooden huts with thatched roofs, built by peasants who could not afford to live in town, dotted the basin. Katelyn swerved onto a rutted trail and came to an abrupt halt behind one of the houses.

A pretty matron emerged at the sound of the engine, her broad smile of welcome a soothing balm to Katelyn's frazzled nerves. Quick, ambling steps brought the woman across the planks of wood that composed a back porch. Before Katelyn had emerged from the Jeep, she found herself wrapped against an ample bosom, close to suffocation. The barrier of the door proved no hindrance. Broad-palmed hands rough with age and festooned with silver and gold rings on nearly every finger pressed her face tight in welcome. Above her head, in muffled tones, Katelyn could hear the rush of queries as though from a distance.

"¡Hola, Katelyn! ¿Que pasa? ¿Quien es tu joven hombre? ¿Donde es Felix?" How are you? Who is your young man? Where is Felix?

Beside Katelyn, Sebastian could feel the shudder that followed the final question. In response, he leaped over the side of the Jeep and walked quickly to their visitor. He bowed deep, then extended his hand. When she responded, he lifted her fingers to his mouth and offered a courtly press of lips to the webbing of lines across the back. *"Soy Sebastian. ¿Como se llama? ¿Es usted Katelyn's hermana bonita?"*

The woman chuckled deep and turned slightly, ready to flirt. Handsome young men did not often cross her path these days, and she believed in taking advantage of opportunity. Especially tall, mouthwatering opportunities who spoke Spanish with a devil's voice. In rich tones that had let her spend her younger years singing to tourists in Lima, she responded in heavily accented English, "I am Senora Martinez. And, no, I am not her sister, you charmer. But I am not too old for company, even so late, if our Katelyn is not your sweetheart." Releasing her young friend entirely, she sidled closer to Sebastian, her hips grazing him thoughtfully.

As she brushed against him with stunning familiarity, Sebastian took the advance in his stride. He continued to hold the beringed hand, and replied, "Our Katelyn has not decided yet what she thinks of me."

Senora Martinez grinned and twisted her hips again, a second intentional graze that had Sebastian taking a quick step away. At his retreat, she laughed delightedly. "But you think of her."

"Senora!" protested Katelyn.

"Hush, *gata*." To Sebastian, she offered, "She is a bright one, but too deep in the books. Babies do not come from books, I tell her. But she doesn't listen." Senora Martinez draped an arm across Katelyn's shoulders. She shifted her hand to grip Sebastian's and led them both forward. As they crossed the crude wooden planks, she questioned in Spanish, "Why have you come to see me tonight?"

"I need answers," replied Katelyn in the same language. "About Tio Felix."

"Come inside. Sit." She opened the screen door and led them inside the small house.

The kitchen they passed through was neat as a pin and the size of a postage stamp. On the wood-burning stove, a pot filled with spices bubbled cheerfully. Scents danced through the snug space and drifted into the living quarters she led them to. The front room was all of a piece, living room and dining room combined. A low sofa decorated in swatches of bright, printed fabric sat against the wall. Two chairs faced the sofa, also covered in greens and golds and reds.

Against the far wall, a small wood table hewn from the forest hardwoods had been paired with three handmade chairs. A squat vase sat in the middle, its porcelain painted with geometric shapes. Cabinets filled the room, shelves stacked with pottery and glass. Despite the humble façade, the interior of Senora Martinez's home bespoke taste and elegance and some means.

Taking his time, Sebastian surveyed the walls, which held well-framed photos of laughing

children and smiling adults who all shared
the same nose as the lady of the house. In more
than one picture, a thinner, lovelier Senora
Martinez stood onstage, lighted by fluorescent
cams, her lips a pouting ruby as she sang. "Cabaret?" he asked with a smile.

"*Sí.*" Senora Martinez sauntered to her favorite, surrounded by a silver frame, and lifted it
from the wall with ease. She turned and held
the photograph out to Sebastian. In the image,
she wore a slick imitation of a dress that mirrored the ruby lips, with an abbreviated hem
that in any era would have stopped a man's
heart. She perched on a grand piano, dark hair
swept up into a riot of curls, accented by kohl-
lined eyes. Behind her, a man hunched over the
ivory keys and tried not to stare.

Sebastian whistled, low and appreciative.
"They must have lined up for miles to see you."

Senora Martinez preened and fluttered her
lashes. "In my day, I was quite the draw in
Lima. Men would travel for miles to see me. I
was known as *La Hechicera.*"

"The Enchantress," Sebastian translated.
"Given these legs, I know why." He stared at
the picture more closely, focusing on the piano
player. "This is Felix, isn't it?"

With a sly smile that spoke volumes, she took
the photo from his hands. Tracing the whorls in
the silver, she said simply, "He has magic
hands."

"Oh, Senora." Katelyn came to join them,
stricken. Stroking the older lady's arm gently,

she broke the news. "Tio Felix is gone, Senora. I
thought you knew. He was hurt—"

"Murdered." Sebastian interrupted baldly.
"Men came into his home and killed him. And
they are after Katelyn now."

"Sebastian!"

He shrugged. Looking down at the senora, he
caught and held her eyes. In the brown that glistened with sorrow, he found what he expected.
Resignation and knowing. "Senora Martinez is
a woman of the world. She will not be surprised
by death. Plus, she knew what Felix did for a
hobby. Didn't you?"

In an echo of his shrug, Senora Martinez
turned away to replace the photo, her hands
not quite steady. Katelyn watched as she missed
the nail twice. With a searing look at Sebastian,
she quietly took the photo and returned it to
the empty space on the wall.

Undaunted, Sebastian lightly clasped Senora
Martinez's hand and led her to the low sofa. He
squatted beside her, stroking the wrinkled skin.
"You and Felix have been close friends for decades, no?"

"*Sí.*" She lifted her head proudly to meet his
inquiring gaze. "We grew up together in Canete.
My parents cleaned house for his. Tended the
gardens and drove the Estrada family around."

"But you and Felix didn't care about stature,
did you? You were in love with each other."

A soft blush bloomed on the wide cheeks.
"Ah, we were in love once. Very young and *stu-
pido*. When I was sixteen and he was seventeen,

we ran away to Lima. I sang, and he played."

"Why didn't you ever tell me?" Katelyn asked softly. "All of these years?"

Senora Martinez lifted her hands, the stones sparkling in the light. "This was before. Long before Felix met his Mirella and I met my Josef."

"Before he began his quest," Sebastian added. "While you were in Lima, he began to collect objects, didn't he? Beautiful, priceless pieces."

Senora Martinez stiffened, her eyes sharp and cold. "I do not know—"

Sebastian lithely gained his feet and strode to the curio cabinet. Opening the glass doors, he lifted the priceless objects. "This statue? Aztec. This pottery? From the Tepeu, a seventh-century Mayan dynasty." He rubbed a length of fabric that rested beneath a row of bronze items. "On the black market, this swatch is worth a great deal, given that it was used to swaddle the dead in Nicaragua, before the Spanish came."

She studied him closely. "How do you know this? Are you an archaeologist?"

Katelyn chortled, the sound short and strangled. "He's a thief, Senora."

"Yes, but I know my trade." Returning to his position beside the sofa, he continued, "Senor Estrada was not a thief, though, was he? He was a collector. Probably started while you lived in Lima. But he became hooked and began to stray farther and farther afield. You loved him and stayed with him as long as you could. Until his hobby became an obsession."

"He would leave for days at a time. Then weeks." Senora Martinez knitted her fingers together and laid them in her lap. "Always, there was something he had to find. I grew tired of waiting, of being kept in Lima. My voice was good, but I would not become a star."

"You are honest with yourself, Senora Martinez." Sebastian cocked his head to the side. "Most are not. We like to believe our own lies."

"It is a curse, this honesty." She reached out and ruffled Sebastian's hair. "An affliction you seem to share."

"Only on Thursdays." To distract, he asked, "Tell us about your husband."

Senora Martinez wasn't fooled, but she complied. "I met Josef, and he did not mind my past. After a time, we returned to Canete. He bought this land, and we made our lives here."

Katelyn asked, "He didn't care about your friendship with Tio Felix?"

"No, *una poca*. After all, Felix introduced us. Josef was his, how do you say, gate?"

Sebastian chuckled, "Fence. Josef was his fence."

She nodded at the translation. "Ah, yes. His fence. The noble Felix wouldn't sell what he found, but he did have family heirlooms that funded his adventures. He asked Josef to watch after me, the first time he left Peru to go abroad. By the time he returned, I was married to him. Felix became godfather to our first, Luisa." She turned to pat Katelyn's cheek, her face somber. "I will miss your uncle. He was a good man."

"I know." Katelyn paused, then asked, "Do you know what he was looking for recently?"

"*¡Madre de Dios!*" With an exclamation, Senora Martinez levered herself up. Startled, Sebastian rose to help her stand. She pressed past him, agitated. "How could I forget? I am growing old in my brain. Wait here. I have something."

As she hurried from the room, Katelyn studied Sebastian in silence. The silence lengthened, and she never broke her oblique gaze. Sebastian shifted uncomfortably under the scrutiny. "What?" he asked testily. "Do I have something on my nose?"

"A bit of brown, perhaps," she teased, rising to join him. "You were very kind to her."

"I'm not an ogre, Kat."

"No, you're not, are you? Nor nearly as much of a scoundrel as you'd like to be."

"Come over here, and we'll test your theory."

Katelyn rose, but instead of joining him, she wandered over to the array of photographs. "I've been in this house a dozen times. I never noticed."

"Don't beat yourself up, Doctor. People see what they expect. Not much else." His tone was only slightly bitter though he didn't notice it. "Show them the obvious, and they won't look any further."

"Hmm," came Katelyn's noncommittal reply.

Before Sebastian could press her, Senora Martinez returned, brandishing a leather journal. She spoke quickly, excitably. "Felix came to see me weeks ago, before his last trip. He asked me to take this, to hold it for you, Katelyn, in case anything should happen."

"He knew he was in danger?"

Senora Martinez shook her head. "I don't know. Felix would come to me off and on, bringing this *diario.* He would tell me to keep it for you, if anything happened to him. Then he would return, safe and sound." "He would bring me a trinket or a vase, always beautiful. We would drink coffee and speak of our beloveds. And of Lima."

"May I?" Sebastian reached out to take the diary, but Katelyn pinched it from Senora Martinez's fingers first.

"Later," she demurred.

Sebastian narrowed his eyes, and seeing the tension between them, Senora Martinez demanded of him, "Tell me about these men who killed Felix."

"They want something that Felix found. A manuscript."

"The Cinchona."

Raising an annoyed brow, Sebastian muttered, "Does everyone know about this damned thing?"

Senora Martinez cuffed his shoulder in sympathy. "The Cinchona was Felix's greatest obsession. He would not tell me much, but he began searching for it when we lived in Lima." She moved past him to the Incan statue. "He found this in Bolivia. On his return, he heard about a prize that would make man immortal. Called the Cinchona."

"Immortal?"

"A myth, of course." Katelyn spoke over Senora Martinez's response. Now was not the time for Sebastian to learn the truth of the Cinchona. Not until she was certain of his loyalty. "But the real story of the Cinchona is its path to the Incan gold, right, Senora?"

Senora Martinez replied, "The Cinchona is many things, Katelyn. Wealth, long life, happiness. But if Felix did find the manuscript, and he was killed for it, why are these men after you?"

"Because they believe she has it," Sebastian explained flatly. He bowed again to Senora Martinez. Quickly, he described the men who shot at them at the cave, led by Enzo. "These men may come to you, Senora. Do not tell them that you've seen Katelyn."

"Of course not." She nodded briskly. "You two will stay here tonight. Felix's secrets can wait until morning."

Chapter 9

"We need to report in." Enzo halted on the winding trail, and his companions immediately followed suit. He held out his hand, and a wiry young man produced a large phone, twice the width of his palm. The tangled thicket surrounding them would have blocked most cellular signals, but he had a sat phone for just that reason.

Without a word, the boy turned to face the way they'd come and trained the Steyr Aug rifle on the opening. Slender, almost spindly, he had a gamine face that would have done justice to a courtesan. Doe eyes sported a heavy fringe of black lashes that women cooed over. The wide, almost feminine mouth was a natural deep rose that framed brilliantly white teeth with a charming gap between the overlarge front incisors. His olive complexion explained the straight fall of ebony hair and the broad, flat cheekbones. He looked sixteen at

most, was actually twenty-two. Rafael Bena-
mor caressed the butt of the rifle with a lover's
touch, his dainty fingers playing over the rifle
sight.

"Do not shoot unless I command," ordered
Turi Avilar, the final member of the party. His
nut brown skin gleamed with sweat from hiking through the rugged terrain. He did not enjoy the heat of Latin America, preferring his
normal environs of South Philly. "Shoot anything else before we find the girl, and I'll make
you more like her than you can imagine."

Rafael giggled and shifted the barrel to aim
at Turi's chest. "Whatever."

Before he could blink, the boy found himself
pinned to the tree behind him, a wicked blade
pinning his pants to the bark, dangerously near
his crotch. When the boy looked as though he
would retaliate, Enzo spoke.

"Behave, Rafe. Turi can do things with a
blade that would make Satan tremble. I would
not like to have him demonstrate. Understand?"
Enzo spoke in a calm, reasonable tenor that
sent shivers along Rafe's spine and scared him
worse than the knife protruding from between
his legs.

"Yes, sir," he muttered, prying the blade from
the bark.

The sat phone chirped, signaling that Enzo's
call had connected. Into the silence, he said,
"Reporting in."

"Yes?" Helen reclined in her office chair, her

nails drumming the arm impatiently. She'd expected his call hours ago. Waiting was her least favorite activity. "Do you have it?"

Enzo straightened his shoulders, forgetting that the woman couldn't see him. "Not yet."

"Then why are you calling?" The question was brittle and loaded with threat.

"I tracked Caine to a hotel in the south. He refused our help."

"Is he still alive?"

"Yes." Enzo touched his throat, his breathing still difficult. "The woman is with him. I told him I would help break her, but he insists on working alone. He said he hasn't found the Cinchona."

"Do you believe him?"

"Not really," Enzo replied tersely. "He's very protective of the girl. I think he knows something."

"Where is he now?"

"We followed them back to Canete." Enzo didn't add that they'd been ditched by the woman's driving. "We'll keep an eye on them."

"No more waiting. Bring them in. Use our police contacts."

"I will." He signaled Turi, who came to his side, tucking the knife he'd taken from Rafe back into its sheath. At Enzo's motion, he pressed his ear to the opposite side of the phone.

Helen spoke briskly, turning over the plans in her mind. "Return to the town. Let the locals know that this man and woman are responsible for Estrada's death. I'll send you their photos shortly." She ended the call and swiveled around to face Marguerite Seraphin.

Helen had chosen her cohorts carefully, selecting three men and one woman who possessed the daring and the resources to share her vision. Clifton Burge was likely sitting in the dank hole where he spent most of his waking hours, fretting about an outcome she had already assured. For their parts, Jeremy Holbrook and Vincent Palgrave had retired to their hotel rooms hours before, each claiming work.

A shrewd judge of men, Helen had learned from the security details assigned to the men that neither had stayed in his suite. Holbrook, it seemed, possessed a weakness for the whorehouses of London's West End and a particular proclivity for redheads. Palgrave was given to equally prurient adventures, but in bathhouses rather than brothels. London offered anonymity to the American and the Kenyan businessmen that neither could find at home. Still, Helen mused, they should have realized that anonymity was a luxury no amount of currency could purchase.

She slid the minutes-old surveillance of them across the slick marble, its black sheen dully reflecting the light, but Marguerite merely tapped the glossy paper with a blunt forefinger. "Blackmail."

"Insurance," Helen corrected. Her smile was razor-thin and knowing. "They seem to be anxious, and we cannot risk attacks of conscience."

"Call it what you will. But if I discover a telephoto lens or a tail, I have my own insurance." Marguerite sipped at a cup of iced coffee. "What is the status?"

"We have one casualty," Helen announced grimly. Only in the way long fingers clamped down on the ceramic handle of the Miessen did she reveal her frustration. "And the manuscript is still missing."

"What of your recovery specialist? And why the second team?"

"As much as I value Sebastian's skills, this project requires a brutality that has never been his strong suit. I cannot afford to count on his avarice this time."

"Do you anticipate more collateral damage?"

"Yes. My guess is that Estrada's niece will prove to be a hindrance." Feeling generous, Helen turned her chair slightly and tapped a few keys on the terminal. A photo of Katelyn Lyda appeared on the screen. A fall of mahogany tied into a ponytail curved down a slender back encased in rough khaki. Clear brown eyes took no notice of the camera or anything as she knelt in a wildflower bed, unaware of the surveillance. Stained work gloves covered the hands that dug into earth with relish. "An ethnobotanist. She studies plants and native pharmacology. An unfortunate connection, I think."

"Has she been working with Estrada?"

"Before flying to Bahia? Not to my knowledge. Records put her in touch with him before he died, so she may know what the manuscript is. What it can do."

"Does she have the Cinchona?" Marguerite asked.

Helen steepled her fingers on the sweep of desk. "I don't know what Dr. Lyda has or what she knows, but it's a good bet that she didn't arrive in Canete by accident. Neither Sebastian nor my other team found the manuscript. Unfortunately, the first team found Estrada difficult to persuade and more fragile than they realized." She shifted against the soft caramel leather at her back. "As soon as Sebastian reports success, we can proceed."

"What will you do with him? With Sebastian? You've utilized his talents for quite a while."

"I have, but I don't enjoy loose ends. Anywhere."

The next morning, Katelyn hurriedly brushed past a burro nuzzling a basket of overripe plantains. Her steps were quick, determined. From a yard behind, Sebastian ambled along at a more sedate pace and enjoyed the view. Fascinating, he thought ruefully. He'd never considered how the sway of a woman's hips could be so, well, eloquent. The woman he followed managed to berate him for his prior life, demand his current attention, and promise retribution in the same loping, graceful gait. He'd had nearly an hour to absorb her communications as she dragged him from a hovel disguised as a hardware store to a rustic *pharmacia* with both aspirin and morphine available over the counter to their present locale in the open-air marketplace.

After their three stops, he labored much like the burro they passed, packed down with medical supplies, twine and rope, a hand shovel, pickax, and a gadget that resembled a cross between an olive press and a thumbscrew. During their trek through the market, she'd purchased twigs and leaves and bark with no discernible purpose, as well as foodstuffs he did recognize. The bounty was slung across his shoulders in a handwoven pack offered by Senora Martinez. They'd stored their gear and the Jeep in her barn. Sebastian assumed they'd return for it once Katelyn had finished her shopping expedition.

He'd selected a few items himself, usually when she ranged ahead. "Plan to stop for air soon, sweetheart?" Sebastian drawled the mock endearment and stopped in his tracks.

Not breaking her stride, Katelyn tossed back, "If we are going to follow the Cinchona, we need to be prepared." Because they spoke in English, a few heads turned to observe their progress.

Closing the space between them, he fell into stride with her. "For what? I've read the diary too, and I'm still not sure what it is we're looking for. He mentions a treasure, but nothing about gold."

Katelyn quickened her steps, leaning forward slightly to pick up momentum and avoid his scrutiny. "I haven't finished translating the Quecha," she equivocated. Soon, though, he'd realize there was no gold. When he did, she'd be on her own.

"Tell me what's going on, Kat," he demanded. "Either fill me in, or I'll get the answers I need from Senora Martinez."

Her stride hesitated for an instant, then redoubled. "She told us everything she knows."

"Could have fooled me." Sebastian adjusted the canvas strap that dug into his flesh. He easily kept pace with her, a fact that seemed to tighten the already taut skin at her cheekbones. To test, he asked in an undertone, "You swear you've told me everything?"

The pause was lengthy and damning. "Yes."

"Liar." Seeing a break in the throng, he hooked a hand under her elbow. Katelyn jerked against his possession, but he merely tightened his grip. They were going to have this out here and now.

Without a word, Sebastian pulled her in between two stalls whose owners stood yelling and gesticulating wildly at each other. Neither paid any notice to them as Sebastian pulled her into the shadowed space. "What is the Cinchona? And don't tell me any more stories about Incan gold."

Katelyn stared at him, eyes cool. "That's what it is."

"I don't play well in the dark." Releasing her arm, he took a step away. "And I thought we'd gotten past the bald-faced lie stage of our relationship. Or do you kiss every man the way you kiss me?"

Refusing the flush that crept along her skin, Katelyn retorted impatiently, "You kissed me. And nothing happened."

"Be careful, Katelyn." Sebastian locked his gaze on hers, irritation rising. In marked contrast, his voice grew softer, almost contemplative. "Where is the Cinchona?"

"In my bag."

"No, the real Cinchona."

Caught, she denied it. "I don't know what you're talking about."

But Sebastian did. She had the Cinchona, had retrieved it when she left camp. And spun a tale of Incan gold to keep him with her. Giving a hard laugh, he folded his arms across his chest. One of the packets she bought in a stall poked at his stiffened spine and his pride. Willing to play it out for a while longer, he asked, "What's the plan, Kat?"

"I don't know yet," she muttered with perturbed honesty. "I can't figure you out."

"Need a category for me, don't you? Saint or sinner. Scoundrel, wastrel, thief?" He felt a tendril of sympathy, mixed with the nagging need to impress her that had become more familiar since they met. Battling both away, he gave her a look of derision. "People aren't one thing or another. We are a nasty mix of mistakes and poor judgments and selfish, baser urges that struggle against our better angels."

Which had her confused, Kat acknowledged silently. "I don't know you, Sebastian. I don't know what to do with you."

"I have an idea."

Kat ignored the entendre and plowed ahead. "Other than the fact that you might protect me, I don't know what I'm doing here with you."

"Then why do you stay? Why haven't you run off with the Cinchona?"

"Because your lies and your truth sound exactly the same." She advanced then, head up, eyes bright. "I have no idea what you believe in, but I know there is something. By your own admission, you're not helping me out of loyalty, still you saved my life."

"Stop being melodramatic."

"Then tell me the truth. Why are you helping me?"

Their argument was broken by the sound of approaching men. In the cacophony of the marketplace, the familiar sound of police sirens blared, cutting through the noise. It halted just beyond their position in the alley. Listening intently, Sebastian placed a cautious hand on Kat's arm, his sixth sense in overdrive.

Inching closer to the dueling owners, he heard the rough voice of an officer asking in strident Spanish, "Have you seen these two? They are wanted for the murder of Senor Felix Estrada."

Kat peered around Sebastian's restraining

arm and caught a gasp. Not more than five feet away, an officer waved a flyer with two photographs nestled side by side.

Sebastian's sly grin stared back, side by side with her unsmiling face.

Chapter 10

"What are we going to do?" whispered Kat, her voice low and steady despite the trepidation that had become an almost familiar sensation. The sight of herself on a wanted poster was almost surreal. The police had her picture, and they thought she'd killed her uncle. "We have to get out of here."

"I know." Sebastian spoke almost too low for sound. The only clear route of escape lay behind them, where another aisle shot through the open market. A few dozen passersby stood between them and the nearest cop. Because it was nearly noon, siesta had not begun, and the marketplace was not overcrowded. What he'd give for a carnival right now, Sebastian thought disgustedly.

"We can sneak out that way," Kat murmured, pointing to the exit that lay behind them. When Sebastian said nothing more. "Let's go."

"Hold on," he instructed, and he clasped her arm tightly, to keep her in place. On cue, two more police officers strode past, more posters clutched in their hands. They paused at each stand. He could hear snippets of conversation as the officers described the gruesome death of Senor Estrada. More than once, a horrified gasp followed their announcement, and tears poured from one shopkeeper who had to be helped to her stool. Soon, the news spread through the market, a lightning version of telephone that had Estrada murdered in his home by Bahia's version of Bonnie and Clyde.

Pressed to his side, Kat tensed at every repetition of the story, at every mention of her uncle's name. They were trapped between two stalls, unable to slip out and run to safety. He parted the heavy curtains and scanned the market. With a cautious peek over the crates, he could see rows of stalls in front of them, but only two behind them. The phalanx of police would be heavier if they went out the way they came, so they probably would be safest exiting into the rear aisle and melting into the throng. Apparently, the law enforcement of Bahia would have officers patrolling the market, handing out flyers, but the crowds were thinner on the last two aisles.

Glancing down, he examined his outfit of khakis and a black T-shirt, complemented by Kat's sawed-off shorts and white tee. Yes, they could join the dwindling stream of shoppers, except for the fact that they clearly stood out as gringos. Around them, villagers wore clothes cut from rougher cloth than his designer pants.

Add to that his pecan brown skin, darker than the *morenito* shades that were common in the area, and his unusual height—not to mention the willowy Katelyn, and they might as well be wearing bull's-eyes.

Frustration rose quickly, directed squarely at himself. He knew better than to stride into a village without adopting the local dress or adopting some disguise that allowed him to go incognito. His was a rookie mistake, unforgivable. And it imperiled both of them.

Sebastian hissed out a curse and cast about for another alternative. At the edge of the stall, the fight between the owners had resumed, indicating that the police had moved on. The flyers bearing the damning photos fluttered into their hiding place, forgotten by the combatants. A church bell pealed out, ringing the time as noon. In a moment, the marketplace would empty until after siesta. They had to move now or risk discovery by the stall owners shutting down for the morning.

As he formulated a plan, Kat tugged at his arm. Obeying the silent command, he turned to look down at her. When he saw the curve of a smile, he grinned in response. He had to love a woman who could laugh in the face of certain danger. He followed the path of her gaze and nodded with satisfaction. Behind them, the burro had wandered into their hideway and nuzzled aside the canvas wall of the male shopkeeper's stall. The invasion revealed their salvation. Sombreros had been stacked tall, the wide brims framed by vibrant cloth. Lying beside the hats were ponchos. Because of the temperate weather that could give way to chill, the wearing of a poncho would not be completely out of place and would help them blend, at least temporarily.

The noise of the crowd began to thin, and Sebastian decided it was time to go. He nimbly slipped beside the burro and retrieved two of the hats and the ponchos. When he turned to hand her a hat, Kat tucked a wad of money into his hand.

"Pay for them," she hissed.

Quickly, they dressed in their newly purchased finery. Kat wore a poncho of dulled brown, which did nothing to distract from the toned, tanned length of leg that emerged from beneath the fringed hem. Their disguises would provide only momentary protection, but he hoped it would be enough. Especially if he added a diversion.

Draping an arm across Kat, he whispered his plan. Kat crouched low and hooked an arm around the neck of the burro, who was silently munching on the brim of a hat. At Sebastian's signal, she turned the beast, using his purloined hat as a treat. Sebastian moved into position behind the donkey and with a silent three count, gave the burro a vicious shove.

The animal bleated at the rough treatment and sidled away, careening into the stall owned by the martinet. Canvas caught beneath the flailing hooves and snagged. Frightened, annoyed, the burro tried to rear away, and the material followed. Unable to evade the falling wares from the stall, the burro turned and butted the man's shop, dislodging the poles that held the rows of hats aloft. Cries rose from both booths, followed by the bleating of the burro, as he struggled to free himself from the mess he'd created.

The collapse of the stall elicited screams of irritation and the perfect opportunity. Sebastian and Kat, faces shielded, merged into the gathering crowd. While the burro continued his reign of terror, they rushed into the aisle, weaving between the shoppers. When Sebastian would have run, Kat hissed at him to slow down. "Only Americans run. We do it, and we'll draw attention."

Leaning down, he assented. "Fine. Watch your left side. Keep your head down and an eye out for the police. If you see one of them, squeeze my hand." Sebastian linked their fingers, as much for his signal system as for support.

Her hand was cool but steady in his, and she gripped his fingers tight. They allowed themselves to be swept along, moving with the crowd, shoulders hunched to mask their height. Katelyn absorbed the chatter in lyrical Spanish, picking up snippets of quotidian conversation— mothers chiding bouncy kids to stop running; old men discussing the state of crops and the latest gossip. The swirl of words flowed around her, soothing with their familiarity. Memories of days spent in this very market with Tio Felix settled like a balm.

A rambunctious, giggling toddler forced himself between Kat and Sebastian, and the slight boy tripped over feet, not quite ready for independence. He fell, sliding against the rough street. With seamless transition, the giggles became plaintive wails. Heads turned to discern the source of the cries, and traffic paused briefly.

Kat felt her throat tighten, heart race. Less than fifteen feet ahead, the sage green uniforms of the Bahia police moved through the crowd. At any moment, they too would turn to investigate the source of the weeping screams. She started forward, but Sebastian reached the child first. In an easy move, Sebastian scooped the boy up, removing him from the harm of oncoming traffic.

He judged the child to be no more than two or three years old, with bright, tear-filled eyes and a dusky complexion that was now smeared with dirt. "Hey, now," he murmured to the child, whose wails had only increased after his rescue. "Come on, little man," he urged in gentle Spanish. "Are you hurt? Can you tell me?"

The little boy stared up at the man who held him securely. He pushed a dusty thumb into his mouth and examined his rescuer. "I fell," he announced in his native tongue, looking at the ground as though it had intentionally tripped him.

"Yes, you did. But you did a great job of it."
Lifting a corner of his poncho, Sebastian tugged
out the filthy thumb and wiped at the smudges
of dirt. Undaunted, the boy promptly replaced
it with his other one. Chuckling ruefully, Sebastian cleaned that one too, then tried to im-
prove the rest of the dirty-faced cherub.

"Sebastian." Kat led the man and his passenger over to the side of the street, allowing the
no-longer-interested patrons to continue on
their way. "What will we do with him?" She
sighed deeply. "Should I alert the police? We
can't just leave him."

"Patience, Kat. He has to belong to someone."
Sebastian chucked the round chin that had angled up to watch the strange man in sombrero
and poncho. "Do you belong to someone, little
man?"

"I am Benito. I fell." The string of Spanish appeared to tax the child, and he leaned forward
to rest his head on Sebastian's shoulder. In a
loud whisper, he added, "Momma is going to
be mad. I'm not to run. But I did."

"Well, we can't always do what our mommas
tell us, can we?"

"Sebastian." Kat's note of censure was softened by an indulgent smile that recognized the
kindred spirits. In English, she chided, "No
corrupting the young."

"I'm just giving him another perspective.
Isn't that right, Benito?"

In response, Benito snaked his chubby arms
around Sebastian's neck, dislodging the hat,

which tumbled to the ground. Alarmed, Kat knelt to retrieve it, in time to see the appearance of sandaled feet racing toward them. "Benito!" The sandals belonged to a young woman, her pitch strident and exasperated, the intonation clearly the practice of a frazzled mother.

Sebastian recognized the mix of maternal resignation and embarrassment. Turning, he tucked Benito to his side, the short legs kicking as he squirmed for release. "I believe this is yours," he offered in Spanish, face once again shielded by his sombrero.

Benito's mother accepted the wriggling bundle, apologies tumbling from her lips. "He is nothing but energy," she explained wearily. "Now he has transportation."

Sebastian laughed, and the woman shifted Benito to her hip, balancing her basket on the other. The rich laughter had her fluffing out hair dragged flat by humidity. "I hope he did not disturb."

"No, he did nothing little boys shouldn't," Sebastian demurred, ruffling Benito's damp curls. "The world is wide, and he must know there's a lot for him to see."

When Benito's mother seemed inclined to linger, Kat gave his poncho a tug. "We are late, dear. And our friends may be looking for us," she murmured tightly.

"Oh, yes." With a gallant bow, he bid the woman farewell and offered Benito an encouraging smile. The boy beamed at him and ducked his head into his mother's neck.

"Do you flirt with everyone?" Kat asked under her breath as they resumed their escape.

Sebastian reclaimed her fingers and answered carelessly, "I breathe, my dear."

Kat snorted at his response, but felt her mouth curl reluctantly. Her hand relaxed in his firm hold, the slightly callused grip sending shivers along her skin, shivers she couldn't dismiss and couldn't explain to her satisfaction. Who was this man who had become her partner? He was incorrigible, charismatic, and occasionally sweet. From charming Senora Martinez to rescuing little boys, he shifted from mood to mood, from situation to situation with hardly a break. Her father would have called him a chameleon, her mother would have deemed him a handsome rogue. Kat knew him to be a thief and a liar and a lifesaver and too insightful for her taste.

Winding through the mash of shoppers, she followed Sebastian's lead blindly. Instead of watching the road, she stared at her boots, covered in the plumes of red dust kicked up by the stampede of feet. The rugged leather had tramped over soil on five continents, in hundreds of countries. She would have given anything to be home.

One foot stumbled, and Sebastian caught her around the waist to steady her. "You okay?"

God, no. But Kat bit off the sardonic retort. Tio Felix had handed her a legacy, and its outcome rest squarely on her. "Where are we going?"

"To Felix's house. We don't have a choice."

"All right." His arm about her waist felt solid and strong, and the depression that seemed to creep upon her without warning eased its bite. Kat looked up and confirmed that they had not only passed through the marketplace, they'd wandered along the dirt path that led into the fishing village.

"Hold on to me." Sebastian slowed his pace, eyes scanning the street for cops. The itch that had settled along his spine refused to stop nagging him. The smart move would be to head back to the Martinez homestead and aim for the Ecuador border, manuscript in hand. He could leave Kat with her friend and send her half his reward. But the mystery of the Cinchona had him firmly by the throat, and he couldn't leave Bahia until he'd solved it.

He hated curiosity.

Together, they hurried along, the roadway twisted into the sloping terrain of Bahia, where fishermen and vintners kept painfully tidy homes. Cobblestone and gravel wound through the tiny town, the bricks laid centuries before by Incans and again by Spanish conquistadors.

In Canete, African slaves had added their labor, scratching a town out of sheer cliffs and uncertain climes. Sebastian scanned the village and recalled his plans for the earlier heist. With a short tug, he indicated a path that slanted off to the left. In step, they ducked behind a long, narrow building constructed of wooden slats and a thatched roof. When he clambered over a low fence and motioned her to follow, she swung her legs over the gate, then leaned against the wooden structure.

Across the street, flashing lights swirled busily. Police vehicles blocked both ends of the street, and officers milled about, watching the deserted neighborhood. Sebastian counted the patrol cars and estimated that nearly a dozen of Canete's force were monitoring the streets, awaiting their arrival.

"Follow me," he whispered to Kat, an idea forming. Crouching, he led her into a backyard overgrown with flowers and weeds. The home had little to recommend it, except for its prime location. "Let's go."

Chapter 11

"Can you get us inside?" Kat whispered the question at the back door of an empty stucco house that faced Tio Felix's mansion.

Sebastian refused to acknowledge the insolent question. Kneeling at the back door, he studied the doorframe and noted a simple alarm connected to a fuse box. He searched inside his toolkit. Seconds later, the blue door swung open silently. They crept inside and took up a post at the living-room window to watch the mansion.

An hour later, Kat felt the muscles in her thigh cramp into vicious knots, a sullen companion to the tension that grated at her spine like claws. Outside, spiky rays of sunlight had moved behind teasing clouds that promised rain. The paved road sweated from the afternoon heat, steam rising in a hazy scrim.

"What are they doing in there?" she muttered. Reaching up, she peeled soaked cotton away from her hot skin. The red-and-blue woven poncho had been discarded forty minutes ago, when she began to bake inside the handmade blanket. Like most of the Bahian homes, air-conditioning was a luxury. A fan whirled languidly above them, moving the hot air. When Sebastian shifted his weight, she could hear his knees crack in response. He'd refused to let her move any furniture, had insisted they stay below the windows. With a roll of aching shoulders, she checked Sebastian's position.

He looked relaxed and alert, at the same time. Kat marveled at his ability to do both at once, not that she was surprised any longer. Sebastian Caine managed to occupy opposite sides of every measure. He fascinated her, perplexed her. His studied candor distracted the unaware from his penchant for half-truths. When he gave a direct answer, she was never quite sure if he meant it or if it was another layer to the lies. Everything she knew of him warned her to run, and she couldn't have moved if her life depended upon it.

She was deathly afraid her heart did.

"What are you thinking about?"

Startled, Kat said the first thing that came to mind. "I've never been accused of murder before."

Sebastian shrugged. "You get used to it."

Kat stared at him, thinking about the slick response. He made a wonderful show of his nonchalance, of his lax morality. But she didn't believe it. Couldn't have it be true, when she felt herself falling. She let out a low breath, deciding that now was as good a time as any to find out whether her heart or her head had the right idea. "How? And how do you get used to never being able to depend on anyone?"

"Practice."

"Don't be glib, Sebastian." Frustration had her closing the distance between them. She planted a hand on his chest and curled her fingers against his shirt. "Talk to me."

Against his will, Sebastian bent forward, catching her scent. They'd been hunkered down in the living room, inches apart, and all he had been able to think about was her. The thin cotton that clung to ripe curves. The streak of courage that constantly surprised him. He covered her hand and tugged her closer. Juniper and lavender shot to his head like whiskey, burned in his belly like fire. With his free hand, he traced the line of her jaw in a caress designed to explore. That the glide of skin beneath his fingers brought him a brutal ache was of no consequence. *None at all.* "There's nothing to say. You're just scared."

"No, I'm not. I'm terrified." She slid forward, bringing her tensed body flush against him. Suddenly, she craved. Angling her head, she brushed her mouth across the pulse that leaped at his throat. His skin tasted of salt and man and safety. "I don't know who you are or who I am becoming with you. Tell me how you do this."

"I can't." The vow whispered out of him as she nuzzled, flicked wet heat across his skin. Trailed it up to his ear, where her delicate explorations hardened him in a keen rush. He gasped beneath her touch, grabbed her elbow. Yet, even as he thought to pull her away, he circled her waist, dragging her tighter. "Katelyn—"

She drew away, watching him. Desire warred with the conscience he denied possessing. Sebastian, her chivalrous scoundrel. Because he'd warned her, he wouldn't take. Because she wanted, she would. "A kiss, Sebastian. That's all."

Without waiting for his capitulation, she streaked her open mouth along his cheek, capturing his mouth. Drawn to discover, she nipped at his closed lips, the hard line a challenge. Softly, she laved the satin flesh until his mouth parted on a groan of denial.

"We can't."

"Kiss me, Sebastian. Like before. So I can forget for a moment. Please."

Unable to resist, he bound her against him and dived inside. Urgent now, he captured her teasing tongue, tangled it with his own. Hot, relentless, he savored the lush velvet that met his forays, spurred him to sweep and taste. One hand plunged into the mass of silken strands she'd knotted at her nape. Determined to plunder, he bowed Kat over his arm, her form wonderfully pliant, arousingly strong. Sebastian answered the call of blood that commanded a rhythm echoed by their dancing hips. "Kat."

Twisting against him, she matched his movements. In the endless kiss, she sampled the hard edge of teeth, the black delight of his mouth. She touched him, skimming inside his shirt to feel the ridge of muscle that bunched and leaped beneath her palm. Flat male disks burned against her skin, rose at her urging. When he mirrored the caress, her breasts swelled, sensitive and greedy for more.

Sebastian bore them down to the threadbare rug. Tangling their fingers, he stretched her arms high above her head, stroked them over her body as she arched to meet his touch. Taut, firm globes curved beneath his hands, luring him. Opening his eyes, he broke their kiss, determined to savor more of the lithe, agile body that ranged beneath him. He released one hand to drag her top higher, revealing golden, sunkissed flesh to his rapt gaze. Bending down, ready to yield to the yearning that raged through him, unrelenting, he murmured her name. Turning to taste, his clouded gaze vaguely recognized the muted room.

"I can't. We can't." With an imprecation directed solely at himself, Sebastian wrenched his hands free and rolled aside. When she followed, blindly, he went under again, slanting his mouth against the full, rich mouth for another foray. To touch her, to taste her, this was all that mattered. Still, warnings jingled dimly in his head, and after a moment, he forced his hands to push her away. His voice gruff with longing, "Kat, no."

Surfacing, she lifted heavy lids and focused on the sharply drawn face that demanded attention. Sebastian sat up, pulling her with him. When she looked away, he tipped her eyes to meet his. Staring intently, he glided a soft kiss of regret across her mouth, then set her firmly away. "We've got to be ready to move. And if I touch you again, we won't be going anywhere for a while."

Sebastian inclined his head to the kaleidoscope of lights. Just beyond the window, a middle-aged man sat on the hood of a police car. He had a sagging belly and an amazing bladder. Three Cokes had slipped down his throat, but he'd yet to excuse himself. Instead, he sat sentry, and any movement by them to leave the house would be discovered instantly.

"While we wait, let's look at the diary again."

Kat nodded and twisted to remove the diary from her bag. Now, she thought, she should tell him now that she had the Cinchona. Still, she resisted. "Here."

"Thanks." Despite his irritation, he couldn't argue with her choice not to tell him about the real manuscript, Sebastian conceded. She was smart not to trust him, not to let him in on the truth behind the Cinchona. Tales of Incan treasure fueled the dreams of most treasure hunters in this area, especially in Bahia and Peru. If he hadn't been fluent in Spanish, despite the Quechua, he wouldn't know the diary was a fraud. Knowing himself, he might be lured by the promise of hidden gold.

Unfortunately for both of them, he'd been able to decipher much of the diary. Father Borrero's journal contained no mentions of ancient Incan troves of gold. But it did speak of the Moche and Nazca dynasties—of a secret passed through centuries. Of an Incan treasure too precious to be revealed to the Spanish. In Borrero's words, a secret treasure that his client would pay a king's ransom to own.

"They're leaving!"

Kat's hushed excitement broke him from his reverie. Engines revved, and, one by one, the police climbed into their vehicles and pulled away from the home. The Coke cop was last to return to his vehicle, leaving the three empty cans to roll off and settle against the curb.

As the final car turned the corner, Kat shot to her feet inside the house. Sebastian yanked her back down, his grip on her arm hard and unyielding. Before she could protest, he leaned close, pinning her below the windows. "Stay down until I tell you to move."

"But the police are gone," she protested. The windowsill pressed against her back and she wiggled a bit, and Sebastian yielded slightly. Still, she found herself caged between his thighs, his hard hands clenched around her upper arms. She tested his hold and found it immovable. Having straddled him before, she could attest to the obdurate confines created by his legs. She wasn't going anywhere until he decided to release her.

"What are we waiting for? We need to get inside." Anxiously, she studied Sebastian's rigid profile, wondering why he hesitated. After nearly two hours, the window of opportunity was open at last.

"Not yet." Sebastian didn't look at Kat, instead focusing his attention on the now-deserted street. Like many of the towns in Bahia, rich and poor lived in close proximity, with little distance between. Estrada had built his mansion on the street where he'd grown up, the imposing structure tucked cheek by jowl beside modest homes owned by the vintners and fishermen who composed Canete. Parked were an aging relic of a van, a vintage Ford, and a Cadillac, whose primer peered through faded blue paint.

However, it was the black sedan that idled at the end of the street that captured Sebastian's attention. The vehicle had been blocked by the crowd of police cars and trucks, but he now recognized the car as a Buick, a standard sedan. The type rented to visitors to Bahia at the local airport.

"Kat, don't be alarmed."

His instructions were accompanied by his hand shifting to readjust her position. With efficient movements, and faster than she'd noticed, he had her settled into place, her spine flush against his chest. Kat felt the hard ridge of muscles that ran from shoulder to hip, could almost hear the beat of his heart inside his ribs. She listed slightly, her balance shoddy from the endless crouching. Quickly, she clamped her hands on his rock-hard legs, keeping herself steady. In silence, Sebastian wrapped an arm around her waist, accepting more of her weight.

A dazed breath hissed out.

"You okay?" Sebastian spoke against her ear, the susurration of breath creating delicate tingles across impossibly sensitive skin.

"Fine." Kat forced her breath to even, her mind to focus. "What am I looking for?"

"Down the street. Eleven o'clock. Black sedan."

Kat followed his directions and caught sight of the car. As they watched, the driver's door swung open, followed by the rear passenger door. A huge man, almost as thick around the neck as the waist, emerged from the driver's side. On the other side, a gangly kid, no older than sixteen, she thought, climbed out and stood on the sidewalk. The kid sauntered to the front passenger window and leaned inside.

"It's them." Kat turned to study Sebastian. "The ones that killed Tio Felix."

"I know who they are," he reminded her flatly. "I assume they've been waiting for the same thing we are. For the police to leave and for us to go into the house."

The man and boy walked along the sidewalk,

and the boy kept twisting to check their tail.
They closed the distance, and Kat's fingers dug
into the powerful leg beneath her hand. "That's
the man that killed Tio Felix."

"The big one?"

Kat gave a short nod. He was only ten feet
away, across a narrow street. There was the
monster who'd tortured an old man. In constant refrain, she could hear the caustic demand
for answers and the screams when Tio Felix
refused to give them what they wanted.

Her muscles bunched, and Kat surged forward, but Sebastian clinched her rigid frame
tight. "Don't! Kat, honey, listen to me. They see
you, they'll kill you." He spoke quickly, urgently, trying to break through the haze that he
knew swirled inside her. Vengeance had a way
of clouding judgment and stalling coherent
thought. "Kat, baby, don't. We'll get them. I
promise. We'll get the men who hurt Felix. I
swear."

Impotent, furious, she struggled to break
free. "You promise? That's supposed to satisfy
me?" Kat craned her neck to face him, the movement awkward and painful. Like the swarm of
emotions that threatened to topple her. Anger,
untamed, demanding anger, insisted on release. "What are your promises worth, Sebastian?"

Sebastian simply watched her. Loosening his
hold, he answered her without inflection. As
though he could no longer stand to touch her,

his arms fell completely away. "I don't make promises I intend to break."

"And what about the ones you don't intend to break? What about the ones that become tiresome?" Kat teetered again, but she steadied herself, unwilling to touch him. The storm of rage passed, leaving only emptiness and a hollow that begged to be filled.

But Sebastian Caine, despite the strong hands and the soulful eyes that invited her deep, was no one's salvation. She clutched the fabric of his shirt in her fist. "When your client or these men or someone else pays you to betray me, what then? What will you do?"

He smiled then, a cool, inscrutable curve that chilled Kat to the bone. Sebastian heard the doubt and the longing. Something loosed inside him, and he wanted to quell her distrust. Satisfy the yearning that flashed in eyes glazed with the shock of loss that had not yet settled. Tugging her fist away from his shirt, he smoothed the rumpled fabric. Unable to do either, he gently set her away from him. "I'll do my job."

Kat refused to be mollified by the vague pledge. She heard something, wanted to hear a vow that would ease the ache of grief. "Which one? Which job will you do? The one you've been paid for?"

He didn't have to answer her, Sebastian reminded himself. No debts, except the ones he felt like paying. Maybe he'd promised Felix to find Katelyn, but he'd made no assurances about later. Guarantees, vows, promises—words that tied a person down. Made easy choices infinitely harder. Made living without regret impossible. No regret, he repeated silently, his cardinal rule.

Yet, in the time he'd spent with Katelyn, he learned that she wouldn't be satisfied with less than his oath. Damned if he'd give it. Narrowing his eyes, Sebastian bit out, "The men who killed Felix will pay, Katelyn. Trust me. Don't trust me. Doesn't matter. It's not about you."

Katelyn studied him, watched as his jaw clenched, the tendons straining along his neck. She didn't know exactly what payment he would mete out. For once, the pacifist in her didn't care. Instead, she leaned forward. Without a word, she brushed her lips against the flat line of his. A whisper of touch that sparked deep inside her and she drew away, feeling as though she'd kissed flame.

"What was that for?" The gruff question escaped before Sebastian realized he asked.

"Thank you." Kat arched her throat and stared out the window at the afternoon sky, the blue pure and brilliant. Clouds drifted easily, meandering across. A condor swooped low and called to its mate. "It looks the same," she murmured.

Sebastian followed the flight of the bird, ignoring the arousal that speared through him from one simple sweep against his mouth. A mouth that craved more of that fleeting contact. More of the hot, silky depths he'd tasted that morning. Instead, he focused on her statement. "What looks the same? The sky?"

"Yes. Like it did when I arrived. How can it look the same? Everything else is different."

Sebastian couldn't agree more. He hadn't signed on for this, damnit. His contract was clear and simple. And within reach. But, for once, he needed to know more than the location of his target and his fee. Her fault. Turning, he asked, "What is the Cinchona, Katelyn?"

The bald question caught her off guard, and she slowly lowered her head. "I told you. It's a manuscript that leads to Incan treasure."

Sebastian shook his head. He was tired of hearing it and the pithy explanation. "Three men don't kill an old man in his home and hunt his niece for the myth of gold. If they're smart, they don't return to the scene of the crime and wait out the police. We're being hunted, Kat, and I deserve to know why."

Kat didn't look up. She hadn't expected him to challenge her lie. She wasn't used to telling them. Men like Sebastian dealt in feints and half-truths. "The Incas' gold would be worth millions today. The diary—"

"The diary doesn't talk about gold, Kat. Father Borrero does mention ancient dynasties. The Chavin and the Nazca and the Moche. They predated the Incas by nearly half a millennium. And they are native to Peru, not Bahia."

Impressed despite the trap she found herself in, Kat forced herself to think quickly. "It's the diary of an explorer. He must have studied the various cultures along his route to the gold."

"I'm not a scholar, Dr. Lyda, but I do read Spanish pretty well. Borrero wasn't some Spanish conquistador explorer. Half the text of the diary is in Latin, which I also read a little because of my mother's mistaken belief that Catholic school might ease the devil out of me." Sebastian snaked out a hand and snatched the pack that had been shoved behind her with his gear. Before Kat could protest, he yanked out the diary and held it up. "The man who wrote this wasn't an explorer, Kat. He was a priest, who was scared and confused and who'd found something so big, he tried to encode it. What is the Cinchona?"

"The diary is the Cinchona, like I told you." She set her mouth. "If you've read the diary, you know about it."

"No." Sebastian retorted. Before she managed to counter, he held up a hand for silence. He eased around Kat to check out the pair who had gone into the house. The boy ambled down the sidewalk, arms loaded with a bundle wrapped in fabric. Close behind, the big man loped along, his arms filled with booty as well.

"They're stealing his things," Kat gasped.

"Very specific things." Sebastian concurred. As they watched, the skinny boy dived into the backseat. With a heavy jerk, the older man opened the front door and wedged himself inside. Soon, the car engine turned over, and the sedan merged onto the street. Sebastian shook his head when Kat gave him a questioning glance.

Kat said nothing more. Instead, she checked Sebastian's narrowed gaze and tried to follow its line of sight. Ahead of them, the sedan turned right.

"Not yet."

Less than ninety seconds later, the sedan circled the house for a second time. Then a third. After ten more minutes of circles and pauses, the black sedan rolled down the street, no turns.

Sebastian stood and helped Kat to her feet. She stretched muscles that threatened to spasm. When she bowed back, arching her back in a deep U curve that looked as alluring as it did painful, Sebastian turned away to gather their supplies.

Once he decided it was safe to turn around, he handed the canvas pack to Kat. "We've got an hour at the most. We need to get inside, get what you came for, and get out."

"Sure."

"And while we look, you are going to tell me the truth about the Cinchona, aren't you?"

Kat stood motionless. The truth was, she didn't know much more about the Cinchona than he did. Nevertheless, she'd sworn to her uncle that she would deliver it to people who were not Sebastian's clients. Eventually, their divided loyalties would require a sacrifice.

It wouldn't be hers.

She bobbed her head once in assent. "I'll tell you what I know, which isn't much. The Cinchona is a guide. To immortality."

Chapter 12

"Immortality?"

"That's what Tio Felix told me. But before he had a chance to explain, the men came. I took the manuscript and the diary and ran. The rest of the answers have to be somewhere inside the house."

With Kat taking the lead, they crossed the street quickly. Next door, a redbrick house squatted on a postage-stamp yard decorated by a festoon of wildflowers. A suspicious dog of indeterminate breeding sniffed the air as they sprinted past. The animal sent up a cautionary howl. Sebastian glared at the hound, who subsided into offended whimpers.

Despite the sophisticated security system inside, Estrada had not bothered with the rudiments of gating off his home. A low hedge of green separated the two properties. Only the neighbor's dog watched their progress as Sebastian tapped Kat's elbow and guided her around to the rear entrance he'd used the night before. Black slate echoed dully as they crept toward the door.

Mountain orchids bloomed in profusions of magenta and tangerine, standing in heavy clay pots along the walkway. The walkway wound through the center of the wide sweep of yard, which contained the most remarkable garden he'd ever seen. In the night, Sebastian had paid scant attention to their presence, intent instead on breaching Estrada's sanctuary.

"Amazing." He paused, scanning the carefully plotted space. Wooden stakes jutted up from the ground, twined with thin wire to cordon off the sections. From his swift count, Sebastian noted more than fifty distinct sections. "Is Felix how you came by your talent?"

Kat nodded. "When I used to visit, we'd spend hours out here. I learned Spanish and Latin from Tio Felix. Told me Latin was the language that plants spoke to each other and that Spanish was the way they talked to the world." The memory brought a sad smile to her mouth. "I learned everything from him."

Not everything, Sebastian corrected silently. If she had, they'd know why the Cinchona was worth having Felix and Katelyn dead. But instead of reminding her, he knelt at the ornate lock, surrounded by scents he'd barely noticed the night before. Now, though, he thought how their scent reminded him of funerals and mourning.

Kat crouched at his side, turned away to scan for visitors. That she'd taken up post without instruction impressed him. Not many—woman or man—would be able to tamp down on the maelstrom that he knew swirled inside her. Grief, rage, distrust, and frustration, with a healthy dose of vengeance. The perfect cocktail for a vigilante. A death sentence for a career criminal. Sebastian glanced at her still profile. Beneath the stark, unyielding beauty lay a conscience that rebelled against the life he'd chosen. Sooner or later, that prickly sense of right and wrong would fight its way out again. *Too bad*, he thought wryly. *She'd make an excellent partner in crime.*

Putting aside his fantasy, Sebastain swung the backpack off his shoulder and onto the flagstone portico. He released the metal clasp and flicked open the canvas flap. Shuffling her belongings aside, he reached down to the bottom of the bag to retrieve his toolkit. The bundle of metal wrapped in black suede felt was seductively familiar against his palm.

Kat glanced over. Sebastian had a case laid on the ground, and he picked over the dull gleam of metal like a surgeon choosing a scalpel. As she watched, he adroitly snapped together two slim rods of tempered steel. When he inserted the pronged tool into the lock, she reached over to stop his hands from releasing the latch.

"What about the alarm?" She spoke in a hushed, tense whisper. "Did you disarm it?"

"No need." Sebastian patted the slender fingers curved around his wrist, their touch cool.

"Our friends managed to wander inside without setting off sirens, which tells me that the police were either careless or unable to figure out how to rearm Felix's system."

"Oh." Kat gave a satisfied nod.

After a couple of seconds, Sebastian smiled and pointedly looked down at the fingers still curved against his skin. "My hand."

Kat snatched her fingers away as though singed. "Oh, sorry."

"No problem." Five seconds later, the satisfying click of release signaled success. In silence, Sebastian swiftly repacked his tools. He rose and tugged at Kat's sleeveless arm. Tucking her behind him, he eased the door open.

Caution urged him to tell Kat to stay outside, but he knew she wouldn't listen. And he needed her inside. Whatever clues hid inside Estrada's house, Kat would be the one to find them. He'd combed the house thoroughly yesterday, with only his new partner to show for his trouble. He pushed the door open wider, into the kitchen.

"What's that smell?" Kat sniffed at the air, nose wrinkled in concentration.

"Blood and bleach," Sebastian answered shortly as he locked the door and shot the dead bolt. He moved forward, feet soundless against the boards. He hated cleaning up after the dead and hated talking about it. When she would have asked another question, he tossed her a look that warned against further conversation.

Blood and bleach. Kat repressed a shudder and

fell silent. Instead, she focused on putting one foot in front of the other as they moved through the wide kitchen. Copper pots gleamed from silver hooks that descended from the ceiling. Black granite stretched around the periphery, interrupted only by the metallic shine of appliances. On her last visit, Kat recalled, she and her uncle had worked together at the center island, making paella and laughing about nonsense.

If she closed her eyes, she could hear the deep rumble that was Tio Felix's laugh, the hearty sound bringing a smile to all who heard it. Why would anyone mute such a glorious sound over a sheaf of papers from centuries ago? It made no sense, she seethed. No sense that he was dead and she was alive and that she was back where it had happened. Where she'd hidden and whimpered and mewled while he died. Flashes of image and sound jumbled in her head. A lifetime of vacations. Snatches of conversations, the Spanish familiar and urgent. Tio Felix.

"My Kat, watch the plants." Strong brown hands lifting a copper pot filled with boiled roots that smelled of cinnamon and sage. Six-year-old Kat watched the bubbling concoction with fascinated eyes. "Plants can give life, can take it just as quickly. The plants know the world, my dear. Listen to them."

"Bahia is not your home, Katelyn. But it is yours. And you belong to it." Sitting in the study, cuddled beside him, a gilt-edged tome spread across their laps. At ten, Kat skimmed the ancient Spanish words mixed with the language Tio Felix called Latin. The shaky handwriting talked of murder and war, appealing to her imagination. "We are born of Peru, but Bahia is not Peru's daughter. Bahia holds life. Remember that."

Kneeling in the garden, hands buried in rich black soil. Thirteen and enamored, she gently scooped out homes for species she'd never seen before. Asking her uncle to tell her why he gardened, why he loved it as she did. In a cascade of memory, she recalled his cryptic answer. "Kat, we may try to bury our sins, but they speak through the earth. In faith, thou shalt find salvation. In devotion, thou shalt find peace. In the least of these, He places eternity."

Kat saw herself at seventeen, cataloging the roots that he laid on the butcher block counter. Her uncle's face wreathed in melancholy. "Tio Felix, why are you sad?"

"Because I have not my own children, and my work isn't done."

"I can do it for you. I can do your work."

"One day, my Kat. One day, if I do not finish it. But you are the daughter of America, not of Bahia."

"I could be. If you want. My mother is from here, so I can be too."

"If I do not finish my penance, it may be meted out before I am ready. Then, my lovely Kat, Bahia will need you. And I will call for you. Will you come?"

"Always."

The memories flooded, receded with such force, Kat collided with Sebastian at the archway leading into the main house.

"Sorry." Kat mumbled the apology, as Sebastian turned on his heel to steady her. Around her, the room dipped and spun.

"Kat?" Sebastian clasped her shoulders firmly, felt a shudder rise through the tight, tense body. "Kat? What's wrong?"

"I'm fine." She lied, swaying. Tio Felix had been telling her then, she realized. He had known even then what would happen to him. That she'd have to finish his penance, whatever it was. No matter what. "I don't know why I've become so clumsy."

"Don't worry about it." Hearing the trembles that cascaded through her voice, Sebastian slipped his hand along her bare arm. Beneath his palms, he felt a chill shiver across her skin that had little to do with the stifled air inside the mansion, the house where she'd seen her uncle murdered.

Sebastian choked off the curse he would have aimed at himself. Katelyn wasn't a professional, used to the smell of death and its cover-up. She was a niece trying to stand in for her uncle, a woman determined to make right the worst kinds of evil. And all he did was snap at her. Instantly contrite, he rubbed lightly at the cold that raised gooseflesh along her skin. "Honey, why don't we sit down?"

Without waiting for a response, he guided her

into the first room he saw, a small sitting room with a low settee covered in lush aubergine velvet. Lowering her onto the surface, he knelt beside Kat, taking her hands in his. He chafed at the frigid skin. "Do you need some water?"

Kat shook her head. "I'm fine. I'm fine." But she lied. Tio Felix had been working on something for nearly twenty years. And the Cinchona was at the center of it. A manuscript that he begged her to return to its people. People she didn't know. For reasons she didn't understand. She wasn't fine, she was terrified. The men who killed him had been after him for years. Now they were after her.

"Kat?"

"I'm okay." Willing the assurance to be true, she gulped at air that seemed to escape her lungs faster than she could take it in. When her breath quickened rather than slowing, she felt the return of the light-headedness.

"God, Kat, you're hyperventilating. Here." Sebastian gripped her neck and gently forced her head to lower. "Breathe slowly, honey. In and out. Slow, deep breaths. Come on, you can do that for me, right?"

Kat heard nothing but the hum of nonsense words and the rush of blood through her head. *Dead. Dead. Breathe. Dead. Breathe. Breathe. Dead.*

On the carpeted floor, Sebastian heard a mantra mumbled through the hissing breaths that refused to catch. He'd seen this before, the shell shock that came and devoured a person whole.

Slowly, he stroked the damp tank top that clung to her skin. The dusky complexion paled, and her gasps became harsh stutters as her lungs ceased to draw in sufficient oxygen. Alarmed, he switched tactics. "Kat, listen to me. If you don't start breathing, you're going to faint. And then I'll have to give you CPR, which means I might have to kiss you again. Do you want me to kiss you again?"

Kiss. Again. The absurd threat penetrated as his earlier admonitions hadn't. She sucked in another draught of oxygen, then another. She wanted to be fully alert if that happened, not on the edge of a breakdown.

Be logical, Kat, she thought hazily. What did she know now that she hadn't known an hour before? That Tio Felix had a secret so huge his life had been in danger? No, she'd known that for years, had figured it out when she realized that no one else in his life had the elaborate security system that surrounded him. Had known deep in her gut that fear for her was the reason she'd not been allowed to visit recently.

Breathing slowing, she continued. Herbology and botany had been the core of her studies with him on her visits. Where *Cinchona calisaya* grew. What the scrapings of bark and steeped white flowers could do for the human body. And other botanical marvels. Like *Desmodium adscendens*, with its light-purple flowers and green fruits. They'd grown them together. Reputed to be a natural antihistamine and muscle relaxant, with properties associated with pain relievers. Or *Kalanchoe pinnata*, a plant with unusual antibacterial and antiviral properties. Tio Felix taught her to boil the broad green leaves to produce a liquid that could be used for nausea.

The Cinchona manuscript, the years of lessons, they were all connected. To her, to Bahia and to a group of people who demanded an old man's penance. Perhaps the men who killed Tio Felix acted out of revenge for his theft of their legacy. Or perhaps they were like Sebastian, hired guns who knew the secret of the Cinchona, a secret she hadn't learned yet.

A secret she had to find. But she couldn't do it alone. She thought of the night before and of the behemoth of a man who had ransacked her uncle's home. In faith, she thought fatalistically, lies salvation. Sebastian.

"I have it."

Sebastian stilled his hand, which had slipped beneath the dense fall of ebony hair to rub at her nape. "Have what, honey?"

"The Cinchona. I have it." She tilted her head and gave him a long, probing look. "I found it like you thought and hid it in the forest. That's what I went to get. You were right."

Sebastian returned her examination with an impenetrable gaze that had her edging away from his touch. She leaned away, but he didn't let go. Instead, he drew a thin line across the suddenly hot skin, feeling her pulse startle at the caress. He braced his free hand on the cushion, effectively boxing her in his embrace. "Why are you telling me now?"

"Because you risked your life. Because I need your help." She took a deep breath. "You knew I had it. So why haven't you conked me over the head and made a run for it? Why are you helping me?"

As the question had been nagging at him, he shot back, "I'm not helping you. I'm keeping you alive until we find the gold."

Intrigued by the heat in his tone, Kat pressed, "The gold?"

"Yes, the Incan gold buried somewhere in Bahia. The gold you claimed the Cinchona would lead us to."

"You know there's no gold."

Deliberately, Sebastian tightened his hand on her throat then released her. He came to his feet, towering over her on the settee. "That's a dangerous admission to make, Kat. Unlike your namesake, you don't come with nine lives."

"I'm not afraid of you, Sebastian."

"Then you're an idiot."

"You won't try to kill me. I know that."

"Murder isn't my style, no. But I will double-cross you. First good chance I get, I will take the Cinchona and pass go and collect my reward."

"Then why haven't you done it yet? There have been plenty of chances." She lifted her fingers to tick off her examples. "On the cliff. At the hotel or the marketplace. Even at Senora

Martinez's house. You've had the pack with you the whole time."

"And you dogging my heels like a lost puppy."

"Won't play, Sebastian. You're the expert. The master thief. Hired to recover the Cinchona. Coulda ditched me anywhere along the way. You speak Spanish as well as I do. So why are you still with me?"

He stared at her, his glib explanations vanished. Hadn't he been wondering the same thing? Why not take the Cinchona, hop a flight to Miami, and cash in? Turning away, he wandered to the bookcase that lined the far wall of the sitting room. The tomes were lined precisely, their leather spines in a straight, unbroken line. Shelves of gleaming mahogany ran across the length of the wall in four parallel rows. From floor to ceiling, the mahogany broke the shelves into five equal columns. Sebastian swept a curious gaze over the bookcase, noting that the fourth column expanded nearly half a foot wider than the others. That kind of flaw would have frustrated him endlessly, he knew. The devil, and the satisfaction, lay in the details. Dismissing the imperfection, he turned to face Kat, who wore a smug expression that crinkled lines near her wide, glossy eyes.

"Stop smiling at me," he snarled. "I don't know what you think the answer is, but it shouldn't make you grin like that."

"Like what?"

"Like the canary who ate the cat."

Kat released a delighted laugh at the imagery. "I thought I was the cat."

He shrugged. "Metaphor isn't my forte."

"No, stealing is." Kat stood and crossed to stand near him, but was careful not to get too close. She could still feel the soothing, tantalizing weight of his hand on her neck, the gentle strokes along her spine. His touch, as much as his patience, had calmed her panic attack, she admitted. But only to herself. After that stupid kiss and his clear warning, she'd keep her distance. "I haven't had a chance to read it thoroughly yet, but I think the Cinchona is a manual."

"For what?"

"Medicine."

"By Borrero?"

Kat nodded and began to circle the room slowly. "I'd have to read it more closely, but yes, I think it has to be him. The writer was a newcomer to Bahia and Peru. Someone who spoke and wrote Spanish, Latin, and Quechua, plus some Greek. Fluently."

Watching Kat pace, Sebastian noticed the irregular bookcase again. "Do you know how your uncle came into possession of the Cinchona?"

"No." Kat halted near the bank of shuttered windows. "He didn't have time to tell me much last night. I arrived late and drove to meet him here. We'd only spoken for a few minutes when the men arrived. We were upstairs, at his safe. Tio Felix told me to grab the Cinchona but to wait until he called me. He came down to check the door, and he never returned."

"So you came to find him."

"After—" Kat wrapped her arms around her waist. "Later, when I found him, he told me that I had to return the manuscript. He begged me."

"Where are you to take it?"

"I don't know. You arrived before he could finish telling me. I hid again, waited until you went upstairs, then I ran."

"Was there anything else in the safe?"

"Just his diary and cash." She spun around to face Sebastian. "I promised him I would return the Cinchona. But I don't know where I'm supposed to take it."

"Well," Sebastian reasoned, "it's time to find out."

Chapter 13

"Fifteen thirty-eight." Sebastian ran light fingertips over the date, scratched onto the parchment in faded brown ink. Though he knew it impossible, he felt ghostly frissons beneath his hand as he carefully turned the translucent vellum with its sketch of a slender stem bracketed by a broad leaf on either side. Along the stem, two smaller leaves flanked the stem until the thin line curved up into nothing.

They set up camp in the drawing room, hunching over their work space. The Cinchona lay open on a low cedar coffee table. Leather cracked with age as the binding adjusted to its modern readers. Sebastian had taken a seat in front of the manuscript and Kat sat cross-legged beside him. He skimmed the opening lines, which had been centered below the date on the front plate. "From the pen of Father Juan-Carlos Borrero."

Kat noted the border of the page, clusters of

leaves and flowers embossing the edges. Centered just below the signature of Borrero, a sketch of a flower with five petals, bunched together but unconnected to a cluster of similar, unfurled flowers. She lifted the vellum and laid it over the page again. The stem and its leaves fit perfectly. She traced the image, and murmured, "This is the *Cinchona officinalis*."

Her pronouncement drew his attention to the other sketches that framed the paper. "What about the other plants? Do you know their names?"

Excitement bubbled in her veins, tugged at an idea not fully formed. "This vine is the *ayahuasca*."

"Ay-a-who-what?"

"Aya-huasca. As in *aya* for soul or for dead and *wasca*, which means rope or vine. At least, that's what the plant is called here and in Peru. The *Banisteriopsis caapi* is a malpighiaceous jungle liana usually found in the Amazon, and along the Pacific Coast in Colombia, Ecuador, and here in Bahia."

"You mean the vines in the jungle? I read about them in the travel book on Bahia. They typically start at the base of tree and wind around the trunk, using the tree as a ladder to reach sunlight, right?"

Impressed, Kat nodded quickly. Whatever his faults, Sebastian possessed a rapacious mind for details. Normally, she would have done her research in silence, knowing her nonbotantist companions found her waxings about leaves and bark tedious. In him, though, she sensed an eagerness to learn, a zeal that owed nothing to their mission and everything to the kind of man he was. She reached for the pad and pen he'd secured for her. "In the rain forest, the sun typically can't penetrate the upper canopy, so the vines come to it."

Thinking about the plants she described, Sebastian wondered what kind of manual the Cinchona was. The quina plant he understood. Every overseas traveler had been dosed with the palliative for malaria. He'd needed quinine's curative powers once before. "What about the dead soul vine? What does it cure?"

Her mind spinning, Kat explained, "Basically, the plant is a hallucinogen. But it has other medicinal properties." She jotted notes on the other plants depicted, describing each species to Sebastian. "The artist had a fantastic talent for re-creation. These renderings are of scientific quality. See how he captures the stem lines and the veins along each leaf. If he drew these, he had some education in art from the church."

"So why is Father Borrero drawing native plants?" Sebastian inquired, shifting position to better view the pages. "Do you see a connection?"

Thinking aloud, Kat offered, "According to what I read yesterday, Borrero was a priest in the Jesuit order." She reached over his hand

and flipped through the aged, browned pages. "He traveled to South America with Pizzaro in 1532."

"His diary talks about his time here. He was among a group of monks brought over to help enslave the native population and destroy the Incas." Reaching behind him, Sebastian lifted a volume he'd taken from Felix's stack of books in the great room. Several volumes were stacked near his knee, more spilled across the Fereghan Sarouk rug. The great room or even the dining room would have been more comfortable, but Kat had paled at the mention of going deeper into the house. He hadn't pressed.

"I saw something in one of these books earlier," he explained as he riffled through the tabbed pages. When he found the bold-typed name, he set the book on the surface and read aloud. "Our journal writer was mildly famous. Father Juan-Carlos Borrero. Says here the good priest has been compared to Bartholomé de Las Casas, the Dominican priest who convinced King Charles V to forbid the enslavement of the natives in the West Indies."

Leaning closer, Kat tried to read over his shoulder. "Why the comparison?"

Sebastian tried to ignore the wafting scent of juniper that lingered after their visit to Senora Martinez. Just as he'd spent the previous hours not noticing how despite the heat and humidity and danger, rather than wilt, Kat glowed. And smelled like a fantasy he'd never dreamed.

Clearing his throat, he skimmed the story.

"Pizzaro and his men weren't having any luck finding the famed Incan gold in Peru, so Pizzaro thought Bahia might prove more cooperative. Borrero deserted his order after the massacre of a village of Bahia Incans. Pizzaro's men raped and sacked the village, then set the town on fire when the Incas refused to tell them about a rumored cache of gold."

"My God."

"It gets worse. The men who committed the atrocities were part of Borrero's order."

"They were priests?"

"Of a sort." Fast hands turned the pages, his eyes moving quickly as he absorbed the tale. "Borrero protested to the head of the order, the Brothers of Divinity." Years in Catholic school had taught Sebastian a healthy respect for the discipline meted out by the holy orders. He wasn't surprised that Father Borrero found their methods in the brutal days of conquistadors and conquest too much for his pious soul.

His account of children stripped from parents, of fathers pressed into servitude rang chords that echoed along Sebastian's own ancestry. Africans. Native Americans. The New World had been hell brought to earth for them. The shiver of memory he'd experienced earlier sharpened into resentment. He'd never understood the type of deity that sanctioned evil. Or the people who thought those gods made any sense.

For his part, the relationship Sebastian had with the Big Guy was one of tolerance and bemused indulgence. In his own way, he figured, he balanced the scales for the higher powers. Taking from the obscenely rich to give to the disgustingly wealthy surely earned him a modicum of consideration.

When Sebastian's silence lengthened, Kat shifted closer to see what had captured his attention. "What happened?"

"Hmm?"

"To Borrero? The priest. What happened when he protested?"

Sebastian rotated the text on the smooth cedar surface. He pointed to the final paragraph on the renegade priest. "Unlike de Las Casas, Borrero didn't receive any good marks for his protests. Instead, he was branded a sympathizer to the pagan Incas and the African slaves Pizzaro sent into Bahia. The Brothers of Divinity decided to have Borrero defrocked. The last recorded sighting of him had the good father headed for the jungle. After that, he vanished."

Kat read over his shoulder. "That was 1533, after the Spanish executed Atahualpa."

"Pizzaro had a brutal reign. He kills the Inca and ransacks the countries." Sebastian leafed through a history text that had been stacked among the other books. "Borrero can't take it. He's a defrocked priest who heads into the jungles of Bahia, cut off from his order and the world he knows. He's obviously Spanish. Bahians despised the Spanish and their holy men. They'd brought death with them. Smallpox had killed their leader, Huayna Capac, and a priest had trapped and murdered his successor."

"How did he survive long enough to write the Cinchona?"

"I guess he found a friendly village that hadn't heard about Pizzaro. One that had a strong relationship to nature." He flipped through the pages of the diary. "The Mutambo. This is the section where he starts to write in a mix of Spanish and Quechua."

"The Mutambo? I've heard Tio Felix and other anthropologists mention them, but I don't know much about the tribe. They are one of the indigenous groups, and their descendants have mixed with the rest of Bahia, though they live together somewhere deeper in the country."

"This is what you do every day, isn't it? Think about tribes and villages and families, figure out their connection to nature."

"In my way," demurred Kat. "A tribe, a family, even small villages are the same thing. We all divide ourselves along sectarian lines defined by race or origin or commonalities. I tend to study cultures that have a spiritual connection to the earth. Like the people who sheltered Borrero. The Mutambo."

He turned the page carefully, the delicate rustling slowing his hand even more. The image that stared back at him was of another plant. Again, the rendering was precise and beautiful. Sebastian lifted his eyes to Kat, who watched the page as though it were alive. "What is this one?"

The simple drawing showed a straight stem

with oval leaves and a clutch of berries at the tip. Below, the image featured a small shrub with berries and delicate flowers scattered across the bushes. "Boldo. *Peumus boldus.* According to legend, shepherds in Chile noticed that when their sheep grazed near these bushes, they had fewer digestive troubles. In Peru and Bahia, the leaves are used like an antacid or a laxative." Kat sank down onto her haunches, mind racing. Her scientific training insisted there were connections between the plants that Borrero drew, that the manual contained more than a catalogue. Without a word, she turned through the papers, skimmed the lines of Spanish mixed with Latin.

Sebastian said nothing. Occasionally, as she read, Kat would grunt or mumble to herself. She spoke to him only twice—once to demand a fresh pen and paper and a second time to instruct him to retrieve a volume for her. Outside, dusk settled into pale indigo twilight. With the blinds drawn, the natural light disappeared, leaving gloomy shadows to trickle across the furniture. They'd been inside for more than two hours, Sebastian realized. Too long to stay in one place.

"Kat, it's time to go. We stay any longer, we risk being caught."

She waved him away. "Can't go yet. I need to read this."

"We can take the Cinchona with us. You can read it wherever we camp out for the night."

Kat finally spared him a perturbed look that

questioned his competence. "Tío Felix's books are here. The manuscript is here. I'm here."

"It's dark and you're squinting." He flipped the manuscript cover over onto her hand. "The Cinchona has been around for centuries. You can take any resources with you, and when we find a place to stay for the night, I'll let you read to your heart's content. But it's too dark in here to read now, and we've been sitting in one place for a while. I don't know when our friends or the police might decide to return, and I'd be perfectly willing not to find out."

Kat merely jerked the manuscript closer, brushed the cover open and hunched deeper over the pages. "The information is here, Sebastian. I know it."

With a snort, Sebastian slapped a palm over the page. "And it won't do us any good if we get caught."

"I can't just leave. Not until I know what I'm supposed to do." Kat tried to nudge his hand aside, to no avail. When she yanked at his wrist, he flicked her attempt off easily. "Sebastian. Move your hand."

"No. Get up. Let's go." He nipped the manuscript from her and folded the cover closed. Before she could stop him, he shoveled it and the books on the table into their bag. The secret had kept for five hundred years, it could wait until daylight. "We're leaving. Now."

His spine was on fire with warning and his stomach had more knots than a sailor's jib. Patience slipped out of his tenuous grasp. "I'm not dying for this book, Kat, and I'm not going to prison for it either. Get your pretty butt up, and let's go." He drew his legs in and moved to his knees. "You can either stand on your own, or I'll carry you out of here. Either way is fine with me."

"I can't go yet, Sebastian." With a deep sigh, she dropped her head back, fixed her gaze on the vaulted ceiling with its Nazca painted tiles. Around her, inside her, the history of Bahia flowed and its currents drew her inexorably to the Cinchona. To its secrets. "I can't leave yet because I don't understand. There is something in that manuscript, a secret that my uncle died to keep. Why Tio Felix wanted to find the Cinchona. But I have to keep reading."

Touched by her urgency, he softened, but refused to yield. He wound an escaped brown curl around his finger, tugging gently. "Listen, Katelyn, the longer we stay here, the more danger we're in. I promised Felix I would protect you, and I can't do that if we're going to sit here, exposed."

"The answers are here, Sebastian. Here in his house." She lifted empty hands to gesture at the stack of books that had not been thrown inside the bag. "I have to read what Tio Felix read, see what he thought he saw. This is a lifetime of work, and all of the books I've got to refer to would be hard to carry without a car."

"Your Jeep—"

"Is still with Senora Martinez. And unless you are willing to haul fifty or so volumes in that bag, I can't move." She swallowed tightly, her heart thumping as it did when she was on the verge of discovery. "There's something here, Sebastian. I can't go yet."

Because he'd had the same thought, Sebastian ground his teeth in aggravated demurral. "One more hour. Then library or no, we're gone."

With a grateful bob of the head, Kat dived for the bag. Her impetuous movement elbowed him in the gut. "Oh, sorry."

"Hell, I don't have to worry about thugs as long as I keep you around."

Kat grinned sheepishly and straightened. "I get excited."

Against his better judgment, Sebastian crossed to the Hepplewhite side table and dragged a Tiffany lamp over to Kat's position, setting the base on the floor. The curtains were drawn, he conceded, probably worth the risk of a low wash of light. He yanked on the gold chain that dangled from beneath the dragonfly shade. Yellow spilled across the room.

"It's not much, but it's all you're getting."

"It will do," Kat agreed eagerly as she found the page she'd been reading. Absently, she drew the light up to the surface.

"Down here," he corrected, returning the lamp to the floor.

"Mmm."

He assumed Kat's mutter signaled agreement and gratitude. Turning, he stretched limbs gone numb from squatting and sitting for endless hours. Restless energy surged through him, accompanied by the itch along his spine that had kept him out of jail on many a moonlit night.

A mysterious client, three goons out to kill him, and a gorgeous scientist absorbed by a renegade priest's diary. Too many players for his taste. Retrieving the Cinchona had been billed as a quick, easy job. In and out and off to Fiji.

Like Kat said, something big had gone wrong, and something titanic was yet to come. Kat's immersion in the manuscript addressed one piece of the puzzle. But at the core of this situation rested Estrada's murder. A frantic call to a niece he hadn't seen in fifteen years, made the day before he died. A manuscript written centuries ago that now had at least two well-financed teams out to recover it. And an ethnobotanist who refused to turn away from dull pages filled with leaves and formulas. The linchpin was definitely Felix.

Every action had a trigger, Sebastian believed. That was his own precursor to Newton's other laws. If he was to protect Kat and finish his job, he had to find that trigger. Calling on his own expertise, he recognized that in order to do so, he needed to reconstruct Estrada's final days.

Bending, he removed the palm light from the bag and switched the beam on low. Sebastian let his eyes adjust to the dimness. He wandered out of the drawing room after explaining his intention to Katelyn. Her response was just shy of a snarl at the interruption. He wouldn't take it personally, he decided. After all, the sketches of plants and the mathematical symbols clearly fell into her province. Determining what had preceded Estrada's death was his.

While he methodically searched the ground-floor rooms, questions piled up, adding to the ones he already had. Leaving the study, Sebastian took the wide, curving stairs two at a time. He checked out the three bedrooms on the floor, inspecting each one for clues. Finding nothing, he crossed to the master bedroom. He entered slowly, scanning the room. From the top floor, one window overlooked the water and a second window gave a clear view of the town.

Including the police car headed their way.

Chapter 14

"We need to go."

"We just had this fight." Kat spared Sebastian an exasperated glance as he raced into the room. Turning away, she made a quick notation on the legal pad she'd scrounged up from the library. Plant genus and species, and miniature sketches joined an increasing list of questions across the yellow pages. Kat had learned several of the names a decade ago, in her uncle's garden. "I'm still working."

Sebastian leaned forward and snatched the pen away. He tucked it into his pocket. "Move your gorgeous butt, Doctor. We've got company." With a jerk of his head, he instructed tersely, "Close the manuscript, pack the books you think you need, and come on."

"When can we come back?"

"I don't know. But we've got maybe three minutes to get out of here. No argument."

"I'm not arguing." She held up a hand when he opened his mouth to retort. Speaking quickly, she explained, "I've made it through the manuscript." Pointing to the open pages, she explained, "From what I can tell, the Cinchona isn't a diary. It's a homeopathic recipe book. Formulas for blending native species into medicines."

"I don't care if the book has the alchemist's process for turning lead into gold." He took a mincing step toward her. Kat stood her ground, her face turned up to challenge him. Wry appreciation that she didn't back down mixed with annoyance. He was usually scarier when he was angry. Sebastian gripped her shoulder, forcing her to listen to him. From this moment on, he had one obligation. To keep her alive until he got her safely home. "I promised your uncle and you that we wouldn't join the body count. We stay, we die. It's that simple."

Kat wanted to fight, but his urgency was undeniable. "What do you want me to do?"

"Gather what you think you'll need. I'm going to wipe down our prints. Meet me at the kitchen door in one minute. Okay?"

Kat began to stack the books she'd used as reference. Medicinal texts and the vicious history of the conquistadors. Like Bahia then, she'd been surrounded by death and lies and secrets since arriving. Waves of chill and heat cascaded over her, and she sobbed once, a raw sound that choked her. Wrapping her arms across her belly, she caught back the tears that threatened. She hadn't lied to Sebastian when she said it was too much. But crying wouldn't bring relief, she warned herself ruthlessly. Answers would.

Answers scratched onto parchment by a monk in search of redemption. Like her. Perhaps, if she could solve the puzzle, could figure out why the Cinchona mattered, she would be forgiven.

Sebastian ran up the staircase to retrieve a suitcase. They'd put the books she required inside, and the cases might come in handy later. In hurried silence, he used a hand towel from the bathroom to erase any evidence of his presence. His single motive was keeping Katelyn safe. From everyone—including him.

Despite their attraction, Kat was out of his league. She'd expect—no, deserve, he corrected himself—flowers and poetry and fidelity. Roses and Byron were definitely his style, but staying wasn't. Ever. A woman like her demanded more than he offered anyone.

No, he determined grimly as he hurried down the steps, he'd keep her safe and get her back to the U.S. That's all. Clear her name and get her out of harm's way. He grunted in agreement with his plan as he reached the bottom step.

And dived.

Gunfire shattered glass insets, sprayed the room with bullets. "Katelyn!" The harsh cry ripped itself from him, and he crawled across the marble foyer, then surged to his feet to run. "Stay down, Kat. I'm coming."

As the mahogany frame splintered, he knew it was too late.

Sebastian broke the cardinal rule of escape

by looking over his shoulder. Inside the door, where ornate stained glass had been, a black-gloved hand wielded a rifle that he quickly identified as a Steyr. Next to the disembodied arm, a massive shadow hammered at the door, the wooden frame splintering beneath the weight. Yet, despite the blows that echoed like thunder, the door refused to give way.

As more of the door split open, Sebastian discovered what held the gunmen at bay. A reinforced steel frame with a dead bolt and locks out of reach of the wildly spraying gun. Relief sang through him as he spun around and jogged for the drawing room. Estrada's paranoia had bought them time.

He careened into the drawing room, dragging the case behind him. "Kat? Kat! Damnit, Kat, where are you?" Panic speared inside as he raced around the room, trying to find her. They couldn't have gotten inside so quickly, not without his hearing her. In a steady, searing rhythm, he cursed the delay, the time stolen to neck like teenagers while their killers stalked them. His decision. His fault.

"Katelyn! Where the hell are you?" After his second circuit, he paused, struggling for control. He scanned the room, noted the only points of entry against the outside wall. Yet, the long, damask-shaded windows looked intact, he noted wildly.

He swallowed hard, trying to figure out where she'd gone. The kitchen? A second after the thought, he ran for the door and turned into the hallway that led to the room. Sebastian sped along the corridor, blind to anything but finding Katelyn. Panels of rich, dark wood ran the length of the connecting wall, mirroring the mahogany panels terminating at the foyer. In the kitchen was the back door, a door their pursuers surely knew about.

In uncanny echo of his thoughts, he heard the staccato report of gunfire erupt in the kitchen, heard the clang of bullets striking the copper pots, the tinkling shower of glass. The hallway seemed eternal, his feet mired in quicksand. Frustrated, terrified that he'd failed her, he yelled her name, praying that either she or God might listen. "Kat! Talk to me. Tell me you're safe."

"Sebastian?"

The tinny, hushed voice called his name, and he swore his heart stood still. "Kat?" He whirled around, trying to find the source of her cry. "Where the devil are you?"

"Here." Like magic, a mahogany panel swung open to his left, revealing a closet barely three feet across. She wiggled out, swiping at cobwebs that clung to her skin, dripped from her hair.

Sebastian grabbed her hand, pulled her behind him toward the drawing room. He dropped behind the divan that faced the settee below the windows, and she immediately followed suit. Fear and relief twined into a single emotion, making his words gruff, his face set as stone. "We're trapped, Katelyn. They've covered both exits and I don't remember a garage from my blueprints."

Kat saw the hard, cold man she'd met before and forgot thoughts of comfort. Survival, now. Shatter later. "Blueprints?"

"From my client." Sebastian shut his eyes, calling from memory the blue sheet with its white tracery of lines. He used the moment to calm himself, to stem the terror that had consumed him when he thought her lost. There would be time for emotion later, he thought, shoving aside any consideration other than escape. "The ground floor has seven rooms, right? The study and library are on the opposite side of the foyer, next to the dining room."

Kat admired the cool calculation, the laser focus on escape. No room for sentiment or for a reassuring hug. Live now, wasn't that Sebastian's motto? Willing herself a similar inhuman courage, she replied shakily, "Yes. Plus the great room, the kitchen, and the drawing room. Tio Felix never learned to drive, never had to. Walking made him happy, and the town is small."

"How did he travel around the rest of Bahia?"

She thought hard, trying to recall long ago summers that had blended into memory. Twisting her fingers together, she pictured the infrequent trips out of the city. Lazy summers of study and conversation in a house now under siege. With effort, she fought off the crest of panic with slippery results. "I don't remember a car. We took taxis when I was younger, or rode with Senora Martinez and her husband. They drove."

Sebastian reached out, covered her hand to quiet the anxious motion of her fingers. The contact soothed him, and beneath his touch, her hand stilled. For him as much as her, he opened her fist, linked their hands. Tilting her chin to him, he spoke softly, firmly. "Kat, we're okay for now. The doors have reinforced steel, and the bolts can't be reached by breaking the windows."

Not to be assuaged, she shook her head, brown tendrils sliding down from their prison. Soon, Sebastian would pull away, leaving her to fend off the horror on her own. She should begin now, she thought, jerking at her hands. His fist closed tight, holding her still, unwilling to let go. Kat became quiescent, absorbing even the smallest measure of comfort as she finished his unspoken thought. "But even if they can't get inside, we can't get out, can we?"

"No unless you know how to fly, Dr. Lyda."

Kat gave a nervous laugh. "I skipped my second year of physics. My professor told me I'd regret it."

"Well, then. We just have to think. Between your brain and my cunning, there's a way out." He lifted her captive hand to his mouth, pressed an absent kiss to the fragrant skin. As delicate as porcelain, strong as iron. And so very nearly gone. Convulsively, against his better judgment, Sebastian caught her and yanked her into his arms, buried his face in her throat. "Damnit, Kat. I thought—"

Moved unbearably, Kat hugged him tight, stroked at the fine black strands of hair that curled at his nape. "I heard the gunshots. You told me to hide, and I remembered the closet. Tio Felix and I would play hide-and-seek during my summers. I discovered that one when I was eleven."

Discovered. Hide-and-seek. The phrases nudged at him, demanded his attention. Over Kat's head, Sebastian stared at the row of books that lined the side wall. The row of books with their oddly spaced columns.

Maybe. Maybe, he thought, the old goat kept a few other secrets off of his blueprints. "Kat, were there other secret rooms?"

Kat squinted at his question. "Other secret rooms?" she repeated quizzically. "Besides the closet? Um, yeah. There's a dumbwaiter in the master bedroom that used to open into the great room. And a nook in the guest bedroom where I stayed."

Moving fast, Sebastian approached the shelves from an angle and called up his recollection of the blueprints. Lids closed over his dark eyes as he focused on the layout of this wing. The outer wall ran the length of the house along its rear, spilling into the private garden. He walked forward and counted off the columns of the bookshelf. One. Two. Three. Four. He measured the width, as he had earlier. The fourth column was definitely wider, by nearly a foot. "Help me remove these books."

Walking to stand beside him, Kat began lifting volumes and stacking them on the floor. "What are you thinking?"

"That this column is half again as wide as the others. And that Felix was a canny old son of a gun who would have built himself an escape route. No one who works that hard to keep others out forgets to leave a bolt-hole." He dumped armfuls of encyclopedias to the rug, unconcerned about spines or age. "I think this column is a doorway. And a way out."

Keeping pace, Kat moved more books to the floor, though she was careful to set them gently on the ground. Outside, the shots had ceased, and the thudding was intermittent. "A way out to a tunnel that leads to the beach."

"Yes." Sebastian cleared a full shelf but found nothing unusual. Undaunted, he selected the row above. "The blueprints showed a crawl space beneath this room. On paper, it simply appears as wasted room. But if there's a tunnel, it's the perfect site for smuggling in artifacts that are brought in by boat."

Working in tandem, they quickly cleared the shelves. Sebastian slid his arm behind the last shelf and tumbled the volumes to the floor. A key panel glowed amber, awaiting the entry of a code. "Well, I'll be damned."

Kat started to speak, only to hear the rev of an engine. "Sebastian?"

"Yes?" He focused and heard the sound. A sharp look at the window confirmed his suspicions. "The kitchen. They intend to drive their car into the kitchen." He dragged her to stand in front of the panel. "Enter the code, Kat."

"I don't know it."

"Take a guess. And make it fast."

Without arguing, she typed in a succession of words. Quina. Cinchona. Juan-Carlos. Borrero. She used permutations and variation, all the time aware of the sound of metal crashing into brick and stucco.

A third slam, and a fourth had the foundation beneath their feet shaking. In two more strikes, Sebastian figured, they'd have company. And they'd die. "Come on, Kat. I know you can figure this out."

She exhaled sharply, clearing her mind. Then, as the casement windows rattled violently, signaling the impending arrival of the thugs, it hit her—1.5.3.8.

She pressed the star key on instinct, and the amber flashed bright green. The panel slid open on silent rails.

"Go," Sebastian commanded, turning to gather their stuff.

"My books," pleaded Kat. "They're on the coffee table."

"Move!" Sebastian shouted as he tossed them inside. He had no idea how long the door would stay open. On cue, it began to slide shut. Shoving the bag in front of him, he slipped inside as the kitchen door gave way.

The panel closed, plunging them into darkness. Sebastian turned, yanked the dagger from the bag, and drove the blade into the exposed circuitry. With a sizzle, the wires died.

"What if you're wrong, Sebastian? What if this doesn't lead to the beach?"

"Then, darling, we'll have a lot of time to read your books."

Chapter 15

Fluorescent light flickered unsteadily overhead, filaments crackling as they connected. Ten seconds later, Sebastian stood with his mouth agape. "Well."

"I had no idea." Kat moved first, walking forward to the short flight of steps that dropped down from the landing where they stood. The steps, like the room, shone bright in the room, the result of the metal sheeting that covered every free surface. Which, she thought hazily, was appropriate for a state-of-the-art laboratory. Sebastian cupped her elbow as they descended to the tiled floor. "It's beautiful," she said, swiveling her head to take it all in.

Lab tables stretched across the length of the cavernous space, the silver surfaces glimmering where the light fell. Built as a hexagon, the six walls met at an angle, welded together along invisible seams. Three short walls comprised the rear of the facility, and two longer walls extended along either side, each with doors leading to other sections. The vertical plane immediately opposite the hidden door sported a broad desk with two sleek black computers and a single monitor.

Above the computers, a corkboard held dozens of scraps of colored paper, the scribble across them unintelligible from a distance. Immediately to the right, she noted a workstation with more books piled high, and several notebooks arranged on a low shelf. The wall on the left bore a utilitarian sink with a row of medicine chests at eye level. Beside the sink sat an industrial refrigerator with Plexiglas doors.

She returned her attention to the two computers. "Something's odd."

Fiddling with the shorted-out keypad, Sebastian shot her an amused look. "Odder than a secret bunker with a hidden panel?"

Kat smiled ruefully. "Yes. The computers over there. I'm going to take a closer look."

She hurried forward. After dropping a steel bar into place, sealing the room from intruders, Sebastian followed. At the edge of the desk, she halted. The two computers bore the same logo, but the one without the monitor had a series of slots not found on the hard drive. "Now why would Tio Felix need a server?" she asked.

"To store information he wants to hide. Or to communicate with others without storing his information on a third-party site."

"You know computers, too?"

"Kat." The admonishment was clear.

With a chuckle, Kat approached the desk and confirmed her observation. Wires ran from the hard drive to the server, whose lights flashed in intermittent warning. A cable led from the rear of the server, and a miniature version of the black box showed a row of options. Power. Receive. Send. Activity. Online. Standby. The orange standby light held steady.

Sebastian followed and easily recognized the cable modem. He had seen this type of setup before, in government labs where the data had to be stored off the mainframe in order to avoid hackers. "Your uncle had a very big secret to keep if he played with these." At her look of inquiry, he explained, "This server has three layers of authentication protocol. Randomly generated cipher keys that change every twenty-four hours."

"You've dealt with them before?"

"I've had occasion to require data stored inside one, yes." He ran a hand over the casing, admiringly. "Took me three months to hack my way inside. We don't have that kind of time."

"Can you figure out who he's been talking to?"

"Absolutely." Sebastian dropped down into the Aeron chair that faced the desk and booted the computer into action. "Why don't you finish taking an inventory and let me know what we're dealing with?"

Soundlessly, Kat made her way to the wall to her left, mind whirling. Connected by what

she assumed were magnets, oversized renderings of flora, identical to those in the Cinchona,
decorated the expanse. Turning, she saw that
more images hung on the opposite side. In between, four black slabs of marble crouched in
the center of the lab. Vials and tubes dotted
each table, their glass containers empty. Gad-
gets to measure and weigh and spin and heat
had been placed at precise stations. The surfaces had been recently disinfected and sani-
tized.

"He's been experimenting recently." Kat
sniffed at a vial and set it down. She returned
to the workstation with the fume hood and bottles of various sizes. "These are distillations
from the plants in the Cinchona." The clear liquid in an oblong cylinder had been labeled, as
had several other extractions. "I recognize most
of the labels, but there are some here that I've
never heard of."

Sebastian craned his neck to see where she
stood. The bottles and glasses reminded him of
Frankenstein's lab. At any moment, he expected
a ghoulish man to emerge, hair black with
white tips. Nothing at this point would surprise him. "Are these medicines?"

"For many of the villages in Bahia and Peru,
yes. The cost of modern, synthetic medicines
has become astronomical. Peasants can't afford
the expense or the time it takes to get a doctor's
appointment. Homeopathic remedies have similar effects, can be produced locally, and aren't
regulated."

"Sounds like a good ad for drug abuse to me."

Too used to the comment to take offense, Kat merely smiled. "On the contrary, few of the pharmacological plants have narcotic properties." She scribbled onto the legal pad she'd brought with her. "But I've never seen some of these combinations. A diuretic and an antihistamine." Tipping another vial into the light, she noted the genus on the sheet. "This one blends the local cure for asthma and a vermifuge."

"Excuse me?"

"Vermifuge. It expels worms."

"Nice."

Kat crossed to one of the doors and pushed it open. The humidity struck her first, then the artificial light. "He's got a greenhouse," she called out excitedly. She hurried inside, careful to avoid touching the plants until she'd done her evaluation. "Most of these species only grow in the rain forest."

Deciding to check behind door number two, she entered a room that contained more equipment, including a machine she identified as a computer-controlled capillary electrophoresis system. When she wanted to use one, she had to cajole the head of the department at the local university wherever she was. The expensive machine required a cache of methanol and heat lamps to prepare the plants for extraction. Kat took a few steps to another doorway marked storage, and peered inside. Containers labeled "methanol" waited for use.

On the workstation in the extraction room,

Kat cataloged more than twenty-nine vials, all infusing different plant essences into singular combinations. She'd done similar experiments in graduate school but had never attempted many of Felix's mixtures. The systems of the body rarely benefited from a universal curative. The Holy Grail of scientists was exactly that, a solitary medicine that could address all human ills without deadly side effects.

Scientific minds had generally agreed that the achievement was impossible, and she concurred. Apparently, though, Tio Felix wanted to compound the usefulness of some homeopathic remedies.

Kat dismissed the idea, exiting to return to where Sebastian continued to manipulate the computer. "Making any progress?"

"I'm trying to access his e-mail accounts. Your uncle was deeply paranoid."

"Apparently." She continued her circuit of the room, wondering what else she would learn about her uncle's secret lab.

Along the back wall where they had entered, a row of lockers protruded. Kat disengaged the latch and lifted the handle. The rectangular structure contained a horizontal bar suspending three lab coats. On the floor, two pairs of scuffed work boots sat in a straight line, the same size and brand. Inside the next locker, drawers had been installed. Reaching down, Kat pulled at the handle, revealing boxes of latex gloves. Squatting, she opened the next drawer, which had been filled with equipment.

The final locker was wider and seemed to whir. Kat swung the door gingerly, and found an incubation pod.

With the hum of the lights playing in her ears, Kat stood frozen, bemused and bewildered. She'd discovered a lab more suited to a pharmaceutical company than an amateur scientist.

"Kat. Come take a look at this."

She circled around to the computer monitor and braced herself on Sebastian's shoulder, reading the screen. Frowning, she reread the name on the message. "Dr. Clifton Burge? At the NIH?"

"I've found more than seventy e-mails between them, starting three months ago." Sebastian clicked on the screen and the name descended in rows of text. All with the same subject line. FOUNTAIN OF YOUTH.

Sebastian tapped the mouse to open one of the messages. Scrolling from the bottom, she and Sebastian read an exchange between Felix and Dr. Burge.

TO: Explorer1538
FROM: Burge, Clifton Dr.
RE: Fountain of Youth

I must have proof soon. I have located potential funding for our project, but they will not invest without a demonstration. I could reproduce a sample here if you would send me the formula. You must know that I will not betray you.

TO: Burge, Clifton Dr.
FROM: Explorer1538
RE: Fountain of Youth

Forgive me if I am unwilling to trust in your inherent goodness, old friend. I will provide you with sufficient information to warrant their continued support of the project. I will also require assurances that our agreed-upon terms have not changed. A good faith payment should suffice.

TO: Explorer1538
FROM: Burge, Clifton Dr.
RE: Fountain of Youth

I am not permitted to compensate you for a product that has not been tested. My investors have substantial doubts that you have come into possession of the manuscript. I have no proof that will assuage their concerns. And, please be aware, the U.S. government is not susceptible to extortion. We will purchase your product, should you demonstrate success. You have two weeks to convince me, or our collaboration will cease.

TO: Burge, Clifton Dr.
FROM: Explorer1538
RE: Fountain of Youth

Then two weeks it shall be.

TO: Explorer1538
FROM: Burge, Clifton Dr.
RE: Fountain of Youth

I need your report.

TO: Burge, Clifton Dr.
FROM: Explorer1538
RE: Fountain of Youth

I have the manuscript and the formula. I require a
first installment immediately. As a show of my good
faith, I have attached an image and will send via
post the original, which I am certain you will au-
thenticate. $100,000 in U.S. Currency to Bank of
Cayman Brac, Ltd, Account Number 201-9403-
810-302. Upon receipt of payment, I will release
an additional page as proof.

TO: Explorer1538
FROM: Burge, Clifton Dr.
RE: Fountain of Youth

Document verified. Payment released.

"That's their last communication." Sebastian
closed the message. He remained silent, waiting for Kat's reaction.

"He was selling the Cinchona." Turning, she
propped a hip on the desk, angling to face

Sebastian. Gripping the underside of the metal top, she stared out into the bunker. "Tio Felix dropped out of medical school when his father died of cancer. A year later, my grandmother died from lupus complications. He and my mother inherited a fortune from their insurance policies. Tio Felix returned to Bahia."

"Returned? From where?"

"North Carolina. He attended Duke Medical School."

Sebastian typed in a command that brought up the Duke University Web site. "When was he in medical school?"

"I don't know. I'd guess 1969 or 1970. I doubt they'd keep a record of those students."

"They'd keep a record of graduates, though." With a series of keystrokes and clicks, Sebastian burrowed into the annals of Duke Medical School. "Bingo."

Kat read the screen aloud. "Dr. Clifton Burge, Class of 1972." She raised her eyes to meet Sebastian's speculative look. "Tio Felix and Clifton Burge were classmates thirty years ago, and then they work together to create the Fountain of Youth."

Sebastian shook his head. "I never took Felix for a fool."

Sliding off the desk, Kat shook her head in bemusement. What she'd seen in the extraction room suddenly made sense. Her heartbeat sped up, driven by excitement. "He wasn't a fool, Sebastian. He was brilliant. And probably right."

She felt it then, a mixture of pride and wonder and despair. "Do you know the legend of Juan Ponce de Leon?"

Sebastian swiveled around. "Sure. Came to Florida in the 1500s to find the Fountain of Youth. Died there. Obviously, he realized the Everglades was a swamp and not a magic potion."

The legend of the Fountain of Youth had been told to her by Tio Felix time and again, an object lesson in hunting for the impossible. But perhaps not. "Ponce de Leon was one of the first Spaniards to come to the continent. His party took Cuba and southern Florida, but he died without finding the fountain. But tales of the pool that could stop death continued to make it back to Europe. Decades later, Pizarro had the same goal. He'd heard about the Incas and their empire. About how they lived far beyond mortal years."

"Pizarro wasn't looking for the Fountain of Youth," Sebastian argued. "He wanted the Inca's gold."

"No," Kat corrected, "Pizarro wanted the treasure of the Incas."

His eyes narrowed in consideration. "Treasure isn't always gold."

"It's Tio Felix's answer. His final quest." She remembered the first time he'd shown her how to tap a tree, explaining the books he made her read. She felt again the rush of exhilaration, the same speeding of her pulse as she comprehended the truth. "The Cinchona is the name used for the sap that produces the treatment for malaria."

"Yes, I know."

"It has a second meaning among certain descendants of the Incas."

"What?"

"Life liquid." How had she forgotten? "Father Juan-Carlo de Borrero fled from the Spanish conquistadors and his order because of their treatment of the Incans. He hid with a village hidden in Bahia. The villagers never spoke with others, and they had no written language. But they saved Borrero's life. In return, he offered them a gift. A written history of their lives and their traditions. And their medicines. He called it the Cinchona."

"Are you saying the Cinchona is a sixteenth-century homeopathic guide?" Sebastian didn't bother to disguise his scorn. "Your uncle died for a self-help book?"

Kat recognized the skepticism, had felt it herself only minutes ago. "Tio Felix died for the Cinchona because it contained an ancient secret that Borrero tried to destroy three hundred years ago."

Derision faded as Sebastian read Kat's angry gaze. A manuscript worth millions. Worth a man's life. And a formula that required a hidden bunker and a small fortune in equipment. He took a slow breath. "What is in the manual, Katelyn? What inside the Cinchona was so important that they killed Felix?"

"Life." Katelyn met his gaze with a steady look that dared him to believe. "Father Borrero learned what Ponce de Leon and Pizarro never did. The Fountain of Youth wasn't a place. It was a formula. And it wasn't in Florida. It was here. In Bahia."

Chapter 16

Enzo stood inside the drawing room and stared at the pile of books that littered the floor. Behind him, Turi paced anxiously, constantly checking out his handiwork. The crumpled nose of their rental car poked inside the mansion, and smoke billowed from the engine.

Rafael reloaded the Steyr and the nine millimeter he carried at his hip. Shrugging, he asked, "What should we do now? Cops are probably on the way."

"You think?" The snarl came from Turi, who advanced menacingly. "We freaking *drive* into the biggest house on the block—the house where we happened to murder the owner a couple of days ago." Whirling, he confronted Enzo, his bulk making the motion more of a lumbering turn. His neck ached from the impact of the crash, and his head pounded something awful. This job had been a bitch from beginning to end, and he was ready to go home. No part of him desired to live out the remainder of his wretched life in a Bahia hellhole. Not when they still had time to run. "Enzo, man, they vanished. Check out the panel. Obviously, there was a door or something. Like as not, they're not coming out for days. We can't wait that long."

Enzo contemplated the keypad with its inactive lights. His poking at the digits yielded no welcoming beep or furious rejection of code. Apparently, Mr. Caine and Dr. Lyda had disengaged the wiring from behind. Very smart. Smarter, it seemed, than the mewling giant behind him, whose constant grousing caused him to wonder if Turi would survive their job. The urge to crush his lackey's larynx warned Enzo that the time had come for retreat. After they'd searched the house.

"Make a thorough search of this place. Every bathroom, broom closet, and mattress." Enzo turned to his compatriots, eyes flat and cold. "Before I call this in, we have to eliminate all other possibilities."

"What about the cops?" Turi whined, his hand squeezing the handle of his favorite knife convulsively. "Someone is bound to call the police, what with the racket we've made. I'm surprised we're not already in handcuffs."

"For a career criminal, you are such a pansy, Turi." He murmured the insult, not concerned about the low growl from the man who outweighed him by a hundred pounds. Enzo merely brushed at the collar of his crisp white shirt, straightened his tie. "I will handle the police." Jerking a finger toward the doorway, he instructed, "Go. Now. You have fifteen minutes." When Turi hesitated, the knife sliding from its sheath, Enzo grinned, and added softly, "Or you can die now. Your choice."

Turi let the knife fall into place and ambled out, muttering beneath his breath. If this job didn't pay so well, he'd be on the next flight home. He hated the heat, the humidity, and his partners. Enzo dressed like a dandy and gave orders like a general. Turi hadn't worked with him before, and he sure as hell wouldn't do it again. For the last few days, he'd been forced to hike killer mountains and babysit a man-child who liked to shoot at stuff like he was in a video game. Would do his heart good to cut out Enzo's, Turi considered as he entered the hallway. The image of red, wet blood spilling all over the clean white shirts the guy preferred brought a pleased chuckle as he headed for the staircase.

"You too, Rafe." Enzo pointed to the door. "Check everything."

"Yes, sir." Rafael bounded to his feet with the relentless energy of youth and rushed out to begin the hunt. Enzo noted that the Steyr lay across the purple settee, but the nine millimeter was gone. "No shooting," he called out. With a sigh, he walked to the gaping hole Turi had punched into the wall of the house. Crude method of entry, he reasoned, but effective. Reaching into the passenger side, he retrieved his phone.

"Canete Policia," came the terse greeting.

"Captain Montoya, please. It is his cousin."

"Sí."

The line went dead for an instant, then a booming voice crowded onto the line. "Enzo? What the hell have you done?"

Though the question was in Spanish, Enzo replied in English. He hated using Spanish unless it was unavoidable. His shrink referred to it as self-loathing. Enzo thought it enlightened self-interest. "Your men were supposed to have had them by now. I gave you the photos—told you where to find them."

Montoya knew of his "cousin's" disfavor for their native tongue and his temper, but he didn't care. Speaking in rapid-fire Spanish, he explained, "They weren't in the marketplace, and we didn't see them at the house. I let you go inside to check even. Why did you go back?"

"Because one of the neighbors heard her dog barking and thought she saw something."

"Your response is to shoot the place like an American mobster film and ram a car into building?"

"As the car carries the Canete Policia emblems, I assume you will explain the destruction in your report. And before you reply, please recall the support I have offered to the police to help you find the killers of Felix Estrada. I appreciate your generous loan of the police car to surveil the area."

Montoya sniffed. "Given the damage, I may require additional gifts. In the meantime, I will dispatch a team to provide backup in thirty minutes. Please have your business completed by then, okay?"

"One more item." Enzo caressed the keypad thoughtfully. "Estrada's niece. If she needed to bolt, where would she go?"

"Estrada lived here alone after his parents died. Never married," Montoya replied. "He was well-known throughout the town. However, I would first check with Senora Martinez, who lives outside the city. The girl might know her. Might go to her for help."

Because he had already visited the homestead, he knew exactly where to go. The house had been empty that time, but a return visit was in order. "*Gracias*." Enzo disconnected the line and stared at the wooden paneling. Behind the wall, he knew Caine and the doctor hid from him and his future. Perhaps Senora Martinez would prove more helpful. He strode to the foyer and bellowed, "Turi! Rafael! Come!"

Clifton Burge huddled in his Bethesda office, gulping down a tepid cup of coffee that tasted of acid in his mouth. On his desk, the photo of Felix Estrada, body sprawled and stained with blood, accused him of betrayal. The scientist shoved away from the desk, rising to pace the cramped box he preferred. At his grade, he merited a larger office, one with a view of the city. But sunlight hurt his eyes, and scenery only served to distract.

"Hey, Dr. Burge, aren't you coming?"

A young WASPish man whose name he never

remembered stuck his head inside the office door. Startled, Clifton darted to his desk, bent double, and folded his arms over the glossy, garish photo. "What? What do you want?"

"Didn't mean to startle you, Doc."

"Next time knock." Clifton couldn't recall if he was a scientist or a politico who'd been parked at the NIH because his father gave a hefty donation to a campaign. Either way, the intrusion frayed at his nerves. "Why are you here?"

"Sorry, sir. Bertha asked me to tell you that the 10:00 A.M. meeting's about to start. You know the director hates for us to be late. She's got some big announcement from DC, and all the muckety-mucks from DHS are coming down." In a conspiratorial whisper, he added with the air of a seasoned gossip, "I hear there's been a shake-up at the White House. That the director is getting promoted. Hey, maybe you'll be in line for her job."

The thought of a promotion and more interactions with his colleagues roiled his already tumbling stomach. "I don't listen to gossip," he managed tightly. "You shouldn't either."

Unrepentant, the man chuckled. "It's a national pastime, Doc. Don't be so stiff." He sidled further into the room, looking around. Dr. Burge was an odd duck who'd been at NCCAM for longer than he'd been alive. The dude guarded his office like a vault and acted all suspicious. He had a theory about the doctor, and it involved quiet types, their basements, and body parts. "You coming?"

Clifton sneezed loudly and bobbed his head. Nauseous, anxious, he stammered out, "I'll be there in a minute. Go on without me."

The intruder gave him a questioning look and withdrew slowly. "Sure thing, Doc. I'll save you a seat."

As soon as the door closed, Clifton coughed harshly, the nervous fit of hacking having followed him since childhood. He fumbled in his pocket for a handkerchief and covered his mouth. Soon, the spate of coughing passed. Wheezing instead, he shoved the square of cloth into a plastic sandwich bag that he kept in a drawer. Then he removed an antiseptic wipe from the tub on his desk and scrubbed at the places where his germs might have landed.

Wiping vigorously, Clifton worried over his current situation. The idea had seemed perfect when Felix first told him about the Cinchona. About a collection of homeopathic remedies that would revolutionize modern medicine. All he required was a financial investment to construct the elixir. A paltry sum, given the medicine's promise. Working at the National Center for Complementary and Alternative Medicines, affectionately known by the DC acronym of NCCAM, had been an ideal placement for him. Surely, his division would leap at the opportunity to fund Estrada's research.

Clifton had taken the proposal to his director, who had firmly refused to discuss an ancient manuscript with "some third-world antidotes to lice." Undeterred, Clifton had made use of a web of connections and found an angel investor. Now, his angel had turned demon, and his salvation had been stabbed to death on the floor of his own house.

Coughing again, Clifton feared this might be his last chance, regardless of what his doctors told him. Sickly since childhood, he didn't trust synthetic remedies, knowing they often created more disease than they cured. After all, he'd gone to medical school to understand the various bugs and bacteria and viruses that systematically attacked him, breaking down his immune system. One more bad cold, and he was dead, he knew. He had to have the Cinchona.

He was no hypochondriac, despite his physician's diagnosis. Instead, he was the model candidate for the Cinchona. Since childhood, he'd been prone to disease, and he had only himself to rely upon.

Hunching back against his chair, he stared at Felix's photograph. A friend for thirty years, Felix had promised him a curative that would save him and make him healthy for the first time in his life. And now, because of his actions, Felix was dead, and he was probably next.

Trembling, he reached for the phone. Maybe he should call Helen, he thought nervously. Find out if she sent him the photo as a warning. If she'd talk to him, he could explain that he was still useful. Perhaps, when they found the manuscript, he might be hired by them to synthesize the elixir. After all, he was the leader in his field. Deputy director of NCCAM. Too important to be killed—by thug or germ. Screwing his courage up, he punched in the digits.

"Taggart Pharmaceutical. Where making you healthy makes us happy." The dulcet British tones greeted him with the company's trademark slogan. "How may I direct your call?"

"Helen Cox, please." Clifton gripped the receiver in a slick hold. "I'm Dr. Clifton Burge from the United States Department of Health and Human Services. NIH."

The voice on the other end hesitated, and Clifton reached for the cup of coffee, downing the last dregs. Had Helen told them not to let him ring through? Was she sending her goons to kill him? Like they'd killed poor Felix. "I need to speak to Helen right now," he urged. "It's an emergency."

"Just a moment, Dr. Burge. Ms. Cox is in a meeting and left instructions not to be disturbed. Let me ring her assistant."

With calm efficiency, the receptionist placed him on hold, a suite from Brahms oozing across the line. Clifton sniffed, then sneezed again, and added a choppy cough for good measure.

"Yes?" Another syrupy voice came on the line. "Dr. Burge?"

"I want to talk to Helen." Sitting up stiffly, he tried to inject vigor into his tone. "Right now. This instant!"

The assistant merely replied in the same saccharine voice, "Ms. Cox is unavailable at the moment. She is meeting with clients and cannot be disturbed. However, I will certainly deliver your message at my earliest possible convenience."

"Your convenience?" The vigor slid quickly into a shrill whine. "I must speak with her now. Do you hear me? Now!"

"I understand your desire, Dr. Burge. However, as I explained, Ms. Cox is not accepting interruptions at the moment. I will pass on your urgency to her. Is there anything else I may assist you with?"

"I want you to know that I intend to report your insubordination to Helen," sniped a defeated Burge, his shoulders slumping forward.

"That is your prerogative, Dr. Burge. My name is Rhonda Minnear. Please have a nice day. And know that at Taggart Pharmaceuticals, making you healthy makes us happy."

Clifton held the phone aloft, listening to the drone of a disconnected call. Inside his head, the drone became a buzzing that pounded at his temples and disrupted his thoughts. "They've already decided to kill me." He muttered his suspicions to the empty cube, and the part of him that suspected a conspiracy of germs shrieked to him. Run, they told him in a cadence brooking no argument. Disappear where Helen and her minions can't gut you like they did Felix.

His body a vibrating wire of angst, Clifton gathered his badge, his Kleenex, the emergency packet of wipes and the Redweld filled with his communications with Felix. Shoveling them into his briefcase, he hesitated over the photograph. Perhaps if he left it, the authorities would use it to find Helen and save him. But he trusted no government, certainly not after years of working for one.

Dropping his briefcase, he flipped the photograph over and filched a marker from the jumble on the desk. In bold, sharp strokes, which said nothing of the man writing, he wrote out the words that had already killed him.

HELEN COX. MARGUERITE SERAPHIN. JEREMY HOLBROOK. VINCENT PALGRAVE. CINCHONA. FELIX ESTRADA. BAHIA.

There, he thought with satisfaction as he screwed the cap into place. His insurance policy. But he couldn't take it with him, and he couldn't afford to leave discovery to chance.

His mind raced for alternatives. "Someone else must know. Someone powerful. Someone not afraid of the pharmaceutical companies." Thirty years of not attending meetings and studiously avoiding interpersonal contact had left him ill equipped for the moment. He reached for his coffee cup and found it empty.

Empty. Vapid. Like his director. A woman with no vision, no foresight. A woman who'd not miss him at all. But she would, he trusted, try to score political points by turning his cryptic photograph over to the FBI or CIA or Homeland Security or one of the many agencies charged with stopping what had already begun.

Satisfied with his choice, he picked up the photograph and rummaged around for an interoffice envelope. With vengeful motion, he dropped the photo inside and scribbled the director's name on the cover. He hurried out into the hallway and shoved it under a stack of mail on the receptionist's desk. "Ignore this, you insipid cow."

He returned to his office, preparing his escape. A knock at his door jarred Clifton from his preparations. He barked at the closed door, "What?"

The door swung open, and a uniformed officer waited on the threshold. "Dr. Clifton Burge?"

"Yes." Struggling not to vomit, Clifton stood stiffly. "Can I help you?"

"Come with me, please." The middle-aged woman with her buzz-cut hair and charcoal skin did not raise a badge for his inspection. "You may leave your belongings."

"Am I," he paused as the question emerged on a squeak. "Am I under arrest, Officer?" He peered around her, hoping to see a crowd gathering. Some disruption to save him. But the staff had been summoned to a meeting. The meeting he declined to attend like a thousand before. "Are you here to arrest me?"

"Dr. Burge, please come with me. Now, sir." She took a solid step inside the office, her hips and shoulders filling the space in the doorway.

Nut brown eyes, flat and impassive, watched him closely. "Bring your briefcase, if you'd like."

Like a condemned prisoner, he came from behind the desk, head bowed. Another man would have run, tried to evade the officer, but Clifton had been born without the survival instinct. Not his genes, not his cells, not his brain. Dutifully, he shuffled past the woman, who made a half turn to allow him to pass. When another might have bolted, her restraining hand on his arm was unnecessary.

"This way, Dr. Burge."

The walk across the NIH campus, in the April sunshine, took less than ten minutes. The ride across town to an abandoned building was fifteen. Twenty-five minutes to regret a friendship and an obsession. They drove in his car, the lady and her partner. He sat on the back seat and coughed fitfully, in between sneezes.

In the alley, the lady escorted him to the front seat and pushed him inside. The shot fired, abrupt and fatal. As he died, Clifton gawked at the officer, stunned he was dead.

The germs had killed him in the end.

Chapter 17

"What are you doing, Kat?" Sebastian yawned, his jaw cracking with the effort. The hours blended together, marked only by the clock on the computer. Felix had also outfitted the lab and the house with cameras. Thanks to Felix's paranoia, Sebastian had been able to keep watch on the house while Katelyn fiddled with the equipment she'd discovered. Kat was in the greenhouse, and he stood in the doorway. "I thought you'd taken all the cuttings you needed."

"I haven't figured out the proportions yet. Borrero used measures like finger width and palm-sized." She lifted a hand covered in white latex. "It will take some time."

"Right now, it's time for bed. We need sleep, Katelyn."

Kat agreed, but she wasn't quite ready to face the conversation about sleeping arrangements. The thought of snuggling into the single cot they'd located sent tremors over her. She sliced off a piece of root and inserted the tungsten-colored stem into a jar. "Why don't you go ahead? I'll be done in an hour."

"Look at me."

She turned, remembering the way he'd kissed her in the drawing room. Worse, though, she recalled how he pulled away. "I'm not sleepy yet."

"You're exhausted." He entered the room, his gaze focused on her. Lightly, he caressed her chin, the softly rounded point lifted pugnaciously. Sebastian understood her reluctance. The narrow cot he'd dragged into the main lab wasn't designed for two. Unfortunately, they'd left her sleeping bag at the Martinez house. "This has been a traumatic day, honey. You need to rest."

"I will. Soon." Pulling away from his disturbing touch, she returned to her pruning. "I'll collect a few more specimens and nap on one of the lab tables."

Sebastian shook his head. The flush on her skin told him that she was recalling their brief kiss in the drawing room. He'd thought of it incessantly. How soft she'd felt beneath his hands, his mouth. How vibrant she'd been, demanding that he kiss her. How he'd pushed her away. One of his few noble moments, and he'd managed to hurt her feelings. Gruffly, he demanded, "Take the cot if you're worried about sharing a bed with me, Kat. I'll sleep on the table."

Hearing something in his voice, Kat angled

her head to look at him. He stood ramrod straight in the doorway, arms crossed. She wanted to sleep with their strength around her, his heat beside her. Embarrassment fled, and she asked boldly, "Did you stop kissing me because of the danger or because you didn't want to?"

Startled, he answered without thinking. "I want you, Kat. There's no question about that. But I'm not going to do anything about it."

She sensed a struggle inside him and wondered at the reason. "Why not?" *Why won't you take what I can offer? Why not me?*

Hearing the unspoken questions, Sebastian grappled with conscience and chose unvarnished honesty. He gripped the sleek shoulders misted by the greenhouse spray. The wet misted her lips, glowed on her skin. Need crashed through him, and for once, he knew he had to resist. For her sake and his. "I may be a lot of things, but I'm not about to take advantage of a traumatized woman running for her life."

In his experience, sex mixed with danger was heady and overwhelming and intensely satisfying. With the wrong woman, it became more— lust looked like love, and mutual convenience seemed like destiny. "You're not the kind of woman for this, Katelyn. I know it, even if you don't." He touched her cheek, the skin impossibly soft. Craving, denying himself, he whispered, "Come to bed, Kat. To sleep. Let me hold you."

Kat felt a swell that threatened to burst through her chest, then the wave settled, gentle and strong. Though she'd never been in love before, she imagined that the flood of need and want and affection and admiration could only be described that way. She petrified him, Kat realized wonderingly. And she loved him. Soundlessly, she raised her head to kiss his cheek. "I'll be there in a minute."

Sebastian backed away, her lips imprinted on his skin. He draped a sheet and the comforter over the mattress. They readied for bed in silence, and Kat slipped in beside him, resting her head against his naked chest. Without speaking, they drifted into sleep, holding each other tight.

Sebastian awoke, hard and ready. Opening his eyes, he found that like the nights before, Kat, like her namesake, enjoyed a sleep position of sprawled abandon. Her thigh tucked itself between his legs, her breath sighing against his throat, and his hands doing in slumber what he only imagined while awake. Aroused, hungry, he nearly accepted her unconscious invitation before he'd wrenched himself into full wakefulness. He surged out of bed and padded across the room to the single bathroom. In what had become a ritual, he availed himself of the icy water in the shower. With limited success.

Kat woke while he showered, and by the time he returned, she was already hard at work. Busying himself at the kitchenette, Sebastian boiled water on the burner and readied the morning's treat of oatmeal and raisins. He lazily stirred the grains into the pot, a habit he'd be more than happy to break if they made it out of this alive. The provisions in Estrada's larder and the lot they bought in the marketplace had been selected for crisis, not for a varied, sophisticated palate. More than once, he craved Senora Martinez's paella and taquitos or the rare experience of Kobe beef prepared by a surly Japanese chef.

Fluorescent lights maintained a permanent midday in the facility, a casino-like atmosphere without the bells and whistles. Instead, he listened to the steady murmurings of his partner as she tried to piece together an ancient mystery that still stunned him.

Sebastian had reread Borrero's diary and, when she allowed him to, he'd checked out the priest's manuscript. According to the diary text, the villagers had found Borrero near death, collapsed in the foothills. They'd nursed him to health and welcomed him into their fold. Five years later, as a gift to the town, he'd recorded their medical knowledge, especially the elixir they'd crafted from a variety of plants found in the Amazon jungle and the Andean mountains.

But his first trip into the Spanish world he'd fled made him realize that should the manuscript fall into conquistador possession, the ramifications would be deadly. Already, a civil war raged in Peru, and its battles threatened to spread into Bahia. Worse, Diego de Almagro, Pizzaro's former partner and current nemesis, caught wind of his discovery and sent a hunting party to find him and steal the Cinchona.

Unwilling to bring harm to his saviors, Borrero hid the Cinchona with other priests who'd abandoned the order. The Brothers of Divinity swore to protect the manuscript and kept it hidden from the Spanish. A feat they managed for more than five hundred years.

Until Felix Estrada found the Cinchona.

Sebastian watched as the grains plumped and thickened. Estrada's quest for the Cinchona might have been fascinating to him if the old adventurer hadn't dragged his niece into this mess. Like her uncle, she was now obsessed. And Sebastian worried over the consequences to her and to him. Because he still had a job to do, one that Kat would vehemently oppose.

Though she seemed to have forgotten, he had not. He was a thief. Nothing more, nothing less.

And the lady was stubborn, headstrong, and brilliant.

Once Kat understood the promise of the manuscript, she'd been scrawling formulas across the whiteboards that hung in Estrada's office, typing code into that monstrosity of a computer they'd uncovered. At the necessary intervals, Sebastian lured her into the makeshift break room for a meal or convinced her to take advantage of the stall shower in the bathroom. Each interruption was met with resistance and a glassy-eyed certainty that a moment of pause would make the Cinchona vanish.

Lucky for him, female vanity at his sniff of disdain and mention of a ripe smell had compelled her to give in after he'd come out of the shower. Using one of Estrada's concoctions, when Kat emerged, she no longer smelled of juniper and lavender or dust and grime. Instead, now, her scent was exotic, unnameable.

And driving him crazy.

Dressed in borrowed clothes from the locker, she should have looked bedraggled in the aquamarine scrubs and one of the ubiquitous black tank tops she carried in her knapsack. Add the stark white lab coat, her hair pinned into an unruly brown mass atop her head and the perpetual squint as she reviewed another stack of notes, and Sebastian could barely take his eyes off her. She uttered Latin phrases like poetry and moved with an alluring competence in a space that grew increasingly too confined for his comfort.

Sebastian set his spoon down on the ceramic cooktop with a muffled thud and glanced over at the object of his wanton thoughts. Too far away to touch, Kat bent over a lab table, cutting at a root with precision. Her slender hands gripped the blade with practiced ease, her concentration complete. The punch of desire he'd grown used to became a boxer's flurry in his gut.

Her lab coat framed the lithe, athletic body that curled against him at night, and the too-large scrubs dipped fantastically low despite their drawstring. A band of caramel skin appeared above the white tie, a tantalizing echo of the flesh that rose above the scooped neck of her black tank. In a flash of blistered memory, he tasted the cool heat again, the silken curves. Sebastian nearly groaned aloud when a brown tendril slithered across her cheek. But it was the steady, sensual grinding of the root by mortar and pestle that mesmerized him like an exotic dancer. He hadn't known science could be so sexy.

He fumbled for sanity and urgently spooned oatmeal into the two bowls he'd found. Setting the meal on a cleared lab table, he ordered brusquely, "Kat, it's time for breakfast. Sit down and eat."

"Just a second." She set the mortar down on the table and lifted the shallow container to sniff. A musty aroma greeted her nose, exactly what she expected from the contrayerva root. According to the Cinchona, it had a diaphoretic effect that combined with flavanoids in other plants to both sweat out and reduce fever. Borrero had described fascinating combinations of roots, leaves, and bark. If she could—

"Kat. Now." Sebastian loomed over her crushed root power and firmly pulled the cup from her grasp. "You've been working for hours."

"I woke up thirty minutes ago," she protested, reaching for the contrayerva. Sebastian
took a long stride away and raised the bowl.
Kat followed the movement with consternation.
"Be careful with that! There's only one more
plant in the greenhouse."

Sebastian lifted the bowl slightly higher,
taunting. "Since we got stuck in here, you have
dissected the manuscript, sniffed at every vial,
and conducted experiments on all manner of
leaf and stem. You sleep for an hour, then jump
up to work again."

"How do you know? You sleep like the
dead."

"I wish. Usually, you're lying on top of me,
and, baby, believe me, I notice."

Kat flushed, embarrassed that he'd been
aware of her body's exasperating tendency to
drape itself across his. Logically, she chalked it
up to her subconscious recognition that Sebastian represented safety and that the firm, hard
body gave off heat like a furnace. Not quite so
logical, however, was her fondness of nuzzling
against the broad, solid chest, lured by the reassuring beat of his heart and the comfortable,
seductive pillow that it formed beneath her
head.

As brazen as she'd been in the drawing room,
Kat wasn't the type to attack handsome men
and demand their favors. Even if the man felt
entirely constructed of sinewy muscle and lean,
sybaritic flesh. Fevered dreams tracked her into

sleep, ones where the deep ache that pulsed inside whenever she thought of him finally found its release.

Nearly had, she thought in silent mortification, after she almost straddled him last night. That time, she'd left their shared bed to study Tio Felix's capillary electrophoresis system, hoping vainly that playing with the geek's dream machine would distract. Instead, she found herself barely able to concentrate, focused instead on the cot where Sebastian wore only the scrubs without a shirt. And where a thin arrow of soft black hair skimmed down a washboard stomach and disappeared beneath his waistband.

No, she admitted ruefully, she hadn't slept much. How could she when her mind was occupied with the task of salvaging her uncle's dream and trying not to attack the most beautiful man she'd ever seen.

More galling though, Sebastian's attraction extended beyond the blatantly physical. Technically savvy, he played the computer's keys like a maestro and made a more than adequate lab assistant. Beneath the glib, facile façade that she didn't dare ignore, her partner displayed a range of talent and a depth of character she knew he'd hate to admit.

The more time she spent with Sebastian Caine, the less she understood about him. And the deeper her attraction grew, edging uncomfortably close to emotions she refused to acknowledge.

Like now, as irritation mixed uneasily with appreciation for the care he took of her. He nagged like a grandmother, pressing food on her when she worked, cajoling her to sleep when she swayed on her feet from exhaustion. Hell and blast, she conceded silently, she had fallen in like with the amoral bandit. She'd have to guard against like slipping hazardously into more.

He'd warned her, and she'd heard his caution loud and clear. No falling in love with scoundrels, despite their better qualities. Conceding defeat, Kat spun away from the lab table and flounced over to the breakfast that steamed gently. She dropped onto the stool and shoved her spoon into the oatmeal.

Sebastian joined her, a smile playing over his mouth. Kat caught sight of the grin, and warned darkly, "Shut up."

"I wasn't saying anything." He swung onto his seat and picked up his spoon. "But if I were to speak, I'd point out that you have a nasty stubborn streak, Dr. Lyda."

"Not all of us can be as malleable as you are. Principles tend to make me tenacious."

"Tenacity is all well and good, but there are limits, even to your formidable constitution."

"I'm eating, aren't I?"

"But you're not getting any rest. The bags under your eyes have bags."

Kat flinched in feminine pique. How dare he point out what the bathroom mirror already told her? Her hair was a tangle that limited a brush's utility. And, yes, perhaps she had dark circles under her eyes, but what type of cad pointed out the obvious. Retreating behind icy indifference, she retorted coldly, "I really don't care what you think of my looks. They didn't seem to disturb you before."

With a grimace, Sebastian realized how she'd taken his comment. "I'm not saying you're ugly, Kat—"

"No, just unattractive. I get it. But having my life threatened does take some of the pleasure out of gussying up for the day. I'm a scientist, not a model, Caine. If you want eye candy, steal from someone else next time."

Annoyed at her self-derision, Sebastian shot his hand across the table and gripped her wrist, knocking her spoon to the table. When her eyes flashed venom at him, he shook his head once. "You know I think you're beautiful, Katelyn."

She jerked at her wrist. "I'm not asking for compliments."

"Well, too damned bad." He tightened his hold, his mouth flattening in temper. "You've got skin like porcelain, with that glow that some women have that makes them luminescent. Those huge almond eyes of yours spit at me and seduce me every time I look, and I become afraid of falling in. Liquid pools of topaz and amber and heat and light. Not to mention that lush, overripe mouth of yours. I could happily die simply kissing you."

"Oh."

"But if you don't slow down, and take better

care of yourself, we're not going to make it out of this alive." Kat opened her mouth to protest, and he raised his other hand to silence her. "I know what we've found. What I don't know is who else is in on this. Dr. Burge for one. My client, possibly. And our friends, who are probably waiting to ambush us as soon as we come up for air. If you're exhausted and tired, they'll use that against us. Against me. I won't risk your life. So as soon as we finish eating, you're going to take a thirty-minute nap while I continue my research online. Then you can return to your experiments. Deal?"

Kat's mouth curved into a tremulous smile. "Why, Sebastian Caine, I think you've just broken one of your golden rules."

"What?"

"Stay the hell away from anyone who might make me forget one or two," she repeated mockingly. "You care about me."

Sebastian released his hold, but she twisted her hand to mesh with his. The contact singed and soothed, and she reveled in the contradiction. "Too late, Sebastian."

Picking up her spoon with her left hand, she began to eat, refusing to relinquish her prize. The giggle that bubbled up inside was tamped down with great effort. Smirking at his frozen expression, she urged smugly, "Eat up. Your oatmeal is getting cold."

Grumpy, mystified, he capitulated, hooded eyes returning to the tabletop, where their joined hands rested. Inside, the frenzied twist of desire shifted subtly into a slow yearning that he resolutely, absolutely ignored.

"Why do you steal?"

Sebastian tensed, despite the fact that he always had a ready answer. This time, though, for the first time, he cared about the listener's reaction. "I like it," he answered simply. "I enjoy the strategy of casing a location, of figuring out the weakest point, and exploiting it. Or the most difficult and surpassing it." Rolling his shoulders, he continued to eat. "A psychiatrist would blame it on my poor childhood."

"Rubbish."

He laughed. "Indeed. Mom and I were poor for a while, then she got a gig as nanny to the most brilliant girl I've ever known."

Ego had Kat pouting until she caught herself. "Who is she?"

"Erin is a professor in New Orleans."

Hearing the obvious affection, ego gave way to a sensation uncomfortably akin to jealousy. Kat took a bite, eyes downcast. "Are you in love with her?"

Sebastian noted the tense question and grinned above her head. "No. Not really. I mean, I do love her, but she's married to a good man. A reporter. She and Gabriel are right for each other."

"I didn't know you were a romantic."

"All good thieves are."

Kat looked up. "You think stealing is romantic?"

"Stealing can be pedestrian, another job. But the best ones are romantics. They love their targets, are willing to risk life and limb and a long prison sentence on the thrill of possessing."

"Men."

"And women." Sebastian thought of Mara, his favorite con artist gone maddeningly straight. Of course, he acknowledged, finding true love and millions of dollars might have that effect on anyone.

"How did you get started?" Not since their dinner in Ballestas had he given her a chance to ask personal questions.

Normally, he avoided conversations about his childhood, but he wanted Kat to know. "Middle school offers more than reading and writing when you live in New York. I used to run a shell game on tourists. Did a little pickpocketing to sharpen my skills."

"Naturally," Kat murmured, drawing Sebastian's self-deprecating chuckle.

"I am a firm believer in practice making perfect."

Her bowl empty, she settled onto the stool to watch him. "Because you intended to be a thief?"

Eyes glinting, he corrected, "A recovery specialist. A master thief hired by the best to retrieve their lost or stolen objects."

"Taking from those who can afford it."

"I've warned you before, Kat. I'm no Robin Hood."

She looked up at him, eyes sparkling. "I know. But you're also not exactly the flint-hearted thief who robs little old ladies of their pearls."

"Unless the pearls are from a descendant of the Imperial Family of Japan. Then, Madame Takamori had to forgive my lapse. Lucky for me, Felix stepped in."

She paused. "You enjoy putting your life in peril?"

"I enjoy living a life that's filled with excitement. We all have our callings, Doctor. Don't tell me you don't savor the rush from a new discovery?"

"Science is different," she countered.

"Why? Because you can study it in school?"

"Because I help people."

"Like the pharmaceutical companies, right? All noble intention and none of the guilt."

"Would you rather live in a world without medication?"

"Of course not, but don't climb onto your high horse so quickly, Kat. Scientists have been the architect of some of the world's gravest tragedies. Hiroshima. Tuskegee. Hell, even Bahia is the fault of some scientist who taught the Chinese to make guns and let them fall into the hands of the Spanish."

"Touché."

"Not to knock your profession, darling. Maybe you do something different."

Kat heard a personal bite, and decided to change tacks. "I try to keep people alive using what's at hand. Native remedies, especially in developing countries, can be critical. Plus, I preserve a part of a culture that might be lost forever otherwise."

"Saving the world, one fig leaf at a time."

"It's a living. And I should get back to work."

Across town, Senora Martinez peered through the peephole at the two men standing on her porch. Beyond the wooden platform, a police car idled, driven by a young man who didn't look old enough to shave. The men did not wear uniforms, and she didn't recognize them, despite her sixty years in Canete. A tall, thin man of middle age and middle features stood half a head shorter than his companion. From the single-breasted charcoal gray suit down to the black oxfords that shone despite the dust, she pegged him as an outsider. A determination that solidified when he spoke to her in Spanish heavily accented by American inflections.

"Hello? Is anyone home? It is the Canete police."

"Yes?"

A lean man with a cat's face lifted a badge for her inspection. "Senora Gabriela Martinez?"

"Yes?"

"I am Detective Selva and my partner, Detective Avilar. We have questions regarding the death of Senor Felix Estrada. Can we come inside and speak with you?"

The glint of gold on the shield caught her eye, and she quietly lifted the chain to latch the door. Her father had served as police chief for twenty years, earning her the friendship of many of the wizened members of the force. The new captain did not know her, but she had many friends. None of whom carried a badge similar to the one waved for her review.

Her husband had taken a fishing trip, leaving her alone but not without protection. She brought the double-barreled shotgun to prop against her leg. "I am happy to come into the police office tomorrow, but I am busy today."

On the porch, she saw the brawny man scowl, watched a hushed conversation that ended with the skinny one raising his hand for silence. Suspicious, she clutched the shotgun barrel with one hand and slowly turned the dead bolt with her other.

"Senora Martinez, this will only require a moment of your time."

"Tomorrow." She picked up the shotgun and leveled the weapon, which forced her to move farther from the door. Pitching her voice sufficiently loud to carry, she instructed, "I will contact the chief of police today and make an appointment."

"There is no need," Enzo protested, his temper rising. Behind the door, his best clue for finding the Cinchona waited. After circling the house, hiding until her husband drove their aging truck out for what he discerned was a fishing trip, Enzo finally had a chance to speak with her alone.

If she cooperated, he probably didn't have to hurt her, though he'd promised Turi some sport if she proved uncooperative. "Please open the door, Senora Martinez. I do not wish to cause you any harm." He lifted his gun.

It happened so quickly, Enzo had no time to react, no time to plan. Like cannon fire, the blast streaked through the door and slammed into Turi's knee. Falling, Enzo heard the clatter of the knife as it tumbled to the porch. The wood door shattered along its panels, splinters flying out in rough-edged shards. A sliver embedded itself in Enzo's cheek, blood welling in a sudden rush. A second shot rang out and, in preternatural instinct, he dived low before it struck him in the face.

"Rafael!" Enzo bellied across to the car, waiting for another blast. He swiped at his cheek, his hand sticky and wet. "Rafael, engine."

The boy had plunged to the car floor, ears covered by his hands. Cursing, burning, Enzo dragged Turi to the vehicle, flung the Taurus door open, and scrambled inside. Though he dearly wished to spray the homestead with cannon fire, he screamed at Rafael to drive.

"Turi?"

"The crazy bitch shot him. Drive." Enzo slumped in his seat, removing himself as a target. He checked the empty road for real police officers. Somehow, he figured, she'd discerned they weren't real officers. A painful error for Turi, a stupid bumble for him. His meanest employee felled by a shotgun. He could have captured her anyway, but his team was making too many mistakes.

When Rafael whipped the Taurus onto the main route, Enzo slid against the blistering leather and sat up straight. "A hospital," he instructed Rafael. "He's bleeding all over everything." Turi's wail added unnecessary emphasis.

"What will we do now? About the woman? Want me to go back and take care of her?"

"No." Enzo closed his eyes, focused on the goal. "She will be gone by now. We leave her until I say otherwise. We will take Turi to the hospital, then head for the Canete Police Department. We have business there."

Chapter 18

"Sebastian, can you go to the storage unit and grab the vial labeled *Tabebuia impetiginosa*: bark: quinoids?"

"Sure." For the life of him, he couldn't have explained half the words in her sentence, but he'd grown used to the hunt for the indecipherable. With quick strides, he entered the temperature-controlled storage unit that they'd discovered and found the bottle she'd asked for. Moving silently, he crossed to the extraction room and stood in the doorway.

Inside, Kat sat at the work space entering instructions into the system, and the odd machine hooked to the computer began its whirring. Breakfast had passed hours ago, and both had opted to skip lunch, for very different reasons. That his had anything to do with cowardice compelled Sebastian to step fully into the room. Kat's sly pronouncement about breaking his third rule might make him antsy, but he wasn't one to retreat. Unless retreat was the more profitable course.

When it came to his partnership with Kat, he couldn't tell yet. But he'd made one decision earlier, an e-mail to Helen. The text was straightforward and to the point.

```
TO:     qi45@pad.intel.net
FROM: mutiny@pad.intel.net
RE:     Finders Keepers

Cinchona is no longer for sale. Will refund money
upon return to U.S.
```

He had never refused to complete a job before, but Kat had been the start of many firsts. So he'd continue on this path and take the necessary course corrections later. He sighed, a quiet, annoyed exhalation and held out the vial. "Making any progress?"

"I think so." Kat continued to review the data on the monitor and nodded in satisfaction. With an absent gesture, she brushed a curl away from her forehead and turned to Sebastian, accepting the glass bottle. The green scrubs rode low on his lean hips and the white T-shirt he wore stretched taut across his chest. Built more powerfully than Tio Felix despite his leanness, Kat understood why some women swooned over doctors. It certainly wasn't simply the brains.

She kept her thoughts to herself and her eyes shaded, her increasingly indiscreet thoughts her own. Given that his question had been the first words he'd spoken since she flirted with him at breakfast, she decided to maintain the peace by focusing on work alone. Probably for the best, she mused. Caring for Sebastian entailed perils she hadn't fully considered. Better for them both to focus on the task at hand and leave romance for a more appropriate time.

After dinner.

With a secret smile, she inserted the tube into a tray and pointed to the vials that had been inserted into the machine and the tray that remained, prepared for extraction. "The Mutambo who saved Father Borrero had incredibly sophisticated medical practices for fifteenth-century peasants. Separately, the teas, juices, and tinctures exceeded the level of care most people get from their general practitioner. What Borrero describes is a method of combining certain chemical properties from the plants and creating a master elixir that can operate as both a preventative and a curative."

"A supermedicine."

"Exactly."

"And now? What exactly are you trying to accomplish?"

"What Tio Felix was working on with Dr. Burge. A stable version of the elixir." She blinked once, then bent low over the vials as she carefully measured out the liquid. "According to Tio Felix's notes, the chemicals reacted poorly each time he tried to find the proper combination. Borrero didn't have access to the sophisticated equipment or even the scientific methodologies used today."

"If your uncle studied medicine, couldn't he—I don't know—just whip up a batch of the Cinchona?"

"Not without causing some chemical reaction that could blow this place up." She indicated a row of vials that she'd been preparing since their arrival. "Each one tries to combine the various plant extracts mentioned in the manuscript. But some of these have evolved on basic levels over time. I won't be able to test out the elixir, but I will at least be able to verify that it is a stable compound."

"When?" Sebastian lightly touched her shoulder, watched her profile as she tipped one green liquid into a beaker containing a yellow concoction. Slowly, she added a deep red using a dropper. "We're on borrowed time, Kat. My client plus whoever hired our friends out there aren't going to be deterred by this bunker forever. If there's another way out, then someone will find it and use it to get in."

"Well," she murmured, setting the beaker on the worktable, "I think I've done it."

"What?" Sebastian looked down at the beaker, the strangely hued mixture an eddy of green and blue and magenta. "Is that it?"

"Unless we explode in the next fifteen seconds, I'd say yes." Amazed, excited, she whirled toward him with a laugh. "We did it! The Cinchona formula is stable. It looks just as Father Borrero described it in the manuscript."

Sebastian caught her around the waist, dipped her in triumph. "You did. I've been a glorified lab assistant."

"An excellent one!" Exhaustion fled, leaving her giddy. "We've done what Tio Felix asked. We have the Cinchona!"

"And what will we do with it now?"

"What he asked. Return it to the Mutambo."

Sebastian held her, asking the question that had bothered him since he understood the purpose of the Cinchona. "Why didn't they do it for themselves? Then? Why leave a miracle cure to the annals of a priest?"

"It wasn't supposed to end there." Because she had considered little else, she explained her theory. "From Borrero's notes, I think the Mutambo had an archaic version of what Tio Felix tried to create, which they called the Cinchona. Borrero and the head of the Mutambo reasoned that the potion, which took three to four years to manufacture for a small dose, could be mass-produced with the proper techniques."

"But the Spanish weren't all that more advanced than the Mutambo, right?" Sebastian queried. "I've read the diary a dozen times over. Borrero spent five years with the Mutambo and offered them the gift of a written record of their medical practices. Then he vanishes for nearly two years, and when he starts writing again, he doesn't mention the manuscript again. He lives with the Mutambo until his death ten years later. But he never talks about the Cinchona again."

Kat had a theory on that as well. "Remember the wars in 1538? If the Spanish had learned about Borrero and the Mutambo, they might have overrun the rest of the continent. A medicine that could heal wounds, fight fever, and make an army nearly invincible."

Sebastian rubbed a thoughtful hand over his chin. "For Borrero, that would have meant betraying the people who saved him."

"His gift might have meant their slaughter," Kat agreed.

"So he leaves the Mutambo to hide his gift." Beneath his fingers, a light stubble scratched at his skin. He hadn't bothered with shaving, though he'd be more comfortable once he did. Felix had a rudimentary setup in the bathroom, more monastic than hedonistic. "That's it!"

"What's it?" Kat demanded quizzically. "What?"

"The answer, Doctor. I know where Borrero vanished to all those centuries ago." Sebastian grabbed Kat and hauled her excitedly up from her chair. Looking inordinately pleased with himself, he led her into the main room and to the computer that accessed the Internet. To see better, Kat stood behind Sebastian, her eyes tired from hours of reading. While she watched, he called up a search engine and typed in *Bahia* and *monastery.* When a list of holy orders and their locations appeared on the screen, there was one entry for the Brothers of Divinity.

Sebastian spun around and grinned up at Kat, reaching up to capture her waist in triumph. "We've got it!" Holding on, he jerked his head toward the screen behind him. "The monastery, Kat. That's where Borrero lived during those missing two years, and that's where Felix found the manuscript."

"Father Borrero went home. Of course." In delight, she curved her hand over his cotton-covered shoulder and squeezed in mute congratulations. "To hide the manuscript and maybe to develop the potion. The order would have had more advanced equipment than the Spanish armies or the Mutambo. I'd bet anything the Brothers of Divinity trained their monks in the medical sciences."

"Army medics." Sebastian relaxed against the chair, flexing his hand along the resilient waist he held. With intention, his thumb drew circles at the wedge of skin exposed by the drooping waistband. The softness lured him, the strength bound him. The combination threatened to undo him. He glided an exploratory touch along her arrow-straight spine, savoring the tiny gasp that sighed out. Catching her inquiring look, he merely added, "Monks were jacks-of-all-trades, weren't they?"

Beneath his touch, shivers fanned across Kat's skin, jellied her knees. She stood between his braced thighs, his fingers splayed low against the curve of her hips, wide along the terribly sensitive expanse of her back. Of its own volition, her hand slid beneath his collar to search. Along his nape to explore. She loved him, the whole complicated package. She needed to be with him. Soon. "They had to be," she murmured. "They were often the most educated of the conquest party. Men like Pizzaro and Almagro had been raised to be soliders, not leaders. In fact, Pizzaro grew up an illiterate swineherd."

Testing, Sebastian drew her deeper inside the V formed by his legs. When she brushed against the iron heat of him, he shifted suddenly, bringing her astride his leg. "Sit down, Kat."

She locked eyes with him, and wordlessly, sank onto his lap. The dark face, usually on the edge of mocking, met her gaze with an intensity that rushed heat into her belly, clenched her hand around his neck. "Sebastian?"

He smiled then, a tender curve of the mouth that owed nothing to mockery, nothing to cynicism. "I've never known anyone like you." He cupped her cheek, tracing the haughty line of bone that brought her beauty into sharp relief. "You're not afraid of anything. Of anyone. Be afraid of me."

Kat laughed, a simple, sultry sound that wound through him and hardened him impossibly more.

"Not afraid? God, Sebastian, I'm terrified. A week ago, I was a scientist. I understood plants and the people whose lives depended on them. I traveled from village to hamlet to tribe and thought I knew the world. I was an idiot."

She slithered forward, drawing his response as his hips surged beneath her once, before he controlled the movement. "I'm afraid of the men chasing us. I'm terrified of the death I've seen, of what my uncle brought me into. I'm scared that my promise to him will get both of us killed." Quietly, she brushed her lips across his furrowed brow, creased in disbelief. "But I'm not frightened of you."

"Kat—"

"Listen to me." She rested her forehead on his, her words a whisper feathering his mouth. "I'm not of your world, no. I can't dance my way past dead bolts and impenetrable security systems."

"But I can. I do." Sebastian wrapped her flush to him, the bodies meshing perfectly. Already, he could feel her beneath him, above him, surrounding him. He tilted her quiescent face to meet his eyes, the promise stark and unyielding. "I'm a thief, Kat. I can make love to you and leave you once we've completed your mission. Do you understand that?"

Kat flattened her hand, covering the heartbeat that thundered in his chest. And with a brazenness she barely recognized, she stroked the ridge of flesh that stood between them. "Believe what you'd like, Sebastian. I'm not afraid."

As he lunged up, sweeping her high in his arms, her lips pressed to the thud of pulse in his throat, Sebastian muttered, "By God, I think I am."

In long, hurried strides, he carried Kat to the spartan cot where they'd slept the night before. Gently, he lowered her to the unforgiving springs, to the thin mattress with its spare white sheets. Ranging his body beside her, he slid his arm around her waist, dragged her lithe, supple form against him.

"Tell me what you want." Sebastian breathed the demand into her skin, her soul.

"You." Kat twisted under him, arched her hips to meet his, intent on merging so there could be no separation. What she wanted was impossible. Absurd. That nothing could come between them, not truth, not lies, not secrets. Her whisper and the dance of need to need urged him to action, to seduction. "This."

He gave in, fusing his open, wet mouth to hers, tasting the heated recesses with a dying man's hunger. Threading his hand into her hair, he surrendered to the erotic simplicity of a kiss. The tangled mating of lips and teeth and tongue. The feral, voracious search for answers. Sebastian enjoyed the act of kissing, the slippery, intoxicating glide of sensation.

He'd never kissed a woman before. Not so his head spun with the scent, the texture, the flavor of her—not so that he could break apart in the act.

In the bright room, he rose above her, determined to see her. His Kat, her body bowed in longing. Elegant, golden lines dipped and flowed, and he thought of a sculpture he'd taken in Senegal, a goddess too ethereal for this world, too earthy for heaven. Lush and delicate, invincible and fragile. His Kat.

Too greedy to wait, he ripped at the worn

material of her top, rending the fabric at the seams. Bending, he licked voraciously at the pouting crests. Creamy, flawless breasts filled his eager hands, his teasing nips drawing them into delicious points that begged for his mouth.

Kat shook with astonished pleasure, her body a taut line of nerves, a mass of sensation. Impossibly, he touched her everywhere, a serration of teeth at her waist as her borrowed scrubs loosened and disappeared, a ribbon of wet heat as he sampled the line of her thigh, the sensitive skin behind her knees, the shadows at her core. Hard, callused hands soothed and skated across her naked flesh. Shocked, overcome, aroused, she reared up, to hold on, to hold fast.

She wanted more, craved all. Turning, she straddled his tight, rigid waist and yanked his shirt over his head, his bottoms down, the cotton dropping to the tiled floor. Laughing, she tormented with tiny, fierce bites at the flat male nipples that rose under her ministrations. When he trembled, she skimmed her tongue over the tangy skin that shivered for her. For her.

The heart that forbid entry drummed, his breath quickening as she marveled at the piquant flavors of steel and flesh. "You want me."

"Always."

Entranced, she sampled the cord of muscle at his waist, the mound at his bicep. Moans broke from the vault of Sebastian's chest, singing her into headier discovery. Panting, she slanted desperate kisses along the mysterious line of hair, this time following its path to the turgid length that jerked beneath her explorations.

"Kat." Sebastian felt his undoing and hauled her away. They rolled together, bodies sliding in exotic counterpoint, angles nestling curves, soft seeking hard. Blood raged and drove him to thrill. To suckle and caress until aches became pleasure became a fantastic despair that consumed them both.

With care, Sebastian readied her, drawing the moist response that swam in his head like a fiery whiskey. He tightened, seduced by the rhythms of snaking hips, the lure of steamy skin whose scent enthralled. Overwhelmed, he struggled for the distance that made sex pleasurable and physical, with no question of commitment. Of love.

He couldn't find it. Could only grasp the lure of advance and retreat, of a joining that seemed endless, weightless, forever. Needing to give her ecstasy, he stroked at the taut nub that slicked beneath his touch. Frantic to devour, he savored her, building a dangerous fire with careful motions, entering in triumph as her nails sank into his skin, demanding speed and consummation.

"More. Sebastian, more." Kat writhed in glorious anguish, too close, too ready.

"Look at me." Sebastian eased out in a slow, endless motion, waiting until her eyes opened, focused their amber passion on him. Unable to stop himself, unwilling to lie, he murmured, "Let me love you."

She cradled his head, brought his mouth to hers, and understood what he didn't yet. "Yes."

He thrust deep, control broken, shattered. Again and again, deeper and hotter and further than fantasy.

With urgency, she accepted him, fascinated by the power, and for a moment, she wavered, wondering if she was prepared. In the next second, she knew she could never be.

Kat moved beneath him, her body too full to stay motionless. Theirs mouths coupled, imitating the dance that frenzied her limbs, wrapping her into him.

Sebastian flew above her, driven to claim and imprint himself forever. He nuzzled her breast, finding the wild beats, and pressed a kiss just there, sealing his fate.

He stretched her, drained her, completed her.

She surrounded him, took him, filled him.

Together, the coming overtook them, flung them beyond the tangle of bodies, beyond the desperate desires of heart. Into everything.

Kat propped her chin on Sebastian's damp chest, the teak flesh stretched taut over ridges of muscle. Sated, she struggled to keep her eyes open, refusing to succumb to the drag of sleep. She turned her head to see this man, now her lover. Lover. A word she'd used to describe men before, but not too often and never like him. Like Sebastian. "Sleepy," she murmured.

"You can sleep, honey." His hand traced idle

patterns along her naked back, his mind racing. Thinking about how natural she felt, beneath his arm, beneath his mouth. A sensation disturbingly similar to contentment wound lazily through him. "But not yet."

"Sebastian?"

Their lips met, and he rolled her beneath him. "Sleep later, Kat. Much, much later." Slowly, methodically, deliberately, he kindled fire, built longing and joined them together, determined to imprint himself on every fiber, every pore.

"Sebastian!"

"Fly with me, Kat." He tasted and reveled in the breaking of her breath as he kissed every secret place. Groaned in delighted agony with the aches she created and eased as she feasted on his flesh.

Again and again, in the dark, they came together, drawn to find answers. To find satisfaction. Finding each other.

Chapter 19

"Katelyn."

Naked, Katelyn inched forward, searching out the solid, sleek engine of a body that had pleased and ravished her for endless, blissful hours. Blindly, she patted at the still-warm place where Sebastian had lain. Her questing hands tapped an empty mattress, and the fog of her mind registered his absence with sleepy dismay. "Where'd you go?"

"Kat, wake up." An ungentle smack to her sheet-covered bottom pushed her into alertness. "We've got company."

Kat's eyes flew open and met the imperious stare of Senora Martinez. Discarded aqua scrubs and a flimsy, torn top dangled from the matron's fist. Mortification washed over Kat in waves, and she jackknifed up, clutching the sheet to her breasts. "Senora. Hello."

The greeting tumbled out, and she wished fiercely that the methanol in the lab would explode and distract the censorious gaze. Kat swept an accusing look at Sebastian, who stood on the other side of the cot, looking smug. He, somehow, managed to be fully dressed and sipping from a cup of coffee. When he offered no rescue, she barely resisted the urge to snarl and instead pulled a ragged cloak of dignity about her. Clearing her throat, Kat smiled wanly at the woman who'd known her since childhood.

"Uh, Senora. I didn't expect to see you."

"That, my dear, is obvious." Leaning in, Senora Martinez dropped the bundle of clothes into her lap. Their eyes met, and Kat could have sworn she saw a twinkle of pride. "You might want to clean up. We have much to discuss."

"*Sí, señora.*" Without waiting for either to move away, Kat scooched to the end of the cot, dragging the sheet with her. One hand clutched the wad of fabric, and standing, she filched Sebastian's coffee away with a muttered comment on his parentage. He opened his mouth to retort, but one look had him stepping away in demurral.

"Senora Martinez, perhaps you'd like a tour of the facility. We can begin way over there." Sebastian extended his elbow to the lady, a courtly gesture that drew her amusement. And her attention away from the fleeing Kat.

After the door to the shower slammed shut, the senora thumped his arm playfully. "You are a scoundrel."

And exactly the right match for her Kat. When she'd come through the tunnel door, she'd caught Sebastian standing near their bed, watching Kat as she slept. One hand wound through the sleeping woman's tousled brown curls, a baffled look playing over his face. In the instant he raised his head at hearing her, she glimpsed a raw terror. In a man like Sebastian, that fear had came from an undeniable source.

"You could have woken her," she chided him now.

"I am a scoundrel, Senora." Sebastian led her to the lab table where he and Kat ate. "But my mother insisted on teaching me manners." He dragged out a stool and helped her to sit. "See?"

"They are not too rusty," she acknowledged, settling onto the high stool. She teetered precariously, then, with a muttered imprecation, stood up again. Her fluffy curves would fare better standing, she decided, rather than falling to the tiled floor. The stools had been made for the hipless, not for women of her proportions.

Felix had insisted upon the barest of essentials in his hideway. Looking around, she remembered the day he'd shown her what his guilt had demanded and his millions had built. That day, like many others, he'd sworn her to secrecy. Oaths she would break today. She looked over at Sebastian, who'd risen gallantly when she stood. "I do not need a tour. You know well that I have seen this place before."

"Given your stealthy appearance, I have to assume you also knew why Estrada constructed it. And that your visit today isn't because of nostalgia." Sebastian walked over to the burner, where a pot brewed. "Coffee?"

"No, *gracias*." Senora Martinez looked around, taking in the place she had last visited ten years before. Her Josef had never come inside, did not know about Felix's exploits. As his best friend, she knew, and because of that bond, she would care for his niece. Glancing up, she watched pensively as Sebastian returned with a black cup that steamed gently.

"I had visitors this afternoon. Three men in a police car."

"Describe them." Sebastian nursed his cup, listening intently.

"A tall one who had a mean look about him, he was the leader. There was a fat one who carried a knife and a boy in the car." Her hands quivered once as she spat out, "The mean one asked about Felix. When I refused, the fat one pulled out his knife and would have come through the door. I shot him in the knee. I had no choice."

He covered the wrinkled fist and squeezed. "They are the men that killed Felix."

"Good. It is good that I hurt him then. But I did not shoot the others. The recoil," she rolled her shoulders where the butt of the gun had slammed. "I had not shot for a long time, not since my grandfather."

"You did well, Senora."

Appreciating the easy acceptance, Senora Martinez patted the young man's hand where it covered hers. "Gabriela. For these times ahead of us, I am Gabriela."

"A lovely name." He glanced at the bathroom door. Sebastian spoke quietly, listening for the roar of the shower. "Kat intends to follow in Estrada's footsteps."

Gabriela pointed to the whiteboards filled with Kat's equations. "She is smart, our Kate-lyn, no?"

"Brilliant. And determined. She's done what he couldn't She figured out the formula and created the Cinchona." Sebastian scrubbed at his eyes, abruptly, brutally tired.

"The elixir was a myth, I thought. Felix knew otherwise. He was a stubborn, foolish man."

"He was right." Dropping his hand to the marble slab, he uttered a curse. "Kat promised him that she'd return the Cinchona to its rightful owners."

"The Mutambo." A woman who understood more of the world than she'd seen, Gabriela understood the shadows clouding the lustrous dark eyes that held hers. The mother in her wanted to soothe, but she too had made promises. "Felix came to see me four months ago. He'd found a diary, he told me, in a monastery. The diary of the priest who wrote the Cinchona. The monks were reluctant to part with their treasure."

"Because they'd sworn to protect it." At her sharp look, Sebastian explained, "Estrada kept a journal." He pointed to the desk and the computer. "On that. He coded it pretty well, hid it under layers of junk, but he wanted a record of his deeds."

"Misdeeds," Senora Martinez corrected blandly. "Felix was no altruist. He was a hot-blooded, passionate, selfish man who blamed himself for deserting his parents and squandering his wealth and youth. Always chasing something better, grander, more exciting. Never standing still long enough to appreciate what he'd found."

"He was in love with you. Until he died."

Sebastian saw the flicker of response, the softening of her mouth. Heard the almost inaudible, "Perhaps."

Giving her a moment, he lifted his cup and drained the contents. He picked up the story, pretty clear on what happened. "Estrada goes to the monastery and convinces the monks to part with the Cinchona. I imagine they were not aware of their revised decision."

She chuckled richly. "No, they were not. By then, Felix had compiled a formidable collection of ingredients. The greenhouse, you have been inside?"

"Yes. Kat tells me that many of the plants only grow in the Amazon. I've never seen their equal."

"Felix loved the beautiful, the exotic. Plants, sculptures, fine art."

Beneath a hooded gaze, Sebastian gauged her reaction. "But he was obsessed with the Cinchona. That's the one possession he died for. Nearly got his niece killed for."

"Not on purpose!" Senora Martinez slapped at the table in disgust. "Felix was a dilettante, but he was not careless with her life."

"The evidence begs to differ."

"I thought you smarter, Sebastian. Evidence tells the story the listener wants to hear."

"Then what is the truth? Isn't that the question of the hour, Kat?"

Kat startled, wondering how he'd heard her when she made no sound.

"Come on. You need to hear this." With a quick, emotionless look, he waved at her to join them.

She'd traded her black tank top for a white one, and the green scrubs rode low on her hips. Her hair curled wildly around her shoulders, the locks dark with water. The wanting he'd imagined sated returned with vicious force. The time, however, for satisfying his baser urges had passed. Reality had intruded when Gabriela Martinez entered the bunker. From now on, he mercilessly reminded himself, Kat and her luscious, agile body was off-limits.

Kat brushed at her wet, lanky hair. She'd brought a limp towel from the bathroom, wishing for a blow-dryer. But if wishes were horses, she thought bleakly, trying not to stare at Sebastian's blank expression. Tension coiled through her, reminding her of his ample warnings. Sex and love were not the same for him. Hadn't he been brutally honest?

She couldn't blame him for the cool stare he

leveled at her because she had no right to expect more.

As she'd been doing since landing in Bahia, Kat shoved aside the tempest of emotion and walked forward. The floor was slick beneath her damp feet, cold to the touch. Halting an arm's length away, she repeated his query. "What is the truth, Señora Martinez?"

"You must understand, Katelyn. Felix blamed himself for not being here for your grandparents. He'd taken his inheritance and frittered it away, playing at archaeology and art and anything that captured his imagination. His one repentance had been medical school, but he'd not been trying hard. Then his father was diagnosed, followed in months by his mother. Your parents offered to return, but Felix was the older son. It was his duty."

"He was too late. They were sick, and he couldn't cure them."

"No one could have." Gabriela shook her head, remembering the arguments with Felix, the pleas for logic. "He got it into his head that if he'd gone to medical school sooner, he might have known they were sick."

"Impossible."

"Of course it was. What he meant was that if he'd been around more, he'd have seen the signs."

Kat mourned silently for the family she hadn't met. "It wasn't his fault."

Unable to stop himself, Sebastian pulled Kat in front of him, her crown tucked beneath his chin. Silently, he plucked the towel she carried from her nerveless fingers and began to dry her hair slowly, methodically.

"Tell her about Borrero's diary, Gabriela."

Senora Martinez moved away, recounting how Felix came to her with his find. "Felix read the diary from cover to cover. Father Borrero's instructions to the monks mandated that the diary and the manuscript remain separated. But there was no mention of where the Cinchona had got to. When Felix started studying Borrero's order, he determined that the Brothers of Divinity had sent the Cinchona to a monastery in Cuzco."

Sebastian continued to rub the water from Kat's hair, her unnamable scent teasing his senses. To distract himself, he asked, "What happened?"

Senora Martinez clicked her teeth together and stopped at the lockers. "In Cuzco, Felix was followed. He got the Cinchona, but in his hotel room, a man attacked him. That's how he knew his secret had been revealed."

"Burge knew where he was going." With a jerk of his thumb, Sebastian pointed to the computer. "I assume Burge tipped off his colleagues."

"Felix needed help from this Dr. Burge. Despite his wealth and his experimentation, Felix was an amateur. But he'd stayed in contact with a friend from medical school. Burge agreed to review Felix's data and help him." Gabriela shook her head. "Felix was worried about whether Burge would reveal his plan. He gave me instructions, in case of trouble."

Kat gave a harsh laugh devoid of humor. "Like being murdered?"

Releasing the towel, Sebastian pulled Kat against him, his arms crossing her waist. She leaned into the embrace, bolstered by his presence. "Senora Martinez, I know what Tio Felix wanted. For me to create the Cinchona and take it to the Mutambo. To return their legacy."

"That's right." She skimmed her eyes over the couple before her, hoping what she knew of Katelyn and what she suspected of Sebastian was true. "Follow me."

Kat moved first, Sebastian's arms falling away. The loss made him hesitate, a forerunner of what would happen when they found the Mutambo. Pushing the grim thought aside, and with the corresponding ache settled near his heart, he followed.

Gabriela led them to the extraction room. The desk that held the extraction system had four drawers. She pointed to the bottom drawer. "Sebastian, reach underneath the desk. There's a key screwed into the base."

He didn't argue. Instead, he lay flat on the cool tiles and scuttled under the massive frame and, near the far right leg, caught sight of the key. "Give me something sharp."

Kat dashed into the main room, found a knife. Returning, she knelt and passed the blade to him, handle first. Sebastian unscrewed the oblong shape and handed out both the key and the knife. From the shape of it, he recognized a safe-deposit key.

Without pause, Kat passed the key to Senora Martinez and helped Sebastian to stand. A tiny thrill coursed through her when he maintained his hold. "What is it, Senora?"

"A safe-deposit box key," replied Sebastian. "The operative question is where is the box."

"I know where it is and what is inside," Gabriela said. "A map, I think. And money. The Mutambo are not friendly to outsiders, but they are not hostile. My Josef has known some of their kin. The village is not on the main roads. You will have to travel along the coast and hike into the country, to where Bahia is crossed by the Amazon."

"There's no way we can get into a bank dressed like this, especially with our friends on the lookout. Exactly how are we supposed to use the key?"

"The bank is not here in Canete. It is east, in Huanco. We should go." She stepped forward and patted Sebastian's cheek. "Are you a sailor, Sebastian?"

"I've been in a boat."

"The runabout is small and motorized." Kat spoke up. "Tio Felix taught me to use it years ago. I've kept it up."

"Well then, we should go." Senora Martinez bobbed her head, pleased. "My vehicle is at the cove, and we will have to walk there from here. You need shoes."

The trio walked into the main area and

Sebastian broke off, going to the computer. "I'm going to download his files. A precaution."

While Kat and Gabriela packed provisions, he logged onto the account he'd established. The yellow envelope warned him of mail.

TO: mutiny@pad.intel.net
FROM: qi45@pad.intel.net
RE: RE: Finder's Keepers

You disappoint me, Sebastian. Deliver the Cinchona in two days or Dr. Katelyn Lyda dies. Not today. Not tomorrow. Not even two months from now. But one glorious morning, as she gardens at her cottage in Miami, an assassin will plant a bullet in her forehead, a bullet you can stop if you keep our bargain. Deliver the Cinchona, and I will still pay your fee and guarantee her safety. Do not disappoint me again.

Taking a deep draft of air, Sebastian surrendered to the coursing of black ice that froze him to the core. Terror grappled slickly with violence, and he wondered about the line between salvation and betrayal, where a secret transformed into a lie that devoured.

To save Kat's life, he'd have to use her and desert her. He'd have to comply with Helen Cox's demand and trade the future of an impoverished community for one woman's life.

The line blurred for him, taunted him. He'd never loved before, never cared about the lines. Then, because he'd crossed so many, he stepped over it. For once, though, the action bothered him on levels he hadn't known he possessed. But as he shunted the disturbing nag of conscience aside, a gaping wound seared him where his heart had been.

There was no help for it, no question. He would betray Kat, rob her of redemption to save her life.

To: qi45@hotmail.com
FROM: cainemutiny@gmail.com
RE: Finder's Keepers

You win. But the price just went up. Ten million for the manuscript and Borrero's diary. With billions awaiting you, I'm sure you won't quibble over price. I'll meet you in Lima on Friday.

With a steady hand, he pressed SEND.

Chapter 20

Helen read Sebastian's e-mail again. His latest demands were steep, but not too onerous. After all, she'd struck her bargain with him before he'd known the true value of his target. Caine was too much the businessman not to seek higher profit. As long as he delivered, the Cinchona was a bargain at twice the price.

Bringing the Cinchona to the marketplace served her purposes sufficiently. Beautifully. A masterstroke to cement her as the rightful heir to the Taggart legacy. Were she more spiritual, Helen would have thought it preordained. Destined.

Had it only been months ago that she received the plaintive communication from Clifton Burge? A silly old man with a fear of death and access to information that had kept Taggart on top for years. A useful partnership, as Burge required an alternate stream of income to his bureaucrat's salary, a way to pay for his hypochondria and penchant for exotic treatments.

The private partnership between Taggart and the NIH had been created when her uncle had done his residency with Burge. And he'd introduced a twenty-year-old Helen to him during her stint in Washington, before she assumed the helm of the family company.

Helen Taggart Cox, daughter of Phillipa Taggart-Cox and Jason Cox. CEO of Taggart Pharmaceuticals. Unless her board meeting in one week resulted in her termination. Taggart had been flying high under her leadership, until recently, when three of their drug trials had resulted in catastrophic deaths, and a pending lawsuit threatened to drown the company in damages.

But in the labs belonging to Taggart and her partners, the Cinchona would save them all. Four companies, each on the brink of ruin. Santé Laboratoire, headed by Marguerite Seraphin, which had not brought a new drug to the marketplace in four years. Its last cash crop, the cancer drug Wynzert, had generic competitors hitting the stores in December. Then there was Gezondheid Corp., the upstart Dutch company led by Kenyan exile Vincent Palgrave. Palgrave had falsified his company's financial records and was in desperate need of a hit to cover his tracks. And Jeremy Holbrook's HolStrum Labs, an American company accused of hiding test results for an AIDS drug, a public relations nightmare that required a distraction. Helen had found the solution for them all, had brought together a team bound by a prisoner's dilemma so taut, no one could afford betrayal. At the light rap at her door, Helen pressed the buzzer and the door swung open to frame Marguerite. "You're early."

Marguerite sank gracefully onto the rich red leather. "I'm interested in our status."

"Sebastian Caine and Dr. Lyda are under control." Helen lifted a Mont Blanc from the desktop, twirling it absently between her fingers. "I have been in contact with my recovery specialist. He has agreed to deliver the Cinchona. We are on call."

"Captured by your other team?"

"No." Helen scowled and lifted a cigarette to her lips. She ignited a black-lacquered lighter, and quickly, pungent smoke filled her lungs and settled her nerves. Enzo had reported in, had told her of Turi's accident. She felt a bit of sympathy, as she enjoyed Turi's penchant for hostility and his ease with knives. "They are on track, in case anything else goes awry."

"But nothing will, no?"

Dragging deeply, Helen puffed out a moue of smoke, the ring evaporating into the chilled air. "No. Caine has the manuscript in hand."

"Where was it? When will it arrive?"

Pleased, Helen became expansive. The Cinchona was her brainchild. Her salvation. "Before our board meeting. In time for our labs to run tests."

"Has Dr. Lyda tested the Cinchona? Is there proof from live subjects?"

"Of course not." She'd thought about the communications between Burge and Estrada, and it occurred to her that the niece might try to accomplish what her uncle couldn't. "Estrada didn't manage it, so I don't see how she could." Helen inclined her head to the doorway, where Palgrave and Holbrook waited in the vestibule. "You know that making the compound stable has been the greatest challenge. Burge tried to help Estrada, but Estrada refused to tell him all of the elements that needed to be combined."

"Could Katelyn Lyda figure it out? Helen, be honest."

"Yes, with enough time, I think she could."

"Then we need to bring them in. Now."

Helen shook her elegant head, the tight coiffure remaining immobile. She possessed sole control over the turn of events, a control she did not intend to relinquish. "We have exactly what we need. There is no cause for alarm."

"What happens now?"

"Exactly what I promised when I brought you all on board. I promised you a return on your investment, and you will have it."

In the years Marguerite had known Helen, their mutual admiration had been tempered by a healthy distrust. Still, she had never had her suspicions confirmed. "Who will deliver the Cinchona? Sebastian Caine?"

"He has not deserted his baser instincts. However, he has upped his price for delivery. I will need an additional $3 million from each of you immediately."

"Fine. I will consult with Vincent and Jeremy."

"As long as they do not interfere," Helen demurred. Sebastian Caine had shown a recent wavering in his amorality, a disturbing trait she didn't quite trust had been quelled. She'd allow Enzo's bumbling hacks to follow them and ensure their arrival in Lima, she would take the Cinchona and redirect the group's investment into her own special R&D account in Zurich.

She pressed the intercom button on the sleek red phone. "Send in Mr. Palgrave and Mr. Holbrook. We have much to discuss."

Senora Martinez drove the truck with a Formula 1 driver's speed, whipping around the tight curves of the highway without regard for gravity or her passengers. Snugged between her and Sebastian, Kat watched the road with terrified fascination. If they made it to Huanco alive, she'd be amazed.

She was amazed to be alive at all. She'd been chased, shot at, shot at again, and in between, she'd solved a centuries-old medical mystery and fallen in love.

With a man who couldn't admit he loved her and never would.

Kat searched vainly for anger, wanting to feel something other than the growing shadows that gloomed inside. But there was only sadness and resignation and that primal urge to be with him again and again and again until reality returned.

Because, Kat admitted wanly, despite the way

he held her hand, or watched her with those piercing, intense eyes or made love to her in the dark of night, Sebastian Caine did not love her.

It was impossible—and imprudent—to believe otherwise. Sebastian wasn't a man to mince words, and he'd warned her more than once that love was out of the question. They were from not only different worlds but diametrically opposite ethical planes.

She wanted to believe she wasn't in love with him either. Falling in love so quickly was the stuff of fairy tales and caprice. A smart, balanced woman didn't succumb to the lure of danger and the romance of adventure.

She didn't brazenly kiss a beautiful, bad man who had stolen from her and her family.

She didn't take a small kindness and spin a fantasy of happily ever after.

She didn't hope that everything she knew to be true wasn't. Which was why loving Sebastian baffled her—she, who valued honesty and morality, bound by heart to a man who glibly decried a belief in either one. He was a self-proclaimed thief and a devout liar. And the one reason she was still alive.

Kat furtively studied Sebastian's stern profile, the gorgeous mouth hard and immobile, the rugged jaw set. The man was a walking, breathing mass of contradictions. He was heroic and loyal and more honorable than most of the men she knew.

More than once, he placed himself in danger

to protect her. More than once, he violated his own rules against caring about others to soothe and comfort her. To save her.

The paradox of him fascinated her, captivated her. He eschewed sentiment, but cradled her in his arms when she whimpered in the night. Forswore obligations to anyone but himself, and yet, here he sat, traveling to Huanco to help her fulfill her pledge to her uncle rather than taking the Cinchona and heading for New York.

The truck lurched around another hairpin turn, tossing Kat into Sebastian. She sprawled onto his lap and gripped at his knee to brace herself. Her other hand splayed across his chest, and because she couldn't help it, she curled her fingers against the beat of his heart. She swallowed once, her pulse fluttering in time with his. Testing, she slid her hand higher, to brush the rigid jawline that seemed hard as concrete. "Hmm," she murmured. "Can't seem to keep my balance around you."

Beneath her touch, Sebastian savored the contact, the gentle heat he knew could explode into an inferno with a stroke, a touch. But their idyll had ended with Senora Martinez's arrival and his betrayal. He no longer had the right to enjoy her scent, to revel in even the briefest contact. His happiness had been forfeit when he accepted Helen's ultimatum.

With more control than he realized he possessed, Sebastian merely wrapped his hands around the taut, narrow waist he'd strung with kisses the night before, and when he wanted to hold tight, he set her away from him. "Grab the dashboard next time."

As quickly as he could, he snatched his hands free and dropped them onto his lap, ignoring the hurt arrowing into the bright, wide eyes. Turning away, he stared out the window, wondering where in the hell he'd gone so terribly wrong.

In his whole damned career, he'd avoided the one, unforgivable sin of a rogue. Never fall for a mark. The moment emotion entered the picture, sanity and smarts vanished. Which was why he had three good friends in his life and no lover who meant more than fun, raucous release.

He'd come close before, tantalizingly close. Until he remembered the trade-off. Give away your heart, he understood, and you give away your edge. All of a sudden, decisions aren't cold and clear, they're hazed up by feelings and promises and the desperate urge not to disappoint. Fall in love, and the woman would sink into you, deep into your skin, into your very bones. She'd cloud your judgment and mess with your head until all you knew, all you wanted was her.

So he resisted. Time and again. And now, in days, he'd lost his edge. Handed it to Kat on a silver platter. Along with his heart.

And as soon as she figured out the truth, she'd crush it and leave him empty.

He had options, he knew. With another

woman, he might have told the truth, asked her to disappear with him. His nest egg was solid. They'd be able to live nicely in Europe, richly in the islands. Even if he retired, he'd take an occasional gig here and there to keep the skills sharp, their lives safe.

But Kat wasn't made for his kind of retirement. Not with her sense of justice, the one that spurred her to fulfill a dying man's wish despite her grief and the peril. No, not his Kat. She'd try to accept him and his work, trying to reform him. With her tenacity, she'd believe it possible. And if she loved him, she'd never admit defeat. Until he'd eroded her trust, broken her spirit. Until she gave in and accepted the man he was. Would always be. And was no longer the woman he loved.

Sebastian rolled down the window, ignoring the blast from the air conditioner. Warm, sultry winds gusted into the car, mingling with the artificial air. The two battled for dominion, the wind bowing to the cold. It wasn't a fair fight. Never could be.

"What are you doing, Sebastian?" Senora Martinez eased off the gas to bark at him. "Put the window up."

Sebastian complied, turning the handle quickly. He clenched his jaw and looked past Kat to Gabriela. "How far to Huanco?"

"Another fifteen minutes or so. We'll stop by a store first, get you two better clothes. You can't go wandering around in those pajamas."

"What about the bank?" Kat asked quietly,

her eyes fixed on the road. "We don't have the identification that matches the safe-deposit box."

"No, but we may yet be able to gain access." Senora Martinez shot a glance at Kat. "Felix wanted you to take the contents."

"What? Why?"

"Because he considered you his next of kin. All of Felix's belongings and possessions belong to you."

"I don't want them."

"Katelyn—"

"No. I will do this for him. I'll return the Cinchona to its rightful owners, but I will not own those other items he stole. I won't profit from his thievery."

"Now, wait a minute—" Senora Martinez began.

"Felix didn't steal, Kat." Sebastian spoke over Gabriela, his tone obdurate and unyielding. "He usually bought his possessions at twice the going rate, just to make sure the artisans were rewarded. Think what you like about your uncle, but he wasn't like me. He was a good man."

Aghast, Kat looked over at Sebastian, her mouth open with remorse. "I didn't mean that you aren't a good man."

He laughed, the sound low and guttural. "Sure you did, honey. And you're right. I'm not a good man. But we've gone over this before." He glanced over at Gabriela, who had slowed the truck even more. Making a decision, he jerked his thumb to the shoulder of the road. "Pull over, Senora. Kat and I need to have a chat."

The truck clabbered over the rough terrain to an area that could generously be called a shoulder. Sebastian unlatched the door and hopped out. "Come on, Kat. Let's go."

Sensing something she didn't quite comprehend, Kat followed as he strode briskly along the trail, winding down into a ravine. Blocked from sight of the truck, he stopped.

Concerned, Kat laid her hand on his shoulder. "I didn't mean to insult you, Sebastian. You're here. Now. Helping me. Only a good man would do that." The slow, mean smirk should have warned her, Kat would realize later.

With a brutal efficiency, he plucked her hand up and released it, as though soiled. He stepped away, held out a hand when she would have closed the distance between them. Shoving aside guilt, he sneered, the cocky grin that infuriated her. "Save the redemption for your uncle. I'm along for the ride because I don't enjoy being double-crossed. Obviously, my client didn't trust me to get the job done and she sent another team after us." To drive the point home, he caught her chin on his fist, raised her eyes to meet the look he trained to slide slickly over her. "I'll help you return the Cinchona because I'm in the mood for revenge. And because you've been good entertainment. Nothing more."

Kat breathed in sharply when their eyes locked. The bitter chocolate darkened almost to obsidian and held as much warmth. She could feel hers moisten, refused the tears. "Nothing more? Really?"

Sebastian leaned close, his voice pitched low, carrying only to her ears. "Look, honey. Last night was fun. Memorable, even. But I warned you before, didn't I?"

Kat took a stumbling step away. "I haven't asked you for anything, Sebastian."

He chuckled insultingly. "But you will. Women like you can't help themselves."

"Women like me." Hurt spun into rage. She barely held in a snarl, and instead ground out, "You mean weak women?"

"Honey, I know you're not weak. You've already proven that." With a flick against her mouth, he drew his thumb along the crest of her cheek. "I mean dreamers like you. Women who weave fantasies to make themselves feel better about their choices. Hell, you don't even know if Sebastian Caine is my real name, Kat. You just think I'm handsome and dangerous and that I can make you feel things no one ever has."

"Like pity?"

Sebastian dropped his hand, and Kat surged forward, eyes flashing. "Pity," she repeated steadily, "because you are so damned afraid that you'd rather lose me than try to be who I know you can."

"What? A solid citizen?" Even to his ears, the scorn sounded less than certain.

Hearing it, hearing him, rage softened, and

Kat touched him, her fingertips grazing his heart. "No. A man who will sacrifice everything for a cause that's bigger than him. A man who lets himself love someone else for a change. But you're terrified of me. Of loving me."

"Bullshit."

"No." Kat felt the tears come, let them fall. "No, honey. You love me, and you can't stand it. Because you know you'll put me first." She reached up then, hauling his mouth to hers. Heat, passion, compassion poured from her into his mouth, into his soul. When his breath vanished, his mouth no longer his own, he begged for mercy, and she twisted against him, denying relief.

His arms imprisoned her, though he was the captive.

Finally, he shoved her away. "Stop it, damn you. I don't want you."

"Liar." The word hung between them. Kat watched him with drenched eyes that measured and found him wanting. "You're such a liar. My God, Sebastian. Until now, I never realized you were a coward too."

Then she turned and walked slowly for the truck.

Chapter 21

Sebastian stood frozen, his mouth tingling, his hands itching to do violence. Not to Kat, but to the Fates that had put him in such a buggered position. Thirty-five years of fiercely guarded independence shot straight to hell. A lifetime of carefree, even feckless existence, answering to no one, and he had to find the one woman who could tie him into knots and unravel him completely, all in the same clear-eyed, soul-searing amber look.

And to be the man she believed him to be, he'd have to betray her. He stopped by a quina tree and, spinning, slammed his fist into the bark. Pain radiated up the bone, and his fist oozed blood from where the bark broke skin. He stared at the tree, realizing that what they carried in the cab of the truck might heal him instantly. Damn the quina, the Cinchona, the whole lot of it, he cursed silently. Everything he'd ever wanted was slipping away, faster than he could bear it.

Out of sight, Sebastian braced his arm against the trunk and rested his forehead on the rough surface. Guilt and love and desire and a desolate aching tore at his breath, bit at his resolve. Maybe, he thought wildly, maybe he hadn't considered all of the angles. Surely, there was a way to outwit Helen and her cohorts. A way to let Kat return the Cinchona and protect her from their wrath. To keep her with him until the aching stopped.

Staring up at the lazy travels of white clouds along the horizon, Sebastian imagined for a moment that there was a way. But he knew better. He knew his client, that her ultimatum was no idle threat.

People feared the military and the mob. But the most highly organized, ruthlessly efficient gang in the world existed ostensibly to heal. Pharmaceutical companies spent billions of dollars in the pursuit of life and squandered millions of lives in the hunt for profit. Complicated, complex moralities that refused a simple label, the tiny nations headed by profiteers like Helen Cox had an army behind them that could wipe out the G-8 in a matter of seconds. Could bring other companies to their knees, make them beg for mercy.

What could he possibly do against those odds? He was one man. Stuck in a forgotten nation, with a scientist, an ex–cabaret singer, and a motley truck as his weapons. He had no choice. No options. Nothing to do but surrender. Swiveling his head, Sebastian watched through the foliage as Kat climbed inside the cab and slammed the door shut. She stared out the front window, refusing, he imagined, to look back and see if he followed.

"That's right, my love. Don't look back." Sebastian spoke softly to the trees, the only audience he trusted. "Whatever's chasing you will catch up soon enough. Unless I can stop them."

Sebastian lowered his head, sucked in a deep draft of air. Still, his lungs felt empty and wrung out. After years of stealing, searching for something to mean more than the next heist, he'd finally found the prize. Found Kat. Only to give her up to save her.

With a cool head and without trying to redeem himself.

The irony twisted through Sebastian, a molten wave of remorse and acceptance. For the first time in his godforsaken life, he'd truly perform an unselfish act, and the beneficiaries would curse him for it. Fitting, he conceded.

But he had never been a good martyr. From his earliest memories, he'd been adept at wiggling out of situations and leaping into others. He made his own choices, his own destiny. For a case like this, an army feared only another force more powerful.

And only sunshine could defeat the enemies of the dark. Sebastian snorted at his own poetry and pushed away from the tree. But an idea coalesced, formed solid and convincing. Satisfied, he turned on his heel and began the climb up from the ravine.

"Do what you have to, Sebastian. Recrimina-
tions are like candy floss," he warned himself
callously. "About as substantial and as memorable." With quick, sure strides, he walked toward the idling truck, mind settled. He had a
job to do, and he was on a schedule. One day to
get Kat to Lima, along with the Cinchona.

He wrenched the door open. "Let's go."

The rest of the drive occurred in silence. In
the cramped space of the cabin, Kat managed to
carve out a wide berth, a yawning space between them that remained even as the truck
lurched around corners. Her fingers dug into
the dashboard, lines of muscle rippling with the
effort to keep her upright as they sped around
corners. When her knuckles showed white from
the strain, Sebastian issued a seething curse.

"Cut it out, Kat. You'll hurt yourself." He settled deeper against the door to give her more
room. If she didn't stop, at the next turn, she'd
go flying through the window. "Look there's
plenty of space. I won't touch you."

Kat said nothing. As if on cue, Senora Martinez took the next curve on two wheels. He slid
into the doorframe and fumed as Kat's nails
sank into the cracked leather. Her arms trembled from the effort, and her legs dug into the
floor for purchase.

"Damnit, Kat. I said cut it out." She moaned
then, a tiny sound that escaped before she broke
it off, the whimper scraping at nerves already
rubbed raw. Angrily, he caught her up and
hauled her into his lap.

"Let me go," she demanded, squirming fiercely.

Beneath her frustrated movements, Sebastian hardened, a nearly perpetual state for him since meeting her. He lowered his head and pressed his mouth against her ear. "Keep moving, and I'll give Senora Martinez a better show than she got this morning." Louder, he warned, "Sit still. We're almost there." Praying he was right, he glanced at Gabriela. "Right?"

She smothered a grin. "*Sí.* Huanco is around the next bend." Deliberately, she barreled around the curve, and Sebastian closed his arms around Kat to keep her from tumbling to the floor. She eased off the gas and pointed to the paved road jutting off to the left of the highway. "That's Huanco."

In short order, she'd parked the truck in front of Huanco's version of a strip mall. The town, population ten thousand, boasted two streetlights and enviable tar paving that leveled the roads for the aging cars in the city. Mariposa's, a stucco building painted a garish pink, welcomed patrons to select from American-designed, El Salvadoran-sewn garments. Sebastian selected a couple of pairs of blue jeans and a third in black. A packet of thick white T-shirts bearing the Hanes label joined a pullover in his basket. He rummaged in a large bin for necessities and kept a furtive eye on his grim companion.

Kat shopped on the opposite side of the store, accompanied by Senora Martinez. She had already found jeans of sufficient length to fit her unusual height, the slim boy cut discovered in the young men's aisle. A couple of tops, patterned brightly in hues she admired, though rarely wore, were added by the senora.

"Such a lovely skirt!" Senora Martinez beckoned to her. Kat reluctantly crossed to where she stood at the arrangement of summery dresses that billowed from their hangers. "Try this on, Katelyn."

"I'm not here to pick out dresses, Senora. I will be working, not dating."

"You will be convincing the Mutambo to accept you. They are traditional people and will not react well to a girl dressed as a man." Certain she'd won, Senora Martinez held up a length of red-and-bronze fabric, the colors blending at the bodice and separating at the skirt.

The wrap-dress had been knitted by hand and seemed to float beneath the senora's hand.

"You must try it on, Katelyn. For an old woman," she added, when Kat began to protest.

Kat sighed, but accepted the dress and the skirts tossed atop her pile. Muttering about interfering busybodies, she stalked into the dressing room and shucked off the scrubs. The tank top fell onto the floor and she worried for an instant that she hadn't bothered with a bra. At her size, a bra was more a fashion statement than a necessity.

Sebastian certainly hadn't raised any complaints.

As soon as the thought winnowed into mind,

she shook her head to clear it. No more, she chided herself. No more thoughts of Sebastian and his refusal to accept that he loved her. He'd made his choice perfectly clear. Despite what she believed he felt for her, he refused to accept it or her. His choice, his decision. Just as she'd made hers. The ache of loss would ease someday, she knew, but not nearly soon enough. She dragged the fabric around her naked body, yanking harder than she intended and heard the seams pull.

"Cut it out, Kat." She repeated his instructions from the truck and clicked her teeth together in pique. "Stop thinking about him."

Swiftly, she wrapped the ties around her waist and knotted them in front. Without a look in the mirror, she flounced out from behind the curtain to confront Senora Martinez.

And promptly collided with Sebastian.

He caught her easily and quickly set her away.

"Sorry." Kat focused on a point over his shoulder, refusing to make eye contact.

So she didn't see his mouth gape open, his jaw tighten as he studied her in the bronze-and-crimson dress. Soft, luxurious fabric draped curves, hollowed contours. The modest bodice framed the swells of smooth, creamy breast in a swirl of color. A nipped-in waist flared into generous hips, and the cotton skimmed down her thighs to halt dangerously just below her knees. From that point, the stunning legs he'd admired from the first day he'd seen them seemed to go on forever. "Buy it."

Before she could retort, he stepped past her and into the adjacent dressing room. Senora Martinez flurried over, beaming. "*¡Muy bonita!*"

"*Gracias,*" Kat responded absently, and turned into the dressing room. Selecting a long skirt in green and a matching top in a floral motif, she took extra time to braid her hair and wind the heavy mass into a knot at her nape. Exiting, she was accosted by Senora Martinez, who pressed earrings into her hands.

"For the bank. It will be part of your costume," she urged, hurrying Kat to the counter.

The aging shopkeeper mumbled over her purchases and tallied the amount on a decrepit cash register. Beside the register, though, an electronic credit card reader blinked imperiously. He announced the total and offered, "Cash or credit," in smooth English.

"We'll pay cash." Sebastian reached past her to pile his selections on the counter. "These are together."

Kat opened her mouth to protest, but a firm hand bit into her arm. Near her ear, he whispered, "We need them to see us as a couple, okay? It's easier."

She subsided unhappily. Having him pay for her clothes vexed her, but there was no help for it. Soon, they exited the shop, dressed in their new finery. Sebastian had selected khakis and a white oxford, the hue a marvelous contrast for his skin. In the sunlight, his skin glowed a

burnished copper, the chiseled features a mask
of obdurate beauty.

Kat tore her gaze away and raced ahead to
the truck. She stored her packages in the bed
with harsh, irritated motions. There was no
way she could bear to spend another minute
in his presence, let alone another night. If she
had to trek to the Mutambo village alone, she'd
be rid of Sebastian Caine by tomorrow sun-
down.

"We can walk to the bank." Senora Martinez
spoke from behind her.

Kat turned quickly, her new sandals kicking
up dust. She looked over the senora's shoulder,
but Sebastian was nowhere in sight. Wanting to
ask, she firmed her mouth in a mutinous line.
"Fine. Let's go."

"Sebastian will meet us there." Senor Martinez unlocked the truck door and flipped over
the bench. She tucked two shopping bags into
the empty space and motioned for Kat to do the
same. "We should put our packages in the truck
and lock the doors. This isn't Canete."

Kat transferred her bags, thinking of her single visit to Huanco. "Tio Felix brought me once,
when I was fifteen. They have a museum here,
correct?"

"Yes. Of the Nazca line that survived in Bahia. Lovely pottery." Senora Martinez secured
the truck and linked her arm with Kat's. "The
bank is down the street, on the next block. We
should hurry, to reach them before siesta."

"Sebastian better not take too long." Kat cast

a suspicious glance around the town square, but did not see him. "Where did he go?"

"Your young man doesn't believe in explanations, I think." The older lady shrugged dismissively. "He'll join us soon, I trust. Certainly, as he has Felix's key."

Kat scanned the town again and saw a tall figure dip into an alleyway. "There he is." She pointed to the tall buildings that comprised downtown Huanco. "You go ahead, Senora Martinez. I need to talk to Sebastian." Without waiting for her assent, Kat hurried down the street.

From force of habit, Sebastian wound between the stucco and wood-framed shops for several minutes before finding a back door that had been left slightly ajar. He ducked into the abandoned storefront, squished in between what he determined to be a grocery and a restaurant. The smell of overripe plantains and sofrito teased his nostrils and reminded him that he hadn't enjoyed a full meal in days. But food could wait. This could not. Inside the store, shelves sagged on rotted wood and dust thickened the floor.

He made his second call to London, breaking every rule of protocol. A voice answered, "Helen Cox's office."

Sebastian paced the empty store, its windows boarded up. He pressed the cell phone close to his ear. "Good afternoon. I need to speak with Helen. Tell her it's Sebastian Caine."

The receptionist sat straighter in her chair,

recognizing the name she'd typed onto wiring instructions around the world. But behind the closed door to Ms. Cox's office sat four of the most powerful men and women in the world, and she had strict instructions about disturbing their confab. Consequences mentioned included hunting for a new job with a permanent smear on her employment record and destitution in London's West End. So, it was with mixed emotions that she replied, "Mr. Caine, Ms. Cox is in a meeting and cannot be disturbed. May I take a message and have her ring you back?"

"No. Walk into her office and interrupt her. She'll thank you."

"Ms. Cox left strict instructions. I am not to patch through any calls. Including important ones."

"Well, darling, we all have our instructions." Sebastian paused, then said reasonably, "Okay, Miss—"

"Miss Lundquist." Gratitude at his understanding softened her vowels, reminding her of the Cockney roots she'd hidden beneath hours of imitating Lady Diana. "Miss Delores Lundquist."

"Okay, Miss Lundquist. Please give Ms. Cox this message. 'Your multibillion-dollar project is about to go up in smoke because your ultra-efficient assistant chose not to deliver my message in a timely fashion.'" He waited. "Did you get all that?"

Deflated, Delores shut her eyes tight and tried to recall where she'd last filed her résumé. "Just a moment, Mr. Caine."

Delores slipped from behind her station and approached the frosted glass door. She depressed the buzzer once, then a second time when there was no response. Eventually, an eternity later, the door slid open to frame the livid face of Helen Cox. "If this building is not on fire, I expect your desk to be cleaned out by five."

She stumbled through her explanations, hoping she'd made the proper choice. In a hissed undertone that did not carry into the office, she explained, "I know you said no interruptions, Ms. Cox, but it is Sebastian Caine. He says it's urgent."

Helen stiffened and cast a glance over her shoulder. Her three companions watched the exchange with varying degrees of interest. Vincent primarily watched Delores's legs, and Holbrook gazed adoringly at Vincent. Marguerite, however, kept an eagle eye on them, the emerald eyes unblinking. Helen gripped Delores's elbow and propelled her into the vestibule. "Put him through to the conference room. I'll take the call there."

With a hurried bob of comprehension, Delores dashed to her station and retrieved the call. "Ms. Cox will be with you in a moment, Mr. Caine."

"Then I will have to tell her how helpful her ultraefficient assistant has been. Have a lovely day, Delores."

Despite the earlier threat, the silky compliment appeased her, and she returned huskily, "Take care, Mr. Caine."

In the conference room, a red button flashed in staccato bursts on the telephone. Helen strode into the area and pressed the door firmly closed behind her. Like every space in the building, the conference room was soundproofed. And like every room, digital devices recorded activities. Helen circled to the audiovisual control panel and disengaged the automatic recording function. This was why she rarely contacted Sebastian using company technology.

Satisfied that their call would be private, she lifted the receiver. Her voice dropped an octave, the tone a sensual invitation a former lover would easily recognize. "Calling so soon, Sebastian? Miss me already?"

"Don't flatter yourself, Helen," Sebastian answered tersely. "I agreed to do as you demanded, but I have some additional terms."

Helen scowled, annoyed by the rebuff. Tone hardening, she scoffed, "This isn't a negotiation. I want the Cinchona in one day's time in Lima. In exchange, your new plaything lives to see another day, and you receive your retirement fund. Isn't that what you used to call it? Especially that night we rolled around in your installment from the Essex assignment." She purred over the memory, images shortening her breath. Sebastian had always been skillful and imaginative. And hers.

"Let's not play nostalgia, Helen. That was a

long time ago." Sebastian didn't regret his alliance with Helen, but he found nothing pleasant in remembering it. However, alienating her served no purpose either. "I can't make it to Lima by tomorrow, not without making Katelyn suspicious."

"That's not my concern. We have a deal. You've tried to renege once already. Don't do it again."

"I'm not reneging, Helen. But we do need to change the drop site. I need you to meet me in Canete. At Estrada's house."

Helen cackled at the thought. "An ambush, Sebastian? Is that your master plan? Lure me to Bahia and murder me to save your girlfriend?"

Not exactly, Sebastian thought. "I don't do murder. You know that. But I can convince Katelyn to pay her last respects to her uncle. At his home. Meet me there in thirty-six hours."

"Where will you be?"

"Pretending to help her fulfill Felix Estrada's last wishes." Sebastian understood better than most that the truth was a more convincing lie than any imagination created. "You'll do a wire transfer to my account for $10 million. I won't tell you to come alone, but if anything seems wrong, I vanish. And the Cinchona goes with me."

"Which leaves Dr. Lyda as fair game."

"I vanish, and you can have her. However, if you're the reason I leave, I'm selling the Cinchona to the highest bidder."

"I'm not worried, Sebastian. You'll play by my rules."

He tightened his hold on the phone and struggled to keep his tone even. "You double-cross me, and Katelyn's death will be the least of both of our concerns."

"Don't be coy, Sebastian. If she didn't matter, you wouldn't be bargaining with me."

"Like I said, Helen, I don't do murder. However indirectly. And we both know I don't fall in love with my marks. This is a matter of profit. Do we have a deal?"

She considered upping the ante, simply to break him, but time was of the essence. "Yes, thirty-six hours, Canete."

"*Ciao.*" Sebastian disconnected the phone and slipped it into his pocket, turning. And stopped.

Katelyn stood in the doorway, her face wreathed in shadow. She took a step inside, the door swinging shut. "You son of a bitch."

Chapter 22

"How much did you hear?" Sebastian intentionally leaned against the wall, ankles crossed negligently. With a careless gesture, he pushed the phone into his back pocket, then crossed his arms against his chest. He had sensed her presence behind him during the call, and he hadn't cared. A betrayed and angry Kat was a damned sight simpler to deal with than the complexity of loving a woman too good for him.

Though he wouldn't have chosen this minute to chase her away, he grudgingly accepted the state of things. Kat would accuse him of betrayal, he'd admit it, and she'd leave him. Because of the love that had sneaked up on him, had twined insidiously inside him, he'd let her.

She stood just inside the store, where he could grab her if she tried to run. In the gray, bleeding dimness, she blocked the exit to the street, in case he decided to escape. Looking at her, Sebastian wished for the first time in his life that he'd chosen another path. Luminous amber eyes held his, their color darkened. He knew the shadows owed little to the overhang of the tin roof above and everything to what she'd probably heard him tell Helen.

Wrong conversation. Wrong time. If he'd been a different man, Sebastian would have cursed his luck or denied the conversation. But he wasn't. So he didn't. "Where's Senora Martinez?"

"At the bank," Kat responded automatically. "I came to find you."

"Well, you certainly did." Shifting his weight slightly, to better watch the street, he repeated softly, the words not carrying beyond them. "Kat, how much did you hear?"

Staring at Sebastian, Kat wondered idly at the science of living on when a heart stopped beating. Surely, the empty cavern that ached in her chest was a scientific marvel. Because she hadn't misunderstood what she'd heard. Sebastian planned to hand over the Cinchona to his client, as he'd always planned. Despite knowing of Tio Felix's sacrifice, of her need for absolution. Stunned, her breath dragging through constricted lungs, she murmured, "I heard enough."

"Enough to know that I've betrayed you?"

A flash of fire caught inside at the easy declaration. Kat took an angry step forward but stopped short of coming within his reach. She had no idea what he was capable of. Not anymore. Her voice husky but strong, she matched his low tone. "Enough to know that you'll never see what's inside my uncle's safe-deposit box."

"Darling, you can't stop me. I've got the key." To taunt her, he fished the sliver of metal from his front pocket and dangled the key before slipping it back inside. "I'll tell them I'm his nephew, come from America to claim his belongings. We both know the bank authorities will be more than pleased to assist me, especially if I sweeten the pot with a couple of thousand dollars."

Kat flinched. "I'll tell them you're a thief. And a liar."

"And I'll point out you're a fugitive accused of killing the owner of the box." Sebastian spoke matter-of-factly, unconcerned. "By the time they sort out the truth, my client will be in town. You can't win here, Kat."

For a moment, Kat shut her eyes, unable to face him. The truth was, he was right. Stupid, trusting fool that she was, she'd let him keep the key. And despite her speed and excellent shape, she couldn't outrace him to the truck. Senora Martinez might try to come to her aid, but at this point, she had no idea what Sebastian was capable of. Everything she thought true of him had been proven wrong.

Including how he felt about her. Last night hadn't been about falling in love or even basic desire. What she'd read as affection had been calculation, pure and simple. Get the gullible novice into bed, lull her into forgetting his two rules.

I don't sacrifice myself for anyone. I don't put anyone's happiness above my own.

The jagged twist of pain forced the humiliating question from her. Her color heightened as she asked, "Why did you sleep with me? For the Cinchona?"

The halting question had Sebastian shifting away from the rough wall. Instinct demanded that he reach out to her and soothe, but he stopped himself in time. Instead, he shrugged. "Didn't you enjoy yourself? I thought I'd done an admirable job on that score. Several times, I believe."

"Bastard."

Sebastian smiled. Deliberately, he closed the distance between them. He needed to touch her again, even in pretense. One last time before he lost the only prize that mattered. Like a blind man, he traced the arrogant jaw, the aristocratic slope of her cheek, the mouth that tempted him to bend. To taste and take and forget his good intentions.

Kat did not pull away from his caress, watching a struggle play out behind the shuttered eyes. Confused by the gesture, she clasped his hand and held it pressed to her cheek. "Sebastian. What's going on? Talk to me."

Love, unfamiliar and unyielding, forced him to drop his hand. He crowded her instead, looming above. "I warned you, Kat. From the first day. I take things. Even from you. You can't be surprised."

She stared at him, rigid and absurdly cold.

"I thought we—that you felt something for me."

"I do, darling. I like you. You're smart and sexy and you've got a body that's worth going to war over. But no woman is worth a million dollars."

"I thought you told whomever you were talking to that the price was ten?"

Sebastian chuckled ruefully, cruelly. "Yes, I did. One million or ten, Kat, it's all the same. Women are all the same."

Resentment surged, snapping into her eyes, steeling her spine. She shook her head once, hard. "How little you must think of me."

"Now you're getting it."

"No. No, you don't get it. Not if you think a few insults and a thanks-for-the-lay speech are going to make me run off. Make me believe that you don't love me."

"I don't."

"Yes, you do." Certainty curved her mouth, lifted her hand to his chest. Beneath her palm, his heart pounded a staccato rhythm and threatened to break free. "My God, Sebastian. You're in love with me."

He shoved her hand away angrily. "I am not. Stop saying that."

The sly smile curved her mouth and she released a charmed laugh. "And for some reason, you plan to make your client believe that you're going to hand over the Cinchona."

"I am," Sebastian insisted, feeling as though his feet had been knocked out from under him. She knew, he thought. How the hell did she know? "I am going to give it to my client and take the money."

"No, you're not. You never were. Not since you saw Tio Felix's body." She grinned up at him, slid her free arm around his waist. "I need you to be brave, Sebastian. Because I'm going to do something that will scare you."

He gripped her arms to push her away, and soon, he thought, he would. "What are you talking about, Kat?"

"I'm going to trust you. I'm not sure what elaborate scheme you've concocted, and I don't know if you'll tell me what you intend to do. I'd be impressed if you did. But it doesn't matter. For the next thirty-six hours—that is the time you gave your client, right?" He nodded automatically, and she continued. "For the next thirty-six hours, I'm going to do what you say, not too many questions asked. You've got my trust, Sebastian."

"I don't want it," he grated out, his fingers sliding beneath the straps of her dress, absorbing the feel of her. The reality of her. "I don't want you to trust me."

"I know. That's why I'm giving it to you. You can't steal it, you can't finagle it. It's a gift, without strings. And I'm not asking for anything in return, a foreign concept in your world, I know. But there you have it. I love you, and I trust you, Sebastian."

Flummoxed, Sebastian glared down at the clear-eyed woman who watched him serenely, topaz eyes boring into him as though she truly understood him. A shiver coursed over his suddenly too-tight skin, a preternatural awareness that his life had been irrevocably altered. He didn't like it. Nor did he like the way his heart seemed to shift in his chest, an abrupt sensation of how he imagined tranquillity felt.

The emotions were alien and overwhelming and addictive. He wanted no part of them. Sebastian scowled, resisting the urge to run. What game was she playing? "I didn't say I loved you, Katelyn."

The retort was harsh, certain, but Kat refused to back down. Turning up the wattage of her trembling smile, she responded, "Doesn't matter. I know you do."

Or so she had to believe. If she was to survive the coming hours, to envision a life where the inky black that crowded inside her dissipated, she had to hold on to the lie she told herself. Sebastian loved her. He wouldn't betray her. Doubt trickled into her thoughts, and to push it away, she laced their fingers and tugged him forward. "The bank will close soon. We've got to go."

"Wait. For a damned minute, wait." On a growled oath, Sebastian spun her to him, dragged her against him. Sinking his fingers into her hair, the sable mass dislodged from its knot. The cool strands burned his skin, coiled around him. Hungry, feral, he dived into the exotic mouth that lied so prettily, promising him dreams he'd never bothered to imagine.

Kat braced for invasion, knowing the demons

that rode him. So when his lips gently parted her mouth, she wondered. When he slipped inside, a delicate exploration that soothed and tempted and begged for absolution, she forgave. In the swirling mist that hazed her mind, she thought she could hear his confession, felt his body melt into hers.

His arms contracted and lifted her. She clung to his shoulders, a moan rising softly between them. Faintly, Sebastian realized the yearning sound came from him. Seeking her tongue, he tangled their mouths, desperate and alive and terrified. *I love you. I trust you.* Her declarations wound inside and spurred him to defy. To cherish.

The contradiction astonished him, and he fought the silken skeins that bound him to her with every whispered endearment, every brush of her lips against his brow, his throat, his avid, questing mouth. Gripping her hips, he lifted her higher and fell back against the solid wall. When she urged him on, he streaked kisses across the taut rise of her breasts, slicked his tongue into the cleft between. Oblivious to their surroundings, he searched for answers, testing the wondrous textures of his Kat. The clean smoothness of skin, the slightly rough invitation of her tongue. Hot and piquant, exquisite and supple, he kissed her and imagined tomorrow.

The image held such clarity, he shook. Kat felt the shudder and lifted her mouth. "Sebastian?"

"I don't understand you."

The ragged question shushed across her damp, aching skin and Kat brushed his mouth in mute understanding. Wriggling free, her legs not quite steady, she clutched his biceps for support. Automatically, Sebastian supported her, fingers clenching on her resilient waist. Kat smiled. "Yes, you do understand me, and it scares the hell out of you." She grasped his hand, palm to palm, twining their fingers. "We've got to go meet Senora Martinez. We've got a busy schedule ahead of us."

Mutely, Sebastian trailed Kat out of the alley, and they walked in tandem down the several blocks to the bank. The broad streets, wider than average, accommodated the roar of aging trucks and cars as well as the occasional cart and burro. Flowering trees, in the second blush of spring, dripped pink and white petals to the ground. Tourists bustled along the cobbled sidewalks to peek into shops and dine on authentic cuisine. The bank stood on the corner of the square, a tall white building with a Bahian flag waving proudly in the slight breeze.

Sunlight glistened on the glass doors welcoming customers. Steering them up the walkway, Sebastian halted, turning Kat to face him. Despite his own actions, the safe-deposit box inside the bank held the last communication from Felix to his niece. Though she hadn't shrunk from a challenge since the day they met, Sebastian regretted the possibility of one more illusion shattered.

According to Senora Martinez, the box contained instructions for returning the Cinchona. Sebastian understood that other secrets usually found their hiding places in banks, especially ones that needed to be hidden from authorities. Felix Estrada had a bevy of secrets, and Sebastian wasn't sure Kat could handle the revelation of another one.

He cupped her face between his palms, trying to read the topaz eyes that met his. "Are you sure about this, Kat?"

Kat nodded once, the wan smile she forced unconvincing. "It's too late not to be. You've already made your deal, and so have I. Both of our futures depend on what's inside that safe-deposit box."

In tandem, they entered the bank, shoes silent on the rose-colored marble floor. White fluorescent lights illumined the interior, glinting off the polished floor and the metal pedestals where customers scribbled digits onto slips of paper. A white teller's counter ran the length of one wall. Three men and two women offered politely professional smiles to visitors and dispatched customers with a brisk efficiency. None of the traditional South American disdain for capitalist speed ruled here. The Banco de Bahia was a wholly Western creation, complete with tricolor signs urging customers to squirrel funds away for their waning years.

Sebastian swept the room in an encompassing gaze and noted Gabriela deep in conversation with a handsome, ruddy man buttoned tight into a black suit and noosed by a black pin-striped tie. With a slight turn, he nudged Kat forward toward the senora's post on the plush leather sofas in the waiting area. Kat apologized in Spanish. "So sorry for the delay. We hope you did not wait too long."

Senora Martinez rose and gestured to her companion. "I had time to talk to an old school-mate I haven't seen since pigtails. This is Senor Jorge Ruiz. He is the new bank manager for this branch. May I introduce my friends Katelyn Lyda and her fiancé, Sebastian Caine?" Gabriela stood beside the distinguished older man, with Sebastian and Kat forming a loose circle.

"Buenos días, Senor Ruiz," Sebastian flashed a look of approval to the preening Gabriela. In another life, she'd have made an excellent op-erative, he decided. "I admire your operation," he said as he shook the man's hand. "A very modern bank."

Senor Ruiz puffed up. "I was transferred here two weeks ago, and we have already whipped the staff into shape."

Sebastian noted the placement of cameras, the bank of monitors that indicated where each patron stood. A security guard prowled the rear of the bank, where customers would examine their priceless belongings. "Excellent facility. I am a connoisseur of banks, and this branch is far more sophisticated than its peers. I may have to make a return visit, when I am not in such a hurry."

Kat nearly choked, and Senora Martinez grinned behind the banker's back.

"Ah, please do. I would be happy to give you a tour."

Gabriela interjected. "But we cannot delay today, Senor Ruiz. They have a flight to home tomorrow."

"Yes, yes." Senor Ruiz nodded sympathetically. "Gabriela was explaining your predicament to me. That you are leaving for the States to marry, but that your family's wedding ring is in your uncle's safe-deposit box."

Kat shot a look at Senora Martinez, who shrugged slightly, as though to say she'd made up the best story she could. Playing along, Kat allowed her eyes to mist, softening her voice. "Yes, and with Tio Felix's passing, he will not be able to bring it to the wedding. I can't believe that he's gone. But if we had the ring—"

Knowing she wasn't wholly acting, Sebastian brought Kat to his side, his hand stroking her shoulder in comfort. "If we had the ring," he picked up, "it would be as if he was with us."

Senor Ruiz strode forward and patted Kat's cheek. "Bank policy normally requires you to provide the account number and other documentation. But Gabriela tells me that you only have the key. And that you discovered your uncle's death."

"*Sí.*"

"What tragedy before such a joyous occasion." He curved his skinny mouth into an indulgent smile. "I am the manager, and circumstances must be considered. If you have the key, I will take you to the box."

Fishing the key from his pocket, he passed it to Senor Ruiz. "We appreciate your accommodation. It has been a trying time, these last few days."

"I can but imagine." Senor Ruiz accepted the key, noting the digits imprinted on the head. His eyes widened. The sequence indicated that Felix Estrada had access to their vaults, a rare privilege extended only to the best of customers. However, no Felix Estrada maintained a vault at his bank. But a Felix Mutambo did. A phantom customer who, according to his assistant manager, shipped items to them for safekeeping every few years but paid a high premium for the privilege. Jorge himself had been inside the vault only once, and the memory of what it contained had fueled dreams of wealth and status.

He aimed a reassessing look at the trio in front of him, each face carefully blank. "How did you come to learn of this key?"

Kat spoke first, her words husky. "At his house. I was cataloging his belongings, and we discovered the key. The wedding ring was nowhere to be found, so I assumed he kept it here."

"In Huanco? Half an hour from Canete?" Suspicion edged into his tone, and Senor Ruiz frowned heavily. "An unusual choice for a man of great wealth, to hide a ring in a vault. And for you to mistake it for a safe-deposit box."

A vault, Sebastian thought grimly. No wonder the helpful bank manager had gotten cold feet. Felix had hidden more than a secret bunker and a murder weapon. He possessed other items sufficiently valuable to warrant a secured hiding place miles from home.

Knowing they were about to lose their access, he decided to cut to the chase. In a conspiratorial tone, he mused aloud, "Senor Ruiz, you must have heard the rumors about your customer. He traveled widely and discovered remarkable treasures. Some of which may have had dubious provenance. I expect the Banco de Bahia enjoys an enviable reputation for its stewardship of its clients. It would surely not do to have us seek court assistance to recover a very small item from among larger prizes, no?"

Senor Ruiz heard the veiled threat of exposure to the authorities, a fate no bank wished for, regardless of how well run. An investigation so early in his tenure would spell ruin. Cutting a look at Gabriela, he noted the slight pallor beneath her skin and the flush of color on her niece. Senor Caine, though, appeared wholly at ease. Absently, he caressed his fiancée, his hand beneath her unbound hair. Jorge was uncertain of the real reason for their visit, but the casual affection spoke of intimacy. And he'd known Gabriela for years, had a passing acquaintance with Felix. Who pretended to also be Felix Mutambo.

If either man named Felix was dead, there'd

be no harm in allowing his grieving kin to open
his vault. That would be his defense, should the
worst transpire. Sucking in a breath, he exhaled
heavily and pointed to the vault doors behind
the guard. "Follow me."

Chapter 23

Gabriela Martinez fell into step behind Ruiz, heart pounding in her ears. Heels clicked on the slick marble, an echo of the sound. She had no idea what would lie behind the vault door, and trepidation skated through her, questioning her choices. The tellers watched their procession with interest, and she forced herself to stare straight ahead.

The presence of the guard at the rear of the bank cemented her anxiety. He carried a gun low on his hip, within easy reach, should Ruiz sound the alarm. She didn't know if it would be necessary, if the contents of Felix's stash would warrant the summoning of police.

Felix had recounted his exploits to her, friend to friend, but the revelation of the vault had come as news. Startling news. To her mind, there were few reasons for needing such heavy security beyond the impenetrable bunker beneath the house he'd built or within the safe in his bedroom. Every reason she could conjure spelled crimes that had to be hidden even from her.

Crimes like murder or possibly worse.

It was that comprehension that lurched her pulse into a frenzied race. In the eyes of the law, she could be viewed an accomplice. Indeed, she'd protected his information—out of loyalty and, were she to be honest, the golden thrill of the clandestine. *But what lies had she protected?* she wondered now, watching Ruiz enter his code into the digital keypad beside the high steel door.

Perhaps, had she been a better advisor, she would have discouraged his obsession or broken her vows earlier. To have known a man her entire life and yet to comprehend so little of him was frightening. As soon as she returned home, she and her husband would have a very long talk about untold stories and private knowledge.

A green light glowed and flashed, and the banker entered a second code that released the locks with a solemn click. He levered the handle down and sidled over to allow the bulky door to swing on hydraulic hinges. Ruiz motioned her forward, and Kat and Sebastian entered behind her, no one speaking in the cool, low-lighted chamber.

She examined three walls with their metal boxes emblazoned with numbered tags. But it was the fourth long wall that caught her attention, spellbound. Like a movie scene, a second man guarded five cumbersome doors, each with a wide wheel and metal spokes.

"Just a moment, please." Jorge Ruiz crossed to a computer and typed in a series of keystrokes. Information flashed onto the flat panel, and he scribbled the contents onto a slip of paper at his wrist.

He beckoned them forward to the second vault. Again, he entered a code on the digital pad and lifted a keycard to swipe in front of a card reader. When the panel beeped imperiously, he spun the vault wheel and yanked the handle to open the door.

"I can offer you thirty minutes, and no more. There is a drawer inside the vault. This key will open the lock." He handed Sebastian the key and bowed slightly. "I do not expect any of the contents not in the box to depart with you."

Sebastian nodded. *"Gracias."* When Gabriela moved to enter, he blocked her path. "Senora, I need you to stay out here."

Kat and Gabriela fixed him with twin looks of surprise.

"I know what is behind this door," Gabriela protested.

"No, you don't. And as long as you stay out here, neither you nor your family will have any part in this." He dropped a hand onto her shoulder. "You have done enough for Felix. Kat and I are American citizens, with better protection should the contents be troublesome. Isn't that right, Senor Ruiz?"

Ruiz studied Sebastian with shrewd approval. "Yes. The laws of our country would have short reach into the U.S., but Canete poses no obstacle."

Catching on, Kat added, "Perhaps you should stay here in Huanco until Sebastian and I return, Senora. Given the excitement at home."

Annoyed, touched by the overly protective gestures, Gabriela gave a sharp nod. "I will contact Josef and have him meet me here." Fishing in her purse, she handed Kat the keys to her truck. "I would hear of your success."

"Yes, ma'am."

With a courtly gesture, Ruiz bowed to Gabriela. "I would invite you to visit with my family, Senora Martinez. While we await your husband's arrival."

Gabriela pinned Sebastian with a quelling look. "Do not let her come to any harm, or you will answer to me."

"Sí."

Unsatisfied, but having no recourse, Gabriela hugged Kat, then turned to follow Ruiz out.

Inside the vault, automatic lights flickered to life, their glow subdued in the gray room. The size of a walk-in closet, the vault was roughly eight by twelve, forcing them to huddle close in the air-conditioned space. Sebastian swiftly inspected the contents and emitted a soft whistle. Statuary fashioned from gold nestled against bronze vessels from China's early dynasties. With his trained eye, he identified a pewter box that had been removed from a Grecian museum nearly half a century ago, the box reputed to be the twin of a second chest in Vatican City, rumored to contain the seeds from Persephone's fateful visit to Hades. He moved quickly among the boxes and the pieces that had been set out for display. More artifacts remained crated, their bills of lading dating back nearly a decade.

"Felix was a very, very busy man." He made the comment as he picked up a burial urn they'd fought over in Egypt. "And extremely prolific. The theft of most of these artifacts have been claimed by other men and women. I never would have suspected Felix."

"All of these items are stolen?" Kat posed the question, not sure she wanted the answer. Her concept of right and wrong had been inviolate a week ago. Now she barely felt the censure that was certainly due. The tempered response worried her, and she frowned. "Tio Felix was a thief too? I thought you said he paid for his collection."

"I thought so too," Sebastian murmured, gawking over a scroll cased in bulletproof glass, the text written in Sanskrit. "But these items are generally not allowed out of their countries of origin, regardless of price. I wonder how—" Sebastian stopped himself, not wanting to destroy any more illusions.

He rose from his position near the scroll and turned in the compact space. Briskly, he gestured to the drawer that sat squarely in the wall and held out the key to Katelyn. "We need the map and the funds. Open it."

She accepted the key gingerly, as though expecting it to bite. When she approached the drawer, she discovered it reached her at sternum level. "Okay." Pushing past the jumble of crates, she jammed the key into the slot and twisted. The metal door popped open, revealing a brass box on a tray. Kat slid the tray forward and tested the key in the second slot. Again, the lock released.

Kat raised the metal lid and breath wedged in her throat. Crisp bills in various currencies stood in precise stacks. A clutch of diamonds glittered in a clear vial. Two passports bore the marks of the United States and Spain. She plucked the documents from the box, flipping to the pictures. Tio Felix stared up at her, the names altered to read Felix Mutambo and Juan de Borrero. Cash, diamonds, and fake documents. But no map.

"It's not here, Sebastian. The map isn't here."

Sebastian came up behind her and reached around to the box. As she watched his hand, he lifted the black tray, revealing a second layer below the first.

A folded document nestled on the velvet base. Kat retrieved the document, still sheltered within Sebastian's embrace. Below the paper, a letter embossed in ornate ink remained along with a Lexar Jump Drive.

"This first," he instructed softly, his mouth near her ear. He lowered his arm to offer a supportive hug, savoring the light shudder that coursed through her body. "Check the map."

She unfolded the page with care, the paper fragile and brittle. Spreading it on the tray, the ends dropped over the sides. Sebastian caught them and gently held the paper taut for her examination. In an instant, she recognized the map of Bahia. "There," she exclaimed, pointing to a red dot positioned between Canete and the point where the Amazon threaded through Bahia. "This must be where the Mutambo live."

The lines wound through foothills and over areas of the countryside where few ventured. Kat traced the winding path, lines furrowing between her brows. "Terrain in southeastern Bahia is notoriously rugged. Despite efforts by the government, paved roads haven't penetrated the entire expanse. The Mutambo welcome the services when they are offered, but the government claims it is too costly to connect this area to the rest of the nation. Chronic poverty separated the Mutambo from their Bahian cousins, and technology has yet to reunite the country."

Sebastian remembered the war vaguely, one of many that had raged in South America. "Why are they so isolated? Is it because the indigenous population mixed with the African slaves?"

"Not exactly. For centuries, yes, they were isolated because of race, but in the 1880s, the government accepted the mélange of Bahia. However, in the 1970s, a civil war broke out. After the war, the federal government cordoned off this area, ceding it to the Mutambo and other groups of the indigenous population, but they did little to provide assistance, despite the cease-fire treaty."

"The Mutambo are freedom fighters?"

Kat shook her head fiercely. "No, but they got caught in the middle. An emblem of the guerillas and a scapegoat for the government. Since the truce a decade ago, neither group has done much for them, and the Mutambo retreated deeper into the land between the Amazon and the Andes. They don't welcome strangers, especially *Norte Americanos*."

"Then we've got our work cut out for us."

"Not the least of which is getting into the area without drawing attention," Kat announced, recalling the terrain from her studies with Tio Felix.

Sebastian concurred. Measuring the distance, he estimated their travel time. "The area is about seventy-five klicks from Canete. Three or four hours from here, with good weather."

Kat twisted to look up at him, her eyes clear and direct. "Then we should get going. Your friends will be here soon."

"Kat—" He began to explain, but stopped the excuse from emerging. Shame writhed through him, despite her unexpected reaction to his betrayal. He'd never thought to be understood quite so well. "You're right, we need to move."

He refolded the map and reached for the second document, handing it to Kat. She flipped a thumb through the wax seal and pinched the letter to remove it from the aged envelope. She read the ancient Spanish quickly, at last understanding. Passing the missive to Sebastian, she explained, "It's a letter from Father Borrero to the leader of the Mutambo. We have to take it with us."

Sebastian continued to cradle Kat between his arms, reading the letter over her shoulder. He grasped most of the text, occasionally asking for clarity on the unfamiliar Quechua phrases. "He knew they would want to see this, to understand."

With reluctance, he shifted away, freeing Kat to place the letter and map inside her satchel. He removed the money and the remaining contents. Should Senor Ruiz get curious or cold feet, Sebastian wanted no proof of Felix's connection to the artifacts. Without the passports, all the banker had was room filled with questionable items and a phantom client who did not use his own name.

When the items were secured, he opened the vault door and led Kat through the bank and out of the glass doors. The sun had dipped slightly during their visit, and siesta had taken hold. They hurried down the steps and headed for the Jeep.

Sebastian acknowledged a prickle of awareness that danced along his spine, and he furtively scanned the scattered parking areas. Two blocks over, on the opposite side of the square, a blue police car idled.

He noted the vehicle and the other cars that surrounded them. Ten yards back, their truck waited in front of the strip mall. Past the police car. Keeping the easy, loping stride he used to accommodate Kat's shorter stride, he imperceptibly slowed them to get a better look. With a sidelong glance that seemed casual, he examined the occupants. A slender man and a skinny boy sat in the front seat, and a large, round head reclined against the rear passenger window.

"We've got company." He murmured the warning to Kat, his grip tightening on her cool fingers. "Don't look at me or over my shoulder."

In involuntary response, her head shot up, but she did not look. Her feet stumbled momentarily, but she quickly righted herself. "Who?"

With an approving smile, Sebastian quickened their pace slightly, the increase barely noticeable. He'd stashed the pistol in his waistband, the black T-shirt he wore covering the slight bulge. The weight reassured him, but the gun was almost out of bullets. "It's Enzo. They're in the parking lot on the square. Blue police car."

Kat frowned. "They stole a police car?"

"Probably borrowed it from an inside friend," corrected Sebastian. "The same one who let them into Felix's house. And who told them about Senora Martinez."

"But how did they find us?"

Sebastian had considered the question already, had known the risks. Starkly, he explained, "The phone call I made. I assume they triangulated my call. The Three Stooges must have already been en route."

"You led them to us?"

"Yes."

"Why haven't they come after us?" Kat fought

the reflex to turn and the grinding of her stomach in distress. Trust, she reminded herself sternly, did not allow for reservations. Her declarations meant nothing if she undermined with nervous queries. Still, the apprehensive question tumbled out before she could stop it. "Are they going to kill us?"

"No!" Sebastian snaked a comforting arm around her waist and tucked Kat into his side. He bussed the loose fall of hair with a comforting kiss. "No, they aren't. Because right now, they believe I am on their side."

"I know you're not." She patted his hand.

"I'm on nobody's side, Kat." *Not even my own*, he raged silently. In a day's time, he'd possess everything he'd ever dreamed about. Everything but the person who mattered most in the world to him. A woman who'd shared her body, her heart, and her soul with him, seeking nothing in return. Determined, he captured Kat's wrist, dragging her toward the car at a breakneck pace.

"Sebastian?" Kat went into a jog, trying to keep up or risk losing her hand. When he didn't answer, she decided not to ask again. The grip on the vulnerable bones wasn't tight, but the fingers held firm. A hasty glance at his profile revealed a saturnine mask, his eyes nearly obsidian. He wound them through the milling crowds of tourists, cutting across the square to the truck.

At the truck, he hauled open the passenger door and boosted her inside. Sebastian stalked around to the driver's side and leaped into the vehicle. The engine turned over on the first twist of the key, and he shoved the gear into place and peeled out of the lot.

Kat half turned in her seat to scan for the police car, which pulled onto the street behind them. She noticed another car, a gray sedan, fall into line behind the police unit. "There's another car," she warned quietly. "Gray Mercedes. Two cars back."

Checking the rearview mirror, Sebastian spotted the tail. The Mercedes was more Helen's style than fraternizing with the police, no matter how corruptible. He drummed the steering wheel, plotting. "How well do you know Huanco?"

Kat shook her head. "Not well at all. Tio Felix and I came here a couple of times, but that was years ago." They merged into the traffic of the main thoroughfare. Cars clogged the four lanes, the drivers a mix of tourists eager to head for the coast for the weekend and residents keen to get home. The truck inched forward lethargically, and the police car and Mercedes kept up the snail's pace. She counted three traffic lights between their car and the turnoff for the highway.

In the expanding silence of the truck, Sebastian sifted through options, discarding them one by one. He faced an intractable problem—a dissatisfied client who demanded her merchandise and forfeit of his soul in the process.

He threaded the truck through the meandering cars, thoughts racing. Helen Cox had tentacles that reached far beyond London, beyond the U.S. If she threatened to kill Katelyn for being with him, she'd find a way to murder her and flaunt the death. But no authority would believe him, and he'd have to explain the whys and wherefores of her hatred.

Confession had never been his strong suit.

Guile and cunning and evading authority, those he handled with aplomb. Soon, he'd have to return Kat to Canete rather than taking her to the Mutambo village. By tomorrow, she'd be on a plane to Miami, and the Mutambo would lose a veritable fortune without ever knowing it existed.

Yet sunshine had always been the best cure for midnight.

"Did you mean it?"

Kat swiveled in her seat. "Mean what?"

"What you said at the store this afternoon. Did you mean it?"

"Yes."

His eyes demanded honesty. "All of it?"

"Yes," Kat smiled, a promise that she wouldn't break. "Yes, love, I did."

Sebastian clasped her hand, believing. "Then I need your help."

Chapter 24

The return to Canete passed quickly. Sebastian and Kat used the passageway to collect what they needed for the journey to Mutambo. They needed to travel light, since the map showed a single point of entry to the village—from a cove on the Pacific Coast.

"Are you sure you've got everything on the list?" Sebastian asked for the third time. He carried the Cinchona and diary in his bag, along with the items from his trusty toolkit. The jump drive with records of Felix's communications with Burge were included as well, as insurance. "Once we get on the boat, we're not coming back until we've finished."

After changing out of her new dress and into the pants and shirt she'd purchased, Kat collected samples of the plants for the Cinchona and essentials.

"I know, I know." Kat placed a vial of the Cinchona elixir in a hollow carved out of styrofoam. The foam chamber sat inside a polyester carrying case that fit neatly inside her satchel. Three additional chambers contained specimens the Mutambo might recognize but few outsiders ever glimpsed. She zipped the contraption and put it in her bag. "Ready."

Sebastian headed for the door and ushered Kat into the tunnel. Their feet scraped the rough gravel as they raced to the boat moored at the other end. Senora Martinez's truck had been parked, the keys in the glove compartment as they'd agreed.

At the edge of the slip, waves lapped at the pier. Following Kat's instructions, he detached the docking lines and climbed aboard. Kat was already in the cockpit. Using short bursts of the throttle, she guided the runabout into the choppy waters of the ocean.

"Ahoy." Sebastian teased, impressed by how easily she handled the boat. It was larger inside than he thought, room for four if they were all friendly. His experience with boats had been limited to necessary escapes. Sailing held little appeal to him, as he preferred the certainty of solid ground. Had God intended him to be on the water, he'd have gills instead of lungs. Sitting, he unrolled the map and took post as navigator. "According to this, the Mutambo live just off a cay between Bahia and Ecuador. We can dock the boat there and reach the village on foot."

"Got it." Kat tossed him a sly look and opened the throttle, engine racing. Above the roar of the water and motor, she warned with a grin,

"Fasten your seat belt, Sebastian. If you like the way I drive a car, you'll love me in a boat."

The runabout glided to a stop and Kat killed the motor. Sebastian fairly leaped from the boat, grateful for the feel of dry land beneath his feet.

"I didn't scare you, did I?" Kat asked innocently, jumping down to stand on the sandy beach.

Sebastian glared at her, waiting for his stomach to stop pitching in distress. "Next time, I drive." When he was certain his legs wouldn't fold beneath him, he lurched forward, muttering beneath his breath.

She'd docked the runabout near the shoreline in a cove constructed of massive rock formations. Blue-green waves rushed onto the shore, the whitecaps tugging at their feet. Together, they jogged inland, feet sinking into the dark sands. Sebastian held Kat's hand as they picked their way along the beach toward the interior.

"We're being watched," Sebastian whispered to Kat. Though the beach was empty, he felt the awareness trickle down his spine beneath the weight of his pack. Fifty feet away, trees swayed in the late winds coming off the ocean.

Kat squeezed his hand in understanding and edginess. Though she made a living venturing into new communities, the stakes this time were impossibly high. "Can you see anyone?"

"Not yet. But I know they're out there." His internal alarm never failed. Plus, Felix's map indicated that the Mutambo inhabited a village six miles inland, close to the Yarapa tributary of the Amazon. The Yarapa was an offshoot of the Maranon tributary that swung near Ecuador. He was certain that beyond the dense stand of trees, the descendants of the Mutambo wouldn't be quite as welcoming as their ancestors.

Squinting into the distance, Kat saw the movement seconds before the men appeared. Sebastian clutched her arm, drawing her to a halt. They stood side by side as first one, then two, then ten men materialized out of the trees.

"Who are you?" A slight man standing in the center of the party leveled a rifle at their position, his Spanish throaty and harsh. He wore a cotton shirt stained with sweat and a wide-brimmed straw hat. On his feet, he sported scuffed boots that had seen much better days. The other men were similarly attired and equally unfriendly.

Speaking the universal language of no resistance, Sebastian tugged Kat's hand up and lifted his hands, palms out. "Visitors. We'd like to speak with your leaders," he explained in Spanish. He felt silly asking to be taken to their leaders like an extraterrestrial, but he couldn't find a better question.

"Names," barked another man, nearly twice as tall as the one holding the gun. "Tell us."

"Katelyn Lyda and Sebastian Caine," Kat offered with a respectful nod. Taking a chance, she added, "We would like to talk about Father Juan-Carlos Borrero."

Whispers streaked through the crowd of men, and three hurried to stand with the main two. The conversation lasted for nearly two minutes, punctuated by guttural shouts and an occasional shove. Finally, the smaller man gestured them forward. "Come with us."

Tucking Kat close to him, Sebastian fell into step behind the men, and the rest of the group circled around them. The men led them between two groves of trees to a clearing where three aged Ford trucks waited.

"I am Huáscar Cajamarca." The older man bowed deeply. "Welcome."

Huáscar opened the door to a black truck with gray primer showing and gallantly assisted Kat inside. Sebastian followed. Huáscar clambered into the driver's seat and more men climbed into the truck bed. He honked the horn twice and set out.

Kat peered out the window as the truck rumbled through the rain forest. Disturbed by the sound, birds cawed madly, answered by other creatures of the forest.

"We do not often get visitors to Mutambo and we are protective of our home," Huáscar said suddenly. "The fighting that happens too near us sometimes tries to come inside. We do not permit it."

Sebastian inclined his head, understanding the reference to the guerilla wars waged in Peru and Ecuador. "I would protect my home too."

Huáscar did not speak again until the trucks reached the village. Adobe structures and wooden huts dotted the town as they descended into a shallow valley. He parked the truck and sounded the horn several times. A few villagers poked their heads out to see what the commotion was about. Children, dusty and rambunctious, raced around a well, under the watchful eye of several women filling their buckets with water. Kat noted the threadbare clothes and the ramshackle buildings.

"Come." Prompted by their driver, Sebastian got out and helped Kat down from the truck. The taciturn Huáscar began walking, and they kept pace. He led them to a yellowish building with a carved sign announcing it as city hall. "Enter."

Sebastian went first, scanning the interior. He noted a simple desk and two low benches and not much else. Oil lamps burned on the windowsill and on the desk. Poverty held Mutambo by the throat. No running water, no electricity.

"Sit." Huáscar pointed to the bench and disappeared behind a door Kat took to be the mayor's office.

"Verbose, isn't he?" She settled onto the bench, legs crossed. For comfort, she turned her satchel to rest in her lap. "I imagine he's conferencing with the mayor."

"I'm just glad he left the rifle in the car," commented Sebastian.

"Did you see their reaction to Father Borrero's

name?" Kat sidled closer, her voice a soft murmur. "I couldn't tell if they were pleased to hear his name or not."

"I'm glad you said it at all. The big guy was ready to pitch us into the ocean." He hadn't been able to make out their argument, but the gist had been clear. Huáscar wanted them to meet the leader, and the big one didn't. Father Borrero's legacy seemed as mixed as every other European's in South America.

The office door opened, and Huáscar appeared. "Come."

With his hand on the small of her back, Sebastian escorted Kat across the floor and into the room where Huáscar waited. Inside, a man of medium build sat behind an identical desk. Black hair parted in the center and swept into two wings laced with gray. His skin was nearly Kat's hue, with deep wrinkles that pegged his age at around seventy.

Two chairs angled toward him on the other side, and he gestured to them. Huáscar stood sentinel, his hat removed. As they sat, he lifted a ceramic pot. "Coffee? Ms. Lyda? Mr. Caine?" He asked the question in heavily accented English.

"Thank you," Kat accepted, and he filled a cup with thick brown liquid drenched liberally with milk.

Knowing she hated coffee, Sebastian decided to follow her lead. He refused the offer of sugar and sipped at the creamy brew. *"Gracias."*

"You are welcome," The mayor continued in

English. "I understand from Huáscar that you both speak Spanish, but I do not often have a chance to practice my English. It is rusty, but good, I think."

"We appreciate the courtesy." Kat sipped at her coffee, used to drinking and eating what she was offered. "And we appreciate your taking the time to speak with us."

"Huáscar tells me that you seek information about Father Borrero." The mayor studied Kat and Sebastian, his gaze hooded. "He holds a special place in our community."

"One of honor?" asked Sebastian.

"One of mystery." Reclining, the mayor explained, "The priest lived with my people for much of his life. However, he left us for a time and stole our most precious secrets. Because my people practice the Catholic forgiveness, we accepted him back into our fold, but he did not repent."

Kat ventured, "We have reason to believe that Father Borrero thought to protect you." She glanced at Sebastian, who signaled her to continue. "Sebastian and I have come to return your secrets to you. The Cinchona." She opened her bag and removed the case. "Look inside, please."

The mayor unzipped the case and stared down at the clear vial and the other plants. With careful hands, he raised each plant, sniffed, and touched the roots and leaves that grew only in Mutambo. Shocked, he lifted his head, wanting desperately for this hoax to be true. "I studied in Lima at the university. Botany, for my people. Since the time when the Spanish came, we have been told a legend of a white man saved by our shaman, and that he in return captured our secrets into pages. Every man in my family line learned about the Cinchona, and we hunted for the recipe, never able to find it again." He handled the vial with exquisite care, the future of his people in his hands. "Are you sure that this is the Cinchona? The elixir of life?"

"Dr. Lyda completed the formula," Sebastian concurred. "It is yours."

The mayor regarded them for a moment, then demanded abruptly in Spanish, "What do you want in exchange? Our village is poor, but we will do what we can to recompense you."

Sebastian shook his head. "No, sir. We don't want anything from you. This is yours. As is this." He brought the Cinchona manuscript out of his pack and laid it on the desk. "The manuscript Father Borrero wrote for your people five hundred years ago. And his diary."

"Why are you doing this?" the mayor asked, curiosity narrowing his eyes. "You could be very wealthy if you kept these things. My people no longer believe that the manuscript existed. Father Borrero and the Cinchona are fairy tales told to our little ones at night."

Kat spoke first, her voice husky with regret. "My uncle, Felix Estrada, stole this from the Brothers of Divinity. They should have returned it to your people long ago. Consider it the penance for many sins."

"However," Sebastian added, "I do have a proposition for you. If you're interested."

"Chief Montoya, thank you for your help." Sebastian stood in the foyer of Estrada's home and walked with the police chief to the dining room. The charcoal gray suit was a welcome respite for Sebastian, after too many days of jeans and T-shirts. The suit had come courtesy of one of their guests for the final act. "We've assembled in here."

Montoya entered the room behind him, studying each of the faces already gathered inside. Three women stood in a loose circle, standing near two men. They stopped speaking when he entered. Montoya recognized the disapproving stares and turned accusingly toward Sebastian. In smooth English, he railed, "I didn't realize you intended to hold a party, Mr. Caine. My agreement with you was to allow Mr. Estrada's niece to collect her uncle's belongings, nothing more. I'm going to have to demand that you all leave."

Sebastian crossed to his company and rested a hand on Kat's shoulder. "I don't think you will, Chief. If I leave here before I'm through, I will have to report to the Bahian federal authorities my suspicions about your operation."

"Suspicions?"

"That you have knowingly assisted American criminals who committed murder in this very house. After all, any lab test will prove that the damage to the kitchen is the result of one of your police cars ramming into the house. And there is the eyewitness who saw a Canete police car in her front yard, driven by one of the criminals while the other two threatened her." Sebastian's smile was thin and menacing. "I expect you will do your part, Chief, if you want to keep your job."

Subdued by the threat, Montoya skulked into a corner of the dining room. "I have another appointment, Caine. This had better be quick."

"It will be." Sebastian turned to the taller of the men standing beside him. "Allow me to make introductions. Mr. Gabriel Moss, editor of the *Bayou Ledger* and a budding media empire in the South. His wife, Dr. Erin Abbott, professor and amateur sleuth." Sebastian glared at the man he considered his brother-in-law. "If I'd known she was pregnant, I wouldn't have asked her to come."

"Well," Erin retorted before Gabriel could respond, "if you ever answered your phone or your e-mail, you'd have known. Some godfather you'll make."

Gabriel hugged her close. "She's been itching to travel before it's too late. Plus, I tried to ditch her, and she threatened to come on her own."

"Besides, it gave me a chance to meet her," Mara Reed added, her hand twined with her husband's. He hung back, observing the gathering. He flexed his fingers against hers, then absently lifted her hand to his mouth.

Sebastian gestured to them. "Mara Reed, my

former business partner, and her husband, Dr. Ethan Stuart."

"When you told me you needed to borrow our plane, Sebastian, I should have expected there was more to it," Mara pointed out. "A man saves your life, and you owe him forever."

Sebastian motioned to Kat, who joined him at the dining-room table. A dress in carnelian swirled around her ankles, the color luminous against her skin. She'd braided her hair into a smooth style that begged for his hands to dip inside. He resisted the urge with effort, but couldn't refrain from stroking his thumb along her bared shoulders. "Helen will be here soon. Everything set up, Gabriel?"

"I've got the feed hooked up in the great room. Get her back there, and we'll be golden," replied Gabriel. "I can guarantee local coverage and a run on CNN."

"Excellent." Sebastian looked down at Kat. Her eyes were steady, but tense, and he wondered if he'd made the right decision. Tipping her face up to his, he asked softly, "Are you sure about us doing this in there? We can use the library or even this room. Just say the word."

"I'm fine, Sebastian," she murmured, reassuring herself as much as him. She rubbed her chin against his hand, savoring the warmth, missing his touch already. "Gabriel said it was best, and they—they've cleaned the room."

Oblivious to the couples watching him, he covered her mouth in a kiss that seared through him. After too short a time, he lifted his head, resting his forehead on hers. "It will be over soon, honey, I promise."

On cue, the doorbell rang.

Sebastian straightened. "Showtime."

He walked to the front door, his steps unhurried. Casually, he twisted the knob and the door swung wide. Sebastian immediately recognized Helen, Enzo, and the teenager he'd seen in the car. Another woman, sharp-faced and thin, stood beside her, and two middle-aged men waited expectantly. At the rear, a heavy, ruddy man leaned on crutches.

"Helen." He stepped back, the gracious host, and invited them inside. "I didn't realize you were bringing friends."

"My partners," Helen explained stiffly, "insisted on accompanying me. Marguerite Seraphin. Jeremy Holbrook. Vincent Palgrave." She pointed to each in turn, the introductions surreally polite. "I believe you've met Mr. Selva and his associates."

"I have." Beneath their feet, the marble clacked as they crossed the threshold. At the entrance to the dining room, Sebastian halted. "Before we go any further, I'll need you to make the wire transfer." He'd set up a laptop on a side table, the screen glowing green.

"First the Cinchona," Helen countered.

"No dice." Sebastian shrugged. "You've come with an army, which makes me think you intend to leave without paying. Give me the money, and you'll get your prize. If I cheat you, shoot me."

Helen brushed at imaginary lint on her Chanel sleeve and sauntered to the computer. Having expected it, she called up the proper screen and typed in her instructions. "Enter your account," she directed tersely.

From memory, he entered the numbers and pressed ENTER. Then he switched to another screen and brought up his account. The transfer amount tripled his previous balance, and Sebastian swallowed a cheer. Instead, he logged out and bowed gracefully. "A pleasure doing business with you, Helen."

"The Cinchona, Sebastian. Now. I have a plane waiting."

"Absolutely. You should get what's coming to you." Sebastian led them down the hallway past the area where he'd scrubbed away Felix's blood. The memory set his teeth on edge, but he controlled his rage with effort. With a flourish, he slid the great-room doors on their runners and stepped inside.

Bulbs popped and lights flashed on the astonished faces of Helen and her cohort. Voices chattered excitedly and a reporter, a pencil of a woman, hurried forward, microphone at the ready. The cameraman trailed behind her, zooming in on Helen. "I'm standing live with Ms. Helen Cox, CEO of Taggart Pharmaceuticals. Is it true, Ms. Cox, that Taggart has formed a consortium to market what is being billed as a wonder drug?"

Furious but trapped by the camera, Helen gritted her teeth, and replied, "Yes, I and my colleagues have formed a collaboration to bring the Cinchona to market." She smiled grimly and introduced her team. "We wanted to announce the development from here, in honor of the man who discovered the Cinchona after nearly five hundred years."

"You mean Mayor Mutambo of the Mutambo village?" shouted another reporter.

Helen whirled toward the voice, her mouth agape. "Mutambo?"

Sebastian stepped forward, Gabriel's camera following. "Mayor Mutambo of the village that actually created the Cinchona. I told the press that you and your consortium have graciously agreed to develop the drug for the tribe. And to give them the patent, in perpetuity. As well as any patents developed on secondary drugs or any derivatives from the Cinchona." He waved to the mayor, who ambled up to the knot of reporters.

"We are so grateful to Taggart Pharmaceuticals for their generosity. The production of the Cinchona will not only save lives, it will bring prosperity to the Mutambo and to the nation of Bahia."

Helen spun to face Marguerite, Jeremy, and Vincent. "I didn't do this, goddamn it! I didn't agree to this. Who did?"

Sensing a meltdown, Jeremy and Vincent said nothing, both grieving the demise of their companies. Marguerite, however, recognized the tall, willowy woman heading for her and Enzo. She stumbled backward, eager to escape.

"Enzo," she muttered, but no one was there. Abandoning pride, she broke into a run, chased by a reporter sensing a new story. She slid across the slick marble and lost her balance. Landing at the feet of five uniformed officers.

"Marguerite Seraphin, you are under arrest for the murder of Senor Felix Estrada and Dr. Clifton Burge." Chief Montoya stood over her while officers helped her to her well-shed feet.

"Helen Cox!" she screamed. "Helen did this. Not me! Tell them, Enzo!" she demanded, wrestling against the officers who tried to subdue her.

"I have no connection to this, Officer. I do not know what she is talking about." Enzo cast his eyes down, hiding a sneer. See how the bitch liked to be ignored. He had sufficient information to trade for a lighter sentence, and Raphael and Turi would make nice patsies.

Soon, Marguerite stood in handcuffs, spewing venom and crying for a lawyer.

Kat watched the drama unfold from the hallway, satisfaction blending with sorrow.

"Make a sound and I'll kill you," Helen said coolly, pressing her gun into the small of Kat's back. "In there," she directed, her head jabbing toward the sitting room.

"Okay." Kat moved slowly, hoping Sebastian would notice her missing. But the sitting-room door closed behind her with a thud, and she was alone with Helen. The woman flipped the lock on the door with an ominous click. Despite the terror crowding in her veins, Kat refused to grovel. "What do you want? The Cinchona's gone, and the police have arrested your friends."

"Which gives me ample reason to take my revenge on you," Helen explained. Bitter eyes took in the room in shambles, books and papers strewn across the floor. "Sebastian shouldn't have tricked me," she offered contemplatively. "Not after everything we've been to each other."

Kat laughed out loud at the pitiable comment. "Are you trying to make me jealous?" Contempt blazed in her eyes, and she replied easily, "Sebastian has made mistakes, God knows, but those days are behind him. Like you."

"Men like Sebastian don't change, darling. What they are is bred in the bone." Helen narrowed her eyes in malicious glee. "A couple of nights in your arms won't transform him, regardless of what the romance novels tell you. He's a thief and a liar, and that's all he'll ever be. It's all he's ever been."

"Whom are you trying to convince?" Kat asked, looking around for any means of escape. The entry to the bunker was sealed shut and the windows to the sitting room would cut her to pieces. "This can't end well for you, Helen. They won't let you leave. I won't."

"Sebastian and I had a deal. He delivers the Cinchona and you live. Given his performance, obviously ten million dollars meant more than your life."

Kat froze. "What are you talking about?"

"His payoff. Didn't he tell you? He had me

wire it to his account before the sideshow started. Out there." She gestured to the hallway with the gun's barrel. "Ten million dollars for your life. I was cheated."

"Sebastian wouldn't do that," Kat protested halfheartedly. "He staged this in order to trap you. Not for the money."

"I told you, love. With men like Sebastian, it's always about the money." She released the safety, frowning slightly. "A deal is a deal."

When the door flew open, Kat dived to the ground just as a shot rang out. She rolled once, her arm on fire. Above her, around her, more gunfire sounded, but she lay on the carpet, blood flowing. She thought she saw Helen's body fall, saw dark-clothed officers swarm inside.

"Katelyn!" Sebastian dropped to the floor beside her, anguish careening through him. His hands shook as he gathered her up. "Katelyn, honey, talk to me. Where does it hurt, baby?"

"My arm. Just. My arm." Fighting through the haze of pain, she tried to focus on the voice, the face of the man she loved. She blinked, suddenly too sleepy to keep her eyes open. "You took the money?"

"What?"

"She told me that you took the money." Kat slurred the question, too overwhelmed to stay awake. "Did you?"

"Yes."

Her mouth quirked into a smile that trembled with pain. "Good."

* * *

Kat lay in her uncle's bed, surrounded by her new friends. Erin fussed over the bandage on her arm, while Mara plied her with juice.

Senora Martinez clucked over her, still astounded that Kat had been shot. "You need to drink. Doctor's orders."

She swatted the juice away using her good arm. "I'm not thirsty." Staring past the end of the narrow bed, she watched the door as she had for nearly two days. But Sebastian didn't appear. Hadn't since she'd regained consciousness. "Tell me what's going on."

Erin saw the heartbreaking look and launched into the day's news. "Mayor Mutambo has accepted an offer from an American company to patent the Cinchona. Gabriel has put together a P.R. team to assist him, and Mara brought in some legal assistance to be sure everything is aboveboard."

Taking the cue, Mara added, "The British government is planning to extradite Marguerite Seraphin, and the U.S. has called dibs on Palgrave and Holbrook. The Bahian authorities have declined to extradite the other three." She sat on the edge of the bed and stuck the straw into Kat's resistant mouth. "Chief Montoya is now a celebrity. Footage of the gunfight has been playing nonstop. Shows Sebastian racing to your rescue and Montoya taking Helen Cox down." Realizing what she'd said, Mara covered her mouth and cursed, "Berkle sticks! I'm sorry, Kat. I didn't mean to bring that up."

Erin gamely rose to her feet and nodded to the door. "Let's give Kat some time to sleep."

"You don't have to be afraid to mention his name," Kat said, smiling wanly. "Sebastian. He saved my life. If he hadn't picked the lock, Helen would have killed me."

"And he's been busy helping the police file charges," Senora Martinez offered enthusiastically. "He'd be here if he could."

"Sure. Of course." She shut her eyes before the welling tears fell. "I think I am tired, okay? I'll just nap." Before the women responded, she turned onto her good side and yanked at the covers. The door closed softly, and she sighed, moisture dampening her cheeks. "Of course."

Twilight had come when she awoke. Kat sat up in bed, dragging her hair away from her face. She reached for the lamp and flicked it on. Then she froze. Pain, sharp as an arrow, twisted inside her.

"You've been asleep for a while." Sebastian spoke from the single chair beside her bed.

His eyes were shadowed, the brown dull in the lamplight. Because she wanted to touch him, she flattened her hand against the sheet. "I don't seem to do much else lately." Abruptly thirsty, she brought the tepid glass of juice to her lips and sipped slowly, marshaling emotions that raged through her, rending her heart. For two days, she'd lain in this bed, waiting for him. He hadn't come. She loved him, trusted him, and it didn't matter. Worse than the tear in her skin from a bullet was the hole he'd left in her heart. So she'd listen to what he had to say and then find her way home. Alone. Swallowing hard, she asked baldly, "Why are you here, Sebastian?"

"To see you." He'd practiced what he'd say to her in his head a thousand times since she'd been shot, knew the words by heart. He'd come too close to losing her already to risk saying the wrong thing. But the sight of her, pale and fragile in the wide bed, chased the carefully planned speech away. "I needed to see how you were doing."

"I'm fine. The doctors say I'll be ready to travel home in a couple of days." She lifted a hand to scrub at her eyes, willing them not to fill. "When are you leaving?"

He leaned forward and clasped his hands together to keep from reaching for her. First, he had to explain what he'd done and why. Why he'd stayed away and why he'd come to her tonight. But he wouldn't finish if he touched her and felt the silk of her skin, the warmth that could burn through him like flame. There would be time, he promised himself. If it wasn't too late. "I haven't decided when I'm leaving yet. Mara and Ethan have offered to fly us back."

Kat flinched at the thought of being trapped for hours on a plane with Sebastian. Wanting what she'd never have. "I don't want you all to wait for me. Senora Martinez can look after me."

Catching her reaction, he countered softly, painfully, "I can take care of you, Katelyn. I don't have anywhere else to be." Fear of a loss he wouldn't survive shuddered through him, leaving only a plea in his mind. *Forgive me. Love me.* "Kat, I have to explain—"

"You don't owe me any explanations," she interjected coldly. She refused to listen to a polite rejection from the only man she'd ever loved. Instead, she'd set him free. Calm, devastated, she explained, "I don't need you to look after me, Sebastian. You've paid your debt to my uncle. We're even."

The cool, impassive tone sent a shiver along his skin and broke his heart anew. "We're even?"

"Done." Kat stared at him, eyes dry and burning. She wouldn't cry over him. Not now. Not ever. She'd offered him trust and love in the midst of secrets and lies, and he'd turned her away. She refused to endure that again. "Our partnership is over. I did as my uncle asked. So did you. We're finished here. No debts, no ties. No regrets. You're free to go, Sebastian." Her throat closed and she fought to finish without a sob. "Please. Go."

The dismissal shot through him like a bullet, breaking him. Too long. He'd waited too long to believe her —to accept that she believed in him. Saw him more clearly than anyone ever had. Searing heat flashed through him followed by a chill that reminded him of death. Could a man die and still feel his heart beat? "Katelyn. No."

Puzzled, she blinked once at the harsh denial.

"Why not? You've gotten what you wanted. The Cinchona. The money. You protected me, saved my life. What more do you want?"

Sebastian surged to his feet, looming over her. Fury, hot and molten, pumped through his veins. "I don't want to be even, damnit. I don't want to be finished." Words tumbled out, but not the speech he'd prepared. When she watched him out of cool topaz eyes, all he could think about was losing. In his mind, he saw her body fall, saw the red rushing out and spilling to the floor. Saw his life ending. He dropped down, kneeling by the bed. Desperate, he grabbed at her hand and set the glass aside with a snap. "I want you. Hell, I'll give away the money."

"What?" She stared at Sebastian, mouth agape. "Why would you do that?"

"To prove myself. To you." He lifted her hand to his mouth, fear driving him to beg, to demand. "I don't know what Helen told you, but I did take the money. For you. For us. For me," he admitted miserably. "I steal things, Kat. It's what I do. What I did. Before you."

"The ten million came after you met me," she reminded him, her words quiet but wry.

"Yes," he acknowledged. "I've been in Mutambo with Gabriel and Ethan. We're setting up a partnership to fund production and distribution of the Cinchona, just in case the pharmaceutical consortium falls apart. There will be a foundation, Kat. The Felix Estrada Foundation. With a five-million-dollar grant from you and me."

Stunned, she stammered, "Half the money? And the other half?"

Sebastian flushed. "I'm new at this charity stuff, Kat. Give me time."

Love filled her, flowed through her, strong and true. "What do you want, Sebastian?"

Holding her eyes, he whispered, "Everything. You." He knelt by the bed, taking her hand in his. "Until I met you, I didn't know they were the same thing." Fumbling in his pocket, he held up a ring, the stone topaz to match her eyes. He'd spent the day hunting through jewelry stores to find the right match. The perfect one. "I'm the thief, but you've stolen my heart."

"Sebastian?"

Suddenly, the words were there, waiting. "I love you, Kat. As much as I imagine the human heart can hold. Then I wait a moment, and I love you more." More afraid than he'd ever been before, he asked, "Marry me?"

Katelyn smiled tremulously. "Isn't this against your rules?"

He nodded, fear receding. "Yes. And that's a promise."

"Why?" She'd told him what she believed, but doubt demanded that he tell her the truth. "Why do you love me?"

Understanding, he gently lifted her wounded arm, feathered a kiss onto her hand. "Because you're brave and loyal and stubborn. Because you can trust a thief." His voice failed him, and he bowed his head. The next words were a whisper against her skin. "Because I want to

spend the rest of my life earning your trust and making sure you never have to doubt me again."

"Those are pretty good reasons." Kat grinned and cupped his cheek. "I love you, too. Of course, I've never met anyone like you before. An honest liar. A loyal thief. Every day with you will be an adventure. Yes, I'll marry you."

With a sigh of relief that quaked through him, Sebastian sat on the bed and carefully pulled her across his lap, raining kisses across her mouth, her cheek, everywhere he could reach. He slipped the ring onto her finger. Tenderly, he soothed her wound with a brush of his lips. "No one has trusted me before. Implicitly. Without wanting proof."

"I've got my proof," Kat whispered, raising her hand, the gem sparkling in the lamplight. "I've got you."

Mutambo and the Cinchona elixir that could be the Fountain of Youth. The rest is as accurate as I could discern.

I welcome your thoughts and feedback, so please contact me at:

selena_montgomery@hotmail.com
www.selenamontgomery.com
P.O. Box 170352
Atlanta, Georgia 30317-0352

Happy reading,
Selena Montgomery

Author's Note

Dear Readers:

Secrets and Lies brought one of my favorite characters into full view, Sebastian Caine. From his first appearance in *Never Tell*, to his heroism in *Hidden Sins*, I've been waiting to fall in love with him. When his "job" takes him to South America and into a web of subterfuge, I knew only Dr. Katelyn Lyda would suit him and the mystery that unfolds. Plus, it offered a brief reunion with Gabriel and Erin and Mara and Ethan, an author's greatest pleasure.

The love story of Sebastian and Katelyn and the mystery of the Cinchona required a special place, born of fact and imagination. My imagined nation, Bahia, is modeled on the actual history of Peru and Ecuador during the time of Pizzaro. I have added the illegitimate Incan son Calcucha, the priest Father Juan-Carlos Borrero, the